She started to pi
gown was wrapped in. Then she noticed something
else. A small object wrapped in tissue paper had
also fallen out. She picked it up and opened the
paper. 'Oh, Mother, what's this?'

In her open palm lay a large brooch, a circle of
diamonds and sapphires set in heavy gold. The
gems twinkled as she held them up to the light.
'It's beautiful,' she whispered in awe, holding it
out to her mother. 'I didn't know you had anything like this!'

The expression on her mother's face made her
stop short. The look of anguish was one Annie
would never forget. Grace was frowning, staring
at the brooch. 'Put it back!' Grace forced out her
words in a hoarse whisper. 'Put it back where it
was! I don't want to see it!'

Tomorrow's Past

EMMA DALLY

WARNER BOOKS

A *Warner* Book

First published in Great Britain in 1995
by Little, Brown and Company
This edition published in 1996 by Warner Books

A CIP catalogue record for this book
is available from the British Library.

ISBN 0 7515 1581 7

Typeset by M Rules
Printed in England by Clays Ltd, St Ives plc

Warner Books
A Division of
Little, Brown and Company (UK)
Brettenham House
Lancaster Place
London WC2E 7EN

To my children,
Rebecca, Alice and Ruth

Part One

CHAPTER 1

❧

A Child is Born

IT WAS A FINE Saturday morning in May, one of those early summer days when the pale blue sky is clear, no clouds can be seen and the sun shines promisingly through a shimmering haze. The air was still crisp with the residue of spring, causing the women on the street to pull their woollen shawls tighter around their shoulders and the men to wonder whether they should still be wearing warm winter vests under their shirts.

Kentish Town Road was busy with shoppers. For those women whose husbands were lucky enough to be in work – and had handed over all or part of Friday night's pay packet – it would be a good meal tonight. Irish stew, perhaps, or steak and kidney pie with lashings of gravy. They might even be able to run to a nice joint of beef for the Sunday roast if they were lucky. For the first few days of the week the food would be relatively abundant. By Friday they would be down to a supper of bread and dripping.

Thirty-five years into the twentieth century, Kentish Town was a shabby, run-down part of north London. It had not always been so. One hundred years before, at the beginning of Queen Victoria's reign, it had enjoyed a brief reputation as a fashionable suburb. High on the hill which runs up to Hampstead and Highgate, Kentish Town had offered green fields and fresh clean air to those choking on the filthy grime in London. However, the popularity of the area had rapidly ended with the coming of the Midland Railway in 1864. The railway extension brought its own dirt to pollute the wide streets and tall villas which had once housed wealthy, genteel families and their servants.

These Victorian dwellings still remained, but since that time many of them had turned into run-down terraces and tenements filled with some of the poorest families.

Some were poorer than others. Respectable working-class families, whose men had skills which kept them in work and who were anxious to improve their living standards, lived alongside those for whom life was a struggle in which they were always the losers. Such people lived on the edge of society, barely part of it at all.

Though most of the inhabitants of Kentish Town were working class, many middle-class families still remained there, tied by their roots to the place where, in better days, their parents and grandparents had been born and brought up. Unlike their friends and peers, these families chose to stay living on the hill rather than depart to the more salubrious villas and gardens in Highgate and Hampstead.

But whatever a person's station in life, the community spirit was strong in Kentish Town. It gave everyone a sense of belonging, a support system, even a sense of responsibility – so long as the community's rules and customs were observed in return.

Regardless of the shifting population, the shopkeepers of Kentish Town always knew what their customers could afford. Bob Worth, the butcher, was one. He knew that he would sell more chitterlings, tripe and lambs' hearts than any good steak or lamb chops. But he still had some customers who could spend more on one Sunday joint than another customer could spend on a week's family cooking.

On the day our story begins his shop was busy. Women of all ages were queuing up and chatting as they watched the master butcher at work, cutting up the bloody meat with his choppers and sharp knives, banging loudly on the wooden block in the middle of the shop. Bunches of furry, glass-eyed rabbits were strung upside down across the window front, above a table piled high with fat sausages and chunky pork pies. Mr Worth worked fast, shifting his vast weight from one foot to another. Behind him, from thick metal hooks set into the ceiling, hung heavy beef carcasses waiting to be cut as the orders came in.

Bob Worth was large and square with heavy, thick brows which hung above his eyes like hairy caterpillars. After his size, his most striking feature was his hands which had the tips of several fingers missing. Customers noticing this for the first time would wonder, as Bob handed over their pound of scrag or sweetbreads, whether one of his fingers was included in the package.

Mr Worth lifted his large head and looked over the counter. 'And what can I do for you, Miss Turner?'

A small child stared up at him with bright grey eyes. She was slight and neatly built. With her well-trimmed brown hair, she was noticeably clean and tidy, dressed in a Fair

Isle cardigan over a white blouse, blue serge skirt, white socks and leather sandals.

'I've come to collect the joint my mother ordered yesterday,' the girl said slowly, as though repeating lines she had carefully memorized. A pink blush crept up her neck as she spoke. 'My mother's not feeling well today,' the girl continued. 'She asked me to pick it up for her and says can you put it on the account.'

Mr Worth nodded and wiped his hands on the bloody apron wrapped around his large belly. Hobbling off to the back of the shop, he returned moments later with a bundle wrapped in white paper.

'It's all ready here, Miss Annie,' he said, 'a nice piece of pork. There's a good amount of crackling on it, your mother'll be pleased to see. I'm sorry she's not well. Please send her my best.'

As the girl left the shop, the women in the queue started to shake their heads.

'That Mrs Turner's been quite poorly lately,' said Mrs Rose to the woman behind her. Mrs Rose was a short spindly woman with thinning yellow hair and a liverish complexion to match. Her stooped frame was frail. She looked as if she could barely carry the large wicker basket in the crook of her elbow, already packed with carrots, cabbage and potatoes from the greengrocer next door.

Mrs Jones nodded. 'Yes, she's been quite ill. She's needed the doctor several times. And it's not just that baby she's expecting,' she added darkly. 'I think there's something else, you know . . .'

Mrs Rose dropped her parcel of meat into her basket. 'Well, let's hope she 'as more luck with this baby,' she said. 'She's 'ad a bad time losing those last ones.'

Mrs Jones sniffed. 'Well, bad luck comes to all of us, whatever our station in life,' she muttered. 'Money won't stop you getting ill health.'

'That's true, Pat,' returned Mrs Rose with a warning sharpness in her voice. 'But, you know, them Turners are a decent family, and I wouldn't wish the death of a child on anyone.'

As Mrs Jones was silenced by her friend, little Annie Turner walked up Kentish Town Road clutching the heavy white parcel to her chest. Her freckled face was set in an expression of intense seriousness. She was thrilled that she had been allowed to go to the butcher's on her own that morning, though she was sorry that it was because her mother had not felt up to going herself. Now, at last, her mother considered her old enough to do the errand by herself without being accompanied by Jack or Clara.

Jack was with his friends and Clara had gone with their father that morning to his office at the piano factory in Camden. He had to sort out some papers. Clara always jumped at the chance to go to the factory on Saturday mornings. While her father worked, Clara was allowed to play on the newly finished pianos, freshly tuned and about to be shipped off to the showrooms the following Monday. She liked to be the first person to play a serious tune on any new piano. She liked to make a first impression on the instrument before it made its way into the world. And as far as her father was concerned, the only time Clara could stay out of trouble was when she played the piano.

Annie pushed a stray lock of hair out of her eyes and smiled at the shopkeepers as she passed. She was feeling so pleased with herself that she did not even feel shy as she normally did. She felt so good and strong that when the little worry about her mother rose in her mind, she was able to push it back again for later. She was determined to enjoy herself for now. Feeling quite bold, she waved to the people on the tram as it trundled up the road towards Parliament Hill and Highgate.

Passing the jewellers, Annie stopped to look in at the window. Her mother had warned her not to dawdle but she could not resist having a quick look at the jewellery, especially the engagement rings – diamonds, with rubies, sapphires or emeralds, twinkling in the sunlight.

With a dreamy look on her face she held her left hand out in front of her, her fingers spread, and turned it one way and then the other. Just looking at the rich blue of the sapphires made her feel warm deep inside her.

'He'll be a lucky man what buys one of those rings for you, luv.'

Annie turned to see Mr Hamilton the stationer standing outside his shop. His bald head was shining in the sun. He had lovely big brown eyes and had probably been a very handsome man in his youth, her mother once told her. He was always friendly to Annie, who thought of him as a kind man.

Annie glanced at him and then looked away, wishing that the blush creeping over her cheeks and neck would disappear.

'You need more paper for your drawings, Annie? There's more for you here whenever you want.'

Annie loved to draw. One day she was determined to be a famous artist. Mr Hamilton provided her with scraps of paper and charcoal whenever he had some going. 'Thank you,' she whispered, staring down at her feet. 'I've got plenty for the moment.'

Mr Hamilton nodded. 'That's fine then,' he said, 'but make sure you let me know when you're running out. We got to encourage the next generation, ain't we? You never know, you could be as famous as that Picasso.'

Annie didn't know what he was talking about. She smiled sweetly at him and sidled away up the road towards home.

Annie decided to walk up Leverton Street on her way back. Unlike most of the other houses in the neighbourhood, the houses in the southern end of Leverton Street were in fact small cottages, with two rooms upstairs and two down. A few had two families squeezed into their small space but most of them housed one family. If the family wasn't too large or if finances demanded, the front room was often let out to a lodger to help with the rent.

Annie loved the colours of the Leverton Street houses, the pale blues, soft pinks and primrose yellows. Although mostly sooty and peeling now, they seemed like fairies' homes. She did not know that these pastel hues were first painted on by earlier Irish inhabitants homesick for the Emerald Isle and the small southern towns they had left behind.

When Annie turned into the street it was jumping with life. Some boys were playing football in the cobbled road, while others were standing in a circle passing a cigarette around. The younger girls were skipping and playing hopscotch, while their older sisters sat on the walls gossiping and giving each other advice about their hairstyles. Occasionally one girl would cast a critical look at one of the boys across the road, lean over and whisper a comment to her friend.

Annie could see Jack and some of his friends from the

grammar school leaning against the wall and swapping
cigarette cards. Jack looked away quickly when he saw his
little sister. Annie shrugged. Now twelve years old, Jack
always disowned her when he was with his pals.

Just then she caught sight of Maudie Sprackling's vast
backside in her doorway. Clad in a floral dress, Maudie's
bottom wobbled and quivered as she scrubbed at her
doorstep with the scouring stone, just as she had been
doing when Annie had passed thirty minutes earlier. She
was doing it several times a day now.

'Maudie's going mad,' Clara had said only that morning. At ten years of age, Clara knew everything about
everyone. 'She's never been the same since her Fred ran off
with Connie Smith.'

Annie felt sorry for Maudie. According to Dolly
Pritchett, moon-faced Maudie had been unable to have
babies and her husband had hated her for not giving him a
son. He had run away one night about eighteen months
ago with the Smith girl from across the street. It had
caused a lot of bad feeling at the time, and some people
even blamed Maudie, which Annie couldn't understand. It
must have been awful for her to go on living right near the
Smiths after that. Annie thought she might have moved
away, but she hadn't.

Poor Maudie now stayed at home, eating and getting
fat, when she wasn't at her job cleaning for the doctor's
family in Highgate. When she wasn't eating, she would get
out her scrubbing brush and have a go at her doorstep for
hours on end.

'She'll scrub it clean away if she goes on at that rate,'
Clara had giggled.

On the other side of the road Mrs Whelan was washing

her front window. Her house was always spotless inside and out. It stood out like a beacon in a street where most of the other houses had not seen a lick of paint for years and buddleia bushes sprouted out of the brickwork. Mrs Whelan liked everything to be clean – she even washed the stucco on the front wall of her house up to shoulder height.

Annie always thought it funny that Mrs Whelan should live next door to the Smith family. With its broken windows and front door falling off its hinges, the Smiths' house was easily the tattiest in the street. Sometimes Mrs Whelan seemed to be itching to give the front of the Smith house a good scrub, too, while she was at it.

Most of the Whelan children were as tight-lipped and proper as their mother, and her husband, a tax inspector, was just a little mouse of a man. He rarely uttered a word. It seemed a miracle that Mrs Whelan had ever produced a daughter like Marie.

Marie was Clara's best friend, and that said a lot about both of them, Annie always thought.

'Hey, Annie!'

Looking up, Annie saw Kitty Challen waving at her.

'Come and 'ave a look at this stag beetle.'

Kitty and her twin sister Betty were poking and prodding at something in the gutter. The hems of their grubby frocks brushed against the dirty cobbles as they crouched in the road.

'Yeah, 'e's a real fighter!' Betty Challen held up the stick with the angry beetle balanced on the end. ''E's got an ugly mug, all right. Looks like Kevin Smith.'

The twins giggled in unison, shaking their blonde heads.

Annie waved. She knew the twins from school and had always been intrigued by their identical looks.

The twins smiled and waved their strange hands. They both had webbing between their fingers and toes, like little frogs. It was because they had been born six weeks too early, Clara had told Annie with great authority.

Annie turned right into Falkland Road and set off for her house. Annie's family lived in one of the tall terraced houses at the end, bang opposite the Methodist church and school. The Turners had the whole house. Annie's father had been born there, as had his father before him. There was lots of space. Everyone had their own bedroom. There was a fine dining room on the ground floor and a large parlour on the first floor next to Frank Turner's study.

Until they died a few years before, Annie's grandparents had lived in these two rooms on the first floor, but when they died, the family spread out freely. The front room on the first floor became the parlour, and then Annie's mother turned the downstairs front room, which was formerly the parlour, into a dining room. 'It's good to have different rooms for different purposes,' she would say.

But the Turner children were aware that theirs was probably the only household north of Leighton Road that had a room solely for eating in. Certainly their living space seemed luxurious compared with what most of their neighbours enjoyed, since Frank, who worked as a clerk in the piano factory in Camden, earned a good enough living to support them all. And although his wife would certainly have liked to follow their friends to the healthier areas of Hampstead or Highgate, Frank Turner wanted to stay where his roots were. 'What was good enough for my father and his father before him is good enough for me. I wouldn't feel at home any place else,' he would say with a light laugh and a sparkle in his fierce blue eyes. 'I'm part of Kentish Town and Kentish Town is part of me.'

When Annie got home she found her mother in the hallway leaning against the piano. A hand supported her back. Her normally serene face was twisted up in pain.

'Annie, put that meat in the ice box,' Grace Turner said weakly. 'The baby's coming. You'll have to run quickly and get Dolly to help. Ask her to get the midwife.'

Annie stared at her mother in horror. Grace Turner was breathing quickly through her mouth like Mr Garcia's horse when it was exhausted. Then her face was screwed up in agony. Annie backed against the door.

Suddenly her mother's face relaxed again. She smiled feebly at her daughter. 'It's all right, love, don't be scared. It's always like this. Now quick, get Dolly, will you?'

Throwing the joint of meat into the ice box in the kitchen, Annie ran down to the corner to Dolly Pritchett's house.

Dolly was peeling potatoes on the table in her kitchen, a huge black cauldron bubbling on the stove behind her. On the floor against the wall, two large baskets of washing waited to be ironed by Dolly and then returned to their owners. Dolly cleaned for Grace Turner five days a week but she also took in washing and ironing for most of the neighbourhood.

Dolly was a vast woman, as wide as a doorway. She had given birth to six children, all of whom had lived, and now they were producing many grandchildren on whom Dolly doted. Her hands and feet were the size of a man's. Her long greasy grey hair was tied up in a bun around her head, and when she walked she swayed from side to side, like Mr Garcia on his way back from the pub.

'Hello, cock,' Dolly said when she saw Annie.

'Mother says the baby's coming and to get the midwife.'

Dolly sniffed. 'We don't need the midwife,' she said. 'Look what happened the last few times the midwife's been. Fat lot of good that did your mother, eh? Besides, the midwife'll be out on her nursings, seeing all the new mums. She probably won't have time to get here.'

Taking off her pinafore, Dolly undid the roller towel from the wall and slung it over her shoulder. 'Come on, then, let's go.' She lumbered out of the house like a moving mountain, with little Annie following behind.

Annie's mother was halfway up the stairs and leaning against the wall. 'It's coming, Dolly,' she gasped. 'I have to get to bed. I hope the midwife'll be here soon.'

Dolly turned to Annie. 'Off you go now, Annie,' said Dolly, giving the girl a pat on the bottom. 'Go out and play. And if you see that father of yours coming home from work, tell him to stay away. He's going to have another mouth to feed by the end of the afternoon. It's quite early by my reckoning but not as much as you was. I'll sort things out here . . .'

Annie watched Dolly help her mother upstairs. She was still hovering in the doorway when Dolly came down again to get a bucket of water from the scullery.

'Off you go, Annie,' called Dolly, lumbering upstairs again. 'Your mum's all right.'

Her mother didn't sound all right at all. Every now and then Annie could hear a howl of misery coming from her parents' bedroom on the second floor. Each time she shuddered. Her mother sounded like an animal.

She sat down on the front doorstep thinking about what

it would be like to have a baby brother or sister. She hoped that this one wasn't going to die like the other two. Annie could just about remember the last time. She could remember her mother sitting in bed and crying. Annie had put her arm around her, as far as it went. She remembered crying but nobody put their arms round her. Nobody seemed to know why those babies died.

The noise from upstairs was beginning to disturb her now. Annie could hear her mother moaning loudly. Then she'd hear Dolly's soothing voice, murmuring to her.

Biting her lip, Annie crept upstairs. She stopped on the landing and peered through the half-open door.

Dolly's huge body blocked much of the view but Annie could see that she was tying the roller towel to the bed rail.

'Pull on this, love,' she was saying. Annie watched as Dolly stroked her mother's back rhythmically up and down .

Her mother was lying on her side on the bed, which was now covered with a mackintosh and newspapers . Annie saw a flash of bare leg. Her mother was breathing loudly and panting. 'Oh dear God,' she groaned. 'Jesus Christ have mercy.'

Annie was astonished. Her mother never swore.

Every now and then Annie's mother let out a low moan and a deep throaty grunt. She was pulling on her roller towel, which was quite taut. Annie watched in awe as the bed rail slowly bent under the strain.

Dolly was bending low over Annie's mother's legs. 'That's it, lass,' she said in a low voice. 'You can push now. Push!'

As her mother let out a low growl which rumbled on,

growing louder and louder until it turned into the most terrifying, blood-curdling scream, Annie shot down the stairs, out of the back door and into the quiet safety of the back garden.

Most of the gardens in Falkland Road were just scrubby bits of open ground, bare patches of hard earth with weeds taking over wherever they could. They were hardly used except for hanging out the washing or keeping a few chickens, as Mr Spratt did next door. Further up the road, Mr Garcia, the rag-and-bone man, kept his old horse in his back garden.

There were few flowers anywhere, for only the hardiest plants could thrive in the filthy London air. And the air in Kentish Town was particularly dirty because of the trains roaring through, belching their black fumes into the sky. It was easy to see why people had to wash their windows all the time – or why they didn't bother. It was a losing battle.

The gardens were divided by low, tumbledown brick walls along which many of the local children liked to scramble. Next door to the Turners, Mr Spratt's chickens scratched around in the dirt and clucked softly, while Marmaduke the cockerel strutted proudly up and down. The chickens weren't laying very well at the moment, Mr Spratt had told Annie the day before. That was too bad, seeing as when Mr Spratt wasn't having one of his 'turns' he was very generous with his chicken eggs. Eating those eggs made up for being woken up by Marmaduke at the crack of dawn.

The Turners' garden was quite different from all the other gardens nearby. The walls were their full height, straight and well pointed, and the garden itself was nicely laid out with a small lawn and narrow borders containing the toughest kinds of shrubs and flowers that could withstand the most difficult growing conditions.

Annie could not bear to think about what was happening to her mother at that moment. Trying to concentrate on the garden and its plants, she pushed past the speckled laurel bush and carefully picked her way round the prickly red berberis which sprawled across the crazy-paving path. Down one side of the lawn, the London Pride was in flower, its tiny pink blooms thrusting stiffly upwards as if competing with the blue bearded irises which had just begun to unfold their soft petals.

At the bottom of the garden was a shed where the gardening tools were kept, and a beautifully crafted wooden hut where Rabbit lived. Annie's father had originally trained as a cabinet maker and had, with loving care, built the hutch for Annie's eighth birthday, the January before. Rabbit was a large black-and-white buck, and he was Annie's friend.

Still fighting back the images of her mother's distress, Annie opened the door of Rabbit's hutch and lifted him out. He never bit her and always seemed pleased to see her.

Annie held Rabbit close and buried her face in his grubby soft fur. His whiskers tickled her bare arms as she held him to her breast. She looked up and around her, at the tall spire of the Methodist church across the road, at the run-down backs of the houses overlooking the gardens. Because it was a Saturday and a fine morning, there was a lot of noise out here as well. Annie could hear people shouting and squabbling through the open windows. Someone was playing an Irish jig on a fiddle and elsewhere a child was screaming.

Annie hugged Rabbit and sighed. She looked up at the

houses in Dunollie Place, which ran at a right-angle up to the gardens. There in the end house, as she had been for the past week, was the little girl staring out of the top floor window. Her sad face peered down at the world below. She had large, widely spaced eyes and short bangs. Annie gave her a little wave but the girl pulled away and disappeared behind the curtain.

Annie sighed. How complicated the world is, she thought. I want to be that girl's friend but she doesn't want to be mine. Yesterday a baby was in Mother's tummy and today it's going to be outside it. Annie suddenly remembered that Dolly had said that the baby was coming early. Did that mean it would also have webbed fingers and toes like the Challen twins? But then why did Dolly say that the baby was not as early as Annie had been? She'd never heard that before. She'd never been told that she had been born early.

There was no holding back those thoughts any longer. The image of her mother writhing in pain flashed before her eyes and the sound of her mother's awful cries rang in her ears. She shuddered again. Well, if that's what having children did, she didn't want to have any, ever . . .

Yet as she thought that, she had in her mind's eye the image of poor Maudie Sprackling scrubbing her doorstep hour after hour just because she didn't have any children. No, Annie didn't want to be like that, either.

CHAPTER 2

The Brooch

THE BABY WAS A little boy named Bobby. He had a crumpled face and tiny black curls squashed flat against his head. He lay in his crib for most of the day. When he was awake, he made strange fluid movements with his hands and sweet snuffling noises through his nose. When he was asleep, he was silent and still. He hardly moved, apart from the slight rising of his chest as he breathed and the gentle pursing of his lips as though he were dreaming of sucking at his mother's soft breast.

Annie loved to sit and watch her baby brother asleep. He was so small and helpless. Then she began to draw him. Hour after hour she would spend trying to capture Bobby's minute features with her stick of charcoal on the paper so kindly supplied by Mr Hamilton. Annie was a naturally talented freehand sketcher, but hours of self-motivated practice had developed the talent she had been born with to an impressive level. Her ability to capture the world on paper was the one thing in her life that Annie felt sure about. She knew she was good at that, if nothing else.

Grace was confined to bed for ten days to recover from the birth. Dressed in a broderie anglaise nightgown, in her younger daughter's eyes she had never seemed prettier. Nor had she seemed so happy, with her skin glowing and eyes sparkling.

Grace was a handsome woman with a strong, slender frame and lean, well-shaped limbs. Her pretty round face was framed with soft, wavy blonde hair which she wore in a short bob. Her eyes were such a dark brown that the pupils were lost in them. Occasionally they gave off a slightly distracted expression, as though her thoughts were elsewhere, but usually they were alert and, like her thoughts, fully focused on her family.

She was always gentle and even-tempered with her family. In those early years, before her circumstances changed, she had endless patience with her children and was always ready to encourage and praise, or listen and advise. Annie loved her dearly.

Grace was regarded as a good mother, even by those who criticized her for appearing stand-offish. She was scrupulously fair to each child – if one had a boiled sweet, the others did too – and she was always available, always there to wipe a salty tear from a red cheek or kiss better a scraped knee. She went out of her way to spend time with her children. As an only child herself, she worried about what it must be like to compete for a parent's attention. She wanted all of her children to feel special in their own right.

During that lying-in period after the birth, Dolly came in every day for several hours. She did her usual cleaning but also the shopping and cooking for the family, teasing Frank good-naturedly when he came in from work, and serving up tea for the family at the kitchen table.

'That baby's the spittin' image of you, when you was a nipper, Mr Turner,' she said, placing on the table a dish of burnt sausages and over-crisp bacon. In spite of their familiarity, Dolly always made it clear that she knew her place in the Turner household. She shuffled back across the room to get the mashed potatoes from the oven. 'I remember those exact same curls when you was born.'

Frank and his children sat around the pine table. Earlier, Frank had opened the window above the sink to let in some cool air. The newly installed black boiler in the corner of the room was very efficient at providing hot water on tap all through the year but it made the kitchen very hot on warmer days.

At the sight of Dolly's lumpy mashed potatoes, Annie's big sister Clara wrinkled her nose and grimaced.

Frank laughed. 'And I've still got those curls, Dolly!'

'Well, you could say that,' returned Dolly with a smirk, 'but there are fewer of them and those that are left have to share yer head with some grey newcomers. Yer dad had the same curls, too.'

Annie raised her eyebrows with interest. She loved to hear about her ancestors. She still had a clear memory of her grandfather sitting by the coal fire in the room upstairs and talking about the old days. She could see the white stubble that had appeared on his chin in the evenings, and the network of blue veins on the backs of his bony white hands, and hear his ancient croaking voice.

'He was a fine man, yer dad, in his heyday,' added Dolly. She stood nearly upright, leaning against the table with a dreamy look in her eye. 'Good folk, they was, yer parents. Always helping people out when they needed it.'

Frank turned to Annie. 'Now, my grandfather, your

great-grandfather, watched this house being built. He
remembered the land being cleared and the walls going
up. He used to have picnics in the field where our garden is.
Imagine that! He could remember when Kentish Town was
just a village on a hill three miles out of London, and
beyond were woods.'

'My grandfather used to tell me about swimming in the
Fleet River as a boy,' chimed in Dolly, not to be outdone.
'He used to catch fish where Anglers Lane is now. That
was before it turned into a disgusting sewer where everyone chucked their rubbish.' She nodded and patted Frank
on the shoulder. 'You know what I like best about you
Turners? It's that you've always stayed here in Kentish
Town when you could easily have taken yourselves off to a
better place, especially since you've done so well for
yourselves.'

Frank laughed. 'Well, who'd ever want to leave old
Kentish Town? It's the only place to live, as far as I'm
concerned.'

The Turner family had deep roots in Kentish Town.
Frank's great-grandfather, Caleb Turner, had come to
London in the 1850s. Caleb was the son of a farm labourer
in Devon but he had been apprenticed to the village car-
penter and went into cabinet making. In the mid-1850s,
with his young wife and son, he moved to London in
search of work. He found there was a good living to be
made in the burgeoning piano-making industry which was
centred in Camden. His son followed in his footsteps, as
did *his* son, Frank's father. Born in 1898, Frank was also
apprenticed to a cabinet maker, and went into employment at the piano factory. But he was an ambitious young
man and wanted to do more than his ancestors before him.

He studied hard at night school to pass the necessary exams to be able to move to the management side of the piano-making business.

Frank was not well-travelled so he could not compare his surroundings with many other places, but Kentish Town always seemed to him to represent the diversity of human life. Unlike his wife, he loved the contrasts that were always before his eyes – the rich villas just streets away from the shabbiest hovels, the dirt and filth of the railway just yards from the fertile fields and sweet-smelling woods of Hampstead Heath.

Frank was a sociable man, and a caring one, too. He was not rich but, thanks to his father, he owned the house he lived in and he was certainly richer than most of his neighbours. It was not uncommon for Frank to reach into his pocket to help someone in need. And he had tried to bring up his children to believe in two important rules: to educate oneself to the best of one's abilities, and to help anyone in a less fortunate position than oneself.

Dolly started to pull on a cardigan ready to go home and leave the family to their tea. She had to try hard to get her sleeves over her fat lower arms. 'Mind you, I'm not sure that Mrs Turner always feels that way. I think she'd like to be higher up the hill. Well now, I'm off. Bye, all!'

With that, Dolly lumbered out of the room and down the hall and, as always, slammed the front door so hard on her way out that the whole house shuddered in her wake.

Bobby was an easy baby and settled enough for Grace to get on with her household tasks as she wished. He fed well and slept well. Everyone described him as a 'good' baby, but the label made Grace laugh dismissively. 'How a little baby can be described as good or bad is beyond me,' she would say. 'But I am glad I have an angel,' she always added with a smile.

Soon life at Number Forty-five with the new baby seemed perfectly normal, and Annie could not remember what it had been like before Bobby was born.

One evening, when Bobby was about eight weeks old, the Turners had just finished their tea. Much to the relief of the family, Grace had resumed doing the cooking so they were now spared Dolly's offerings. That night they had eaten a good meal of pork chops and fried potatoes, followed by stewed prunes and custard.

Clara had already washed the dishes and it was Annie's turn to dry them. She handled the plates carefully but her mind was elsewhere, as it so often was when she did routine tasks. Her thoughts were off in a fantasy of colour and form as she conjured up the next picture she wanted to paint with her new poster paints. As she placed the plates and dishes in the cupboards and sideboard, Frank went outside to fill up the coal scuttles for the boiler and fireplaces. After clearing up the cooking pans, Grace had gone upstairs to her bedroom to give Bobby his evening feed. Jack was in the dining room bent over his homework, his schoolbooks spread out across the table, while Clara practised her scales on the piano. She was waiting for her father to join her playing some duets.

Annie went out into the garden to feed Rabbit and when she returned her father and Clara had already launched into a series of lively tunes.

Annie sat on the stairs and listened to the music for a while. She looked at her handsome father with his broad, smiling face under that head of black curls. Beyond him sat Clara with her thick blonde hair falling down her long straight back as her slender fingers moved gracefully over the piano keys. With their short, straight noses and strong chins, their silhouettes were strikingly similar. They were instantly recognizable to any stranger as father and daughter.

The piano notes rose up the stairwell and filled the house. Annie held her chin in her hands and smiled, quietly tapping her foot and nodding her head in time with the music.

Whenever Frank and Clara played, Annie longed to join in and sing joyfully at the top of her voice. But she knew she could not without ruining it for everyone. She was completely tone deaf. It was so unfair that she should be the only one not to be able to sing a note. Her mother had a sweet voice and even Jack, when he could be persuaded to join in, could hold a tune well.

Perhaps Bobby will be the same as me, Annie thought hopefully.

She climbed up the stairs to her parents' bedroom and peered in through the door. Her mother was in the far corner sitting on the low nursing chair. She was wearing a long dark skirt and a soft cotton blouse which, as she was still feeding Bobby, was half-unbuttoned. Grace was trying to write something with one hand, while Bobby, supported by the other arm, nursed quietly at her breast.

She looked up and smiled warmly at Annie, her eyes glowing with maternal love. 'I'm making a list of things we have to do for Bobby's christening,' she said. 'The vicar's coming tomorrow to discuss the arrangements.'

Annie stepped into the room with an eager smile. She loved to plan things. 'Can I help?'

Grace held out her arm. 'Come and sit next to me here and we'll make the list together.'

Annie sat down on the floor next to her mother and leaned against her legs. For a few moments Grace stroked her brown hair absent-mindedly. 'You're a good girl, Annie,' she murmured.

A warm feeling spread through Annie's body. Praise from her mother meant so much to her. It seemed to fill a space inside her and affirm her as a real person. Grace often praised her children, and equally, too, yet Annie never felt as confident as Jack and Clara seemed to be. However hard she tried to dismiss it, she always had a strange nagging feeling deep inside her that she was different.

'Now, perhaps we ought to look at what Bobby will be wearing. I wonder if you can reach the christening gown. It's at the top of the wardrobe.'

Annie leaped up. 'I'll get it!' Going over to the high mahogany wardrobe in the corner, she pulled open the heavy doors. Then she dragged a chair across the room and climbed onto it.

'There's a big white box at the back of the top shelf there. Just bring it down and we'll open it here. Are you sure you're tall enough?'

Annie reached up. She could just see the white cardboard box at the back of the shelf. It was surrounded by parcels wrapped in tissue paper – her mother's best woollen cardigans put away in mothballs for the summer months, along with the precious Fair Isle caps and mittens knitted long ago by her grandmother.

She could barely reach the white box with her out-stretched arms. Her fingertips brushed it and the box moved slightly. She lunged at it again and the box fell off the shelf and on to the floor. The long christening gown spilled out of its wrapping of tissue paper and spread over her feet.

'Oh, it's beautiful!' exclaimed Annie, picking up the soft white garment and holding it up in front of her. It was made of the finest silk with delicate smocking across the chest and along the cuffs. It was long, and lined with several cotton layers.

'My mother made that gown twelve years ago when Jack was born. You were the last one to wear it . . .'

Grace's voice had suddenly gone soft. Tears were flooding her dark brown eyes.

Annie walked over and placed her hand on her mother's shoulder. She knew that her mother was thinking about the two babies who never got to wear the gown. 'Bobby'll look very handsome in it,' she said quietly.

'Now, let me clear up this mess.' She started to pick up the cardboard box and the tissue paper the gown was wrapped in. Then she noticed something else. A small object wrapped in tissue paper had also fallen out. She picked it up and opened the paper. 'Oh, Mother, what's this?'

In her open palm lay a large brooch, a circle of diamonds and sapphires set in heavy gold. The gems twinkled as she held them up to the light. 'It's beautiful,' she whispered in awe, holding it out to her mother. 'I didn't know you had anything like this!'

The expression on her mother's face made her stop short. The look of anguish was one Annie would never forget. Grace was frowning, staring at the brooch. Her mouth was open, but no words came out.

'What's the matter, Mother?' asked Annie, suddenly afraid.

'Put it back!' Grace forced out her words in a hoarse whisper. 'Put it back where it was! I don't want to see it!' Her lips had paled. She looked almost frightened. 'Please.'

Annie hastily wrapped up the brooch and reached on tiptoe to put it back on the wardrobe shelf.

By now Grace had collected herself. 'I'm sorry, love,' she said. 'I didn't mean to shout at you.'

'But where is the brooch from? Where did you get it?' Annie felt dizzy with questions.

But her mother was shaking her head. 'It's from another life. It was given to me by someone, by the person my parents used to work for. You know my father was the farm manager for some people in the country. They were always kind to my parents. The lady gave me the brooch.'

'But why did she give it to you? She must have liked you a lot.'

Grace sighed and looked down at the floor. 'She just wanted to give it to me,' she replied vaguely.

'But it's beautiful,' Annie persisted. 'Why don't you ever wear it?'

Grace looked back up at her with an expression Annie had never seen before. She looked as though she were wincing in pain. 'Sometimes you can't take things from one life into another one,' Grace said simply. 'It's too dangerous.' Then she turned to stroke Bobby's head. 'Look, Bobby's going to have curls just like his father's,' she said, making it clear that she was changing the subject.

The baby had finished feeding and fallen asleep with his head back and mouth open in a contented stupor. Grace buttoned up her dress and placed the baby in his crib beside the big brass bed.

'Thank you for getting the gown out for me, Annie,' said Grace. 'Now it's time for you to have a wash and go to bed. You've got school tomorrow.'

As Annie climbed into bed half an hour later, her head was spinning with her mother's words. What did she mean, another life? And why can't you bring things from one life to another? And most of all, why was it dangerous? Dangerous in what way?

She lay in bed thinking of that dazzling jewel and trying to work it all out. By the time she finally drifted into sleep, she had reached the obvious conclusion that her mother must have stolen the brooch from the lady who was her father's boss. Why else would she hide it away?

It was not long before Annie did make friends with the little girl she had seen in the window of the house in Dunollie Place. The very next week, in fact, the girl had turned up at Annie's school in Islip Street. She had come after the register, and Annie had watched as the newcomer, now bright red in the face with embarrassment, was ushered into the classroom. She was thin and gawky, with freckles on her nose, but her long face had a pleasant expression, and Annie was impressed by the thick brown plait which fell straight down her back.

As if sensing Annie's interest in the newcomer, Miss Cole, the teacher, asked Annie to look after the shy little girl and show her round the school. Annie had smiled in the friendliest way she could and patted the hard wooden chair beside her to indicate that the girl, who was called Tilly Banham, should sit down.

In no time, Annie and Tilly were best friends. Annie was Tilly's partner when they had to team up for lessons, and played hopscotch or cat's cradle with her in the playground during break time.

Tilly was a quiet girl and did not often speak unless spoken to. But she was quick and clever at school, and watched everything that went on around her. She was happy to have just one friend in Annie, and Annie, who had been bossed around by her big brother and sister for all her life, appreciated the way Tilly looked up to her for guidance.

Annie told Tilly about her family – her new baby brother, big brother Jack, and sister Clara who was two years ahead at school and who was always getting herself into trouble. Indeed, as if to make the point, that same day Clara was given a double detention for throwing a bucket of water out of the science room window into the playground below. Everyone knew that Clara Turner was the naughtiest girl in the school. But they also knew that she was clever. That helped her get away with behaviour that would have got most of them expelled.

Tilly confided to Annie that she was an only child and her parents had lost all their money when her father's business collapsed six months before. Now her father was out of work. They used to live in a big house in Highgate, she said, but her father's debts had been so big that they had to sell their house and move into rented accommodation in Kentish Town. She hinted that her parents were both unhappy. 'And they don't like having to live in Kentish Town,' she added. 'They think it's a slum.'

Annie sniffed. 'There's nothing wrong with Kentish Town,' she said. 'Lots of people here go way back to the time when it was the countryside. Sometimes I pretend it's still the countryside, too. Lots of nice people live here, you'll see.'

'Oh, I like Kentish Town,' Tilly said hastily. 'And I've met you.'

Annie smiled. 'You'll have to come to my house and meet Rabbit,' she said. 'But in the meantime, I can send you messages from my back garden.' Together, the girls devised a sign language so that they could communicate between their houses.

Annie and Tilly began walking home together from school. Annie was pleased not to have to walk with Clara at the moment because her older sister had recently been in the habit of teasing her by making jokes about how different Annie looked from the rest of the family. Only last week Clara had said that Annie had probably been adopted at birth from an orphanage. For some reason her sister's teasing was much more upsetting than usual.

When she could not bear it any longer, Annie had gone to her father in floods of tears and been relieved by his response.

Frank laughed. 'Nothing ever changes, does it! My older brother used to tease me by telling me that I was a changeling – found under a tree on Hampstead Heath. It drove me wild, even though I knew it couldn't be true. I was the spitting image of my father from the day I was born, so I knew it was nonsense but it still upset me.'

Annie frowned. 'But that's the point. I don't look like anyone.'

Frank smiled and put his arms around her. She loved

the smell of his clothes. 'I think you look rather like my grandmother,' he said. 'Your genes have just skipped two generations, that's all.' Frank ruffled her hair. 'You have to get tougher,' he said, 'and ignore the silly things that Clara says. She's just trying to get you worked up. Older brothers and sisters always do that.'

Annie smiled sheepishly. 'Thank you, Dad. I'll remember that.'

With Tilly as her friend Annie was able to steer clear of Clara after school. They walked home slowly, prolonging their time together and talking over the events of that day at school.

One day the two girls were walking up Kentish Town Road when they saw old Mrs Horder and her son Danny standing outside the baker's shop.

Mrs Horder was a tiny little woman with white hair. She always wore long black dresses, and had done since her husband had died a few years before. Danny was her only child. And he was still like a child even though he was at least twenty years old. He was a big boy and towered over his mother, whose hand he always held when they were out in the street together. He seemed to have little control over his head because it was always flopping about on top of his wide shoulders. His thick tongue hung halfway down his chin and this made him dribble constantly. He could not talk but instead he communicated with a series of grunts and snorts.

Some of the local children thought Danny was scary but Annie was not afraid of him. Her mother had told her that there was something wrong with his mind, which meant that he would never grow up to be able to look after himself. She said it was because Mr and Mrs Horder had been nearly fifty when Danny was born. It was sad, and he needed a lot of looking after, which was even harder for Mrs Horder now that her husband was not around to help any more.

As the girls approached, Mrs Horder waved towards Annie. Danny was grunting and seemed to be pulling away from his mother. 'Oh, Annie, dear, I wonder if you can help me . . . I need to go into the baker's to choose a cake for my neighbour's birthday. Danny is too frightened to go into the shop. Something's upset him and I can't persuade him to come in. Would you stay here with him while I pop inside? He'll be quite happy to stay with you and I won't be a minute.'

Annie smiled. 'Of course, Mrs Horder. We'll just wait until you come out. Hello, Danny.' She smiled at the great hulk of a youth who was staring mournfully at the pavement.

Danny grunted, while Tilly, who had only seen Danny from a distance before, stared at him in wonder. With his thick black hair and coarse features, he reminded her of one of the ogres in the Grimm's fairy tales she had been reading. But since Annie wasn't afraid, she tried not to be either.

Mrs Horder was in the shop for a while. There were few shoppers about as the pair waited outside with their charge. Then Annie noticed two scruffy boys coming up the road towards them. They were not from her school but she recognized them anyway, as members of the Torriano gang, which had been causing some trouble in the neighbourhood recently – stealing washing off the washing lines and tipping dustbins upside-down outside people's front doors. The Torriano gang was a group of boys from Torriano School in Torriano Avenue. They were renowned for their toughness and wild ways. The leader of the gang was Roger Knight, who was twelve, and known as the worst tearaway in the neighbourhood.

The boys had seen her, too, and started nudging each other as they approached.

The bigger one started to jeer. 'Look at the idiot boy, then, yer ought to be in a zoo!'

The other boy laughed and together they began to chant: 'Zoo time for Danny, zoo time for Danny.'

Danny was looking quite distressed. He scowled and shook his head violently, then squealed as he backed away. Annie had to grab him by the arm to stop him stepping back off the kerb into the road.

'Go away! Leave him alone,' she yelled. 'He can't help it!' Her fists were clenched tight as she stood her ground.

Now the boys turned on her.

'Ooh, listen to her, then. Talk posh, don't we? You're a hoity-toity one, you are!'

The bigger boy reached over and lifted Annie's skirt. 'Got clean knickers on, then, have we?'

The boys both roared with laughter as Annie danced around the pavement trying to stop them lifting up her skirt again.

'Go away!' she screamed. She looked around, hoping that a grown-up would come and help.

'Go away!' shouted Tilly. She chewed the knuckle of her thumb and jiggled up and down anxiously.

'Go away,' the boys chimed back at her, circling them menacingly.

Suddenly there was a shout. Looking up, Annie saw her brother Jack running towards them.

'Shove off!' he yelled at the boys. They turned and ran up the road. 'You're all right now,' Jack shouted at Annie as he ran past, 'I'm going to get them!'

Annie watched with wide-eyed admiration as Jack ran up the road after her tormentors. The smaller boy darted off down Holmes Road while the bigger one ran on. Jack followed the bigger boy. With his longer legs, he easily caught up with him and tackled his ankles. The boy fell heavily onto the pavement.

Although she was fifty yards away, Annie could see Jack turn the boy over on his back and pound him hard in the chest. The boy was shouting and begging for mercy, but Jack would not stop. 'This'll teach you to pick on people weaker than you,' he hissed. Grabbing the boy by the ears, he dragged him across to the gutter and rubbed his face in a pile of fresh horse droppings in the road.

Jack then stood up triumphantly. Breathing hard, he tossed back his hair, his face red from the exertion.

He sauntered down to join Annie and Tilly by the baker's shop. Mrs Horder was just emerging with her cake in a large cardboard box.

The boy had got to his feet and stood with his hands on his hips defiantly. He yelled down the road. 'Get yer big brother to help out, eh? Well, we can all play at that game!' Then he shook his fist and ran off up Leighton Road towards Torriano Avenue.

'Who is that boy?' asked Tilly. She was still shaking from the experience.

'That was Ian Knight,' replied Jack. 'His big brother is Roger, you know, the leader of the Torriano gang. I don't suppose we've heard the last of them now.'

Annie frowned. 'Thank's for helping us out, Jack,' she

said quietly, 'but don't you think you might have gone a bit far, rubbing his face in the dirt like that?'

Jack shrugged. 'Probably,' he said. 'Who knows? But he deserved it, so who cares?'

Annie and Tilly walked home in silence, each girl reliving the terrifying excitement of the incident in the high street. Annie's arms were still trembling as she turned over and over in her mind the image of Ian Knight shaking his fist at her and shouting out his threats. It scared her out of her wits. She was proud of her big brother but she was also now frightened of what Ian's big brother might do in revenge.

The Turners were regular church-goers and attended the church in Lupton Street where Bobby and all the children had been christened. The older children also attended Sunday school in the church hall. They went after breakfast for an hour before returning home to get ready to go to church with their parents. Annie rather liked Sunday school because she loved Bible stories, and nowadays she was joined in her group by Tilly, which made it all the more fun. And she loved looking after the little ones as well.

One Sunday on their way to the church, Jack mentioned that he had seen Roger hanging around in Leverton Street.

'That doesn't mean anything,' said Clara. 'His greataunt lives there. He's probably just visiting her.'

Annie shivered. It scared her even to think of Roger, the leader of the Torriano gang. She did not know what he looked like but his very name conjured up images of demons and monsters. She slipped her hand into Jack's and squeezed it hard.

Sensing his little sister's fears, Jack for once did not push her away. He squeezed her hand back and then awkwardly placed a protective arm around her.

Clara did a cartwheel on the pavement. It was perfectly timed, with her strong legs following on from her carefully positioned arms.

'Oh, Clara,' said Annie, 'don't you care if everyone can see your knickers?'

Clara tossed her blonde curls and snorted. 'No,' she laughed. 'I don't care a bean. I don't care what anyone thinks!'

Later on, at Sunday school, as Father Gregory read the story about Joseph and his coat of many colours, Annie suddenly began to feel nauseous. Sour liquid rose up in her throat and deposited itself in her mouth. She excused herself, and spat out the sourness in the sink. Then Reverend Richardson suggested that she go home early. He was a kind man and sensitive to the ways children thought and behaved. He had been a hero to the Turner children ever since the terrible day when Clara was caught pocketing the money from the collection plate, and he had been so nice about it and not made too much of a fuss.

Annie was relieved to escape from the stuffy church hall and in spite of her queasy stomach she ran all the way home without looking to the left or right. She was terrified that Roger was out there and going to get her.

But she reached her street quite safely and slowed down to walk the last few yards to her house.

Inside, the house was quiet. That was odd. Annie had expected to find her mother in the kitchen, preparing Sunday lunch.

When she went into the kitchen it became clear that her

mother had been preparing the meal. Large peeled potatoes sat covered with water in a saucepan on the stove. The carrots had been scrubbed and cut into long strips. They too sat in water ready to be boiled. The meat – a plump shoulder of lamb – had been placed in the roasting pan and covered with a blue-and-white checked dishcloth until it was time to put it in the oven. On the sideboard was a large prickly pineapple. This was for pudding, cut into thick slices and served with Carnation milk.

'Mother!' Annie called up the stairs but there was no reply.

It was creepy. Annie began to climb the stairs up to her room. As she reached the second floor, she could hear noises. Her parents were in their bedroom. She continued up the stairs.

But as she approached, the noises coming from their room frightened her. There were moans and shouts coming from her father. Peeping through the crack in the door, she saw a terrifying sight. Her parents were on the bed. Her mother was lying on her back with her father right on top of her, completely naked. He was moving up and down like the dogs in the street when they were messing around.

Annie stood transfixed by the sight and sounds. She had never seen her parents without their clothes on. Her father's white buttocks were moving up and down faster and faster. He started to mutter in time: 'Oh yes, oh yes.'

Then suddenly he collapsed on top of Annie's mother with a great groan, his body shuddering for a few moments until it stopped. He muttered something into Grace's shoulder. It was hard to make it out but Annie could have sworn he was saying 'Thank you, thank you.'

Praying that she would not be heard, Annie started to creep downstairs again. In her mind's eye she could see her father's backside and her mother's expressionless face staring up at the ceiling.

She had almost reached the bottom of the stairs when her stomach lurched. The acid rose in her throat. She let out a little moan which was quickly followed by a fountain of vomit arching out over the banisters and splattering all over the wooden floorboards in the hall. Clamping her hand over her mouth, Annie dashed into the scullery and expelled the rest of the vomit into a tin pail.

As she retched into the pail, Annie heard hurried steps on the stairs. Moments later her mother was beside her. Grace was hastily pushing wisps of hair into place.

'Annie, love, are you all right? We didn't hear you come in.'

Grace put her arm around Annie's thin bent shoulders.

Behind her mother, Annie became aware of her father's large form in the doorway. He looked both confused and concerned but Annie was too busy being sick to notice his expression or the dishevelled state of his clothes, pulled on in a hurry. 'When did you get back, love? Are you all right?'

Annie nodded and waved them both away. 'I just came in a few minutes ago,' she lied. 'I just came in and was sick. I'm sorry about the mess, Mum, I'm really sorry.'

Grace hugged her daughter and glanced back at her husband. Thank goodness Annie had not been upstairs. Frank looked as relieved as she was.

Being sick made Annie feel much better. She did not have to go to church with the family and she did not feel like eating any lunch afterwards, but by the late afternoon

she felt quite normal again. In fact, she felt well enough to
go out into the garden to play with Rabbit.

The minute she stepped outside she knew something
was wrong. The door to Rabbit's hutch was open, and the
hutch was empty.

'Rabbit!' Annie called, looking frantically around the
garden. How could he have escaped?

She found Rabbit behind the shed. He was completely
stiff and cold, lying stretched out on the earth. His head
had been bashed in, his neck broken.

Annie fell to her knees. Sobbing loudly, she hugged the
dead animal to her and rubbed her cheek across his fur.
'Please don't be dead. You can't be dead, you can't be,'
she cried. 'Please be alive!' She jumped to her feet and,
with a great howl of despair, salty tears pouring down her
cheeks, ran to the house cradling the dead rabbit in her
arms.

CHAPTER 3

❧

Maudie

GRACE HAD ALWAYS FOUND it difficult to make friends. Ever since Frank had brought her home to Kentish Town, showing her off triumphantly as his beautiful new country bride, she had always felt like an outsider.

An only child, she had been born and brought up in a small village in Sussex, at the bottom of the South Downs. She met Frank at a barn dance in Chichester. They had been introduced by an acquaintance of her parents whose son had invited a friend to stay for the weekend. He was a lad who worked with their son in London. The two young men had planned a week of sailing in Chichester harbour.

With his fierce blue eyes and head of curly black hair, Frank had literally swept the shy Grace off her feet. He monopolized her all evening, giving no one else a chance to dance with her. In no time, Frank Turner had won over Grace's parents, too. He was, everyone agreed, a natural charmer who exuded friendliness and enthusiasm. His zest for life was catching. He collected friends wherever he went, as though people were attracted to such a happy soul in the hope that some of it would rub off on them.

Frank and Grace had a brief, intense courtship, and were married in a tiny Norman church in the next village. After a week's honeymoon in Hampshire, Frank took his bride home.

Grace did not take easily to London. After breathing pure country air all her life, the dirty streets of Kentish Town disturbed her deeply at first. But her devotion to Frank was stronger than her distaste for the crowded environment, and she quickly came to appreciate the fresher air on Hampstead Heath and in Highgate Woods where, before the children came along, the young couple went for long peaceful walks every weekend.

After her solitary country upbringing, and being a self-contained creature by nature, Grace never felt much need to seek out friends of her own. She was quite happy with the company of her husband and children and the brief everyday contact she had with the local people in Kentish Town Road.

It came as a surprise to her, then, to find how much she liked Marion Banham, the mother of Annie's new friend, Tilly. For the first time in her life, Grace discovered the pleasure of sharing a common point of view with someone other than Frank.

Like Grace, Marion was in her mid-thirties, though the many grey hairs on her head made her appear older. The women got to know each other because of the girls, who spent nearly all their time together, and they soon found that there was a strong bond between them.

Marion was a tall, big-boned woman with strong features. She had brown wispy hair, a slender waist and narrow face which seemed at odds with her thickish ankles and plump arms. Ever active, she walked in long strides everywhere she went, as though she had more energy than she could ever use up in a day. She always seemed cheerful and sane, however hard life became for her. She never lost her temper or panicked, and she could always be relied upon to be sensible.

Marion was proud and strong-minded but not a snob, even though she was quite openly unhappy about her predicament. 'It's having to prop up Geoffrey that I find so hard,' she confided to Grace one day. 'He always used to be so certain about everything. Now he doesn't seem to have any sense of himself at all.'

Marion's husband had sunk into a deep gloom and did little except sit in his room all day and read books. Marion coped well, eking out a living for the family by tutoring. She never complained but it was obviously a relief for her to talk openly to her new friend about her problems. And Grace felt flattered that Marion seemed to respect her opinion about the matters they discussed, and that she trusted her enough to confide in her about her sadness at not having another baby.

'It just never happened,' she said wistfully. 'And that means Tilly is all the more precious. Mind you,' she added, 'in the present circumstances, it's probably just as well that we only have one child.'

The women talked about public affairs, too, and gossiped along with the rest of the world about the abdication of Edward VIII and his love for Mrs Wallis Simpson. 'Just imagine, 1936 will be known as the year when three kings reigned – there's George, Edward, and now his brother George.'

'He must love that Mrs Simpson very much to give up the throne for her,' remarked Grace.

Marion sniffed. 'Yes, I wonder if he'll seem like such a catch to her now,' she added drily.

Annie had been pestering her mother for weeks to allow her to take Bobby out. She helped her mother look after the baby as much as she could, feeding him his stewed carrot and scooping it off his chin and spooning it into his mouth again. She soon learned how to change his nappies, deftly folding the material into kite shapes to get the right thickness in the right places. (Her mother explained that it was done differently for girls.) She even managed to push the safety pin through the layers of towelling without pricking the baby once. And she walked around with him just as her mother did, holding the baby so that he could rest on her hip.

She loved to act as Bobby's mother. It made her feel grown-up and responsible. It made her feel like her own mother. She had always observed Grace and imitated her in admiration. She now brushed her hair in a dreamy fashion, just as her mother did, staring out of the window, lost in thought as her head moved up and down until her hair fell thick and sleek down her back. She copied the way her mother ate her food, taking small pieces and chewing slowly for a long time. She even walked like her mother, in short, springing steps, and had the habit of putting an apologetic hand up to her mouth when she laughed unexpectedly loudly.

At home, Grace had always been happy to let Annie help with Bobby. 'You're my extra pair of hands,' she would say. But in spite of Annie's pleas, Grace had never let her take the baby out in the pram on her own. She never gave a reason, simply saying, under pressure from Annie, 'Oh, when you're a little older. You can do it then . . .'

Annie would fall into a hurt and bewildered silence. Why would her mother not trust her with this one task? It was so unfair.

In the end it was Marion Banham who persuaded Grace to allow Annie and Tilly to take Bobby out in his pram. The two girls had both been pleading with her. Annie was desperate to show Bobby off to the street, and to pretend that he was hers. After all, her mother let her bath Bobby and dress him, and change his nappy. Why not let her take him out, too? The answer was always no. Until Marion intervened.

'Go on, Grace,' Marion said, 'let them take the baby out for a while. They're good girls, you can trust them to look after him.' Marion smiled at Grace. 'It'll give you a bit of a break, too. And you can't be tied to Bobby all your life, you know.'

Grace shrugged her shoulders but then nodded. 'Yes, you're right. I'm not sure I'd trust Clara to be responsible, even though she is older. But Annie's always been a sensible girl and Tilly – well, I certainly trust her.'

Annie's eyes widened with excitement as Tilly nudged her in the ribs. 'You mean we can take Bobby out in his pram? Oh, we'll be ever so careful with him, Mother, I promise.'

'Just round the block,' said Grace. 'Not across the road.'

Annie's face dropped. 'Oh, couldn't we take him down to the shops? Can't we do a bit of shopping for you, Mother?'

Grace hesitated. Then she caught a glimpse of Marion's

raised eyebrow. 'Oh, all right, then. But promise me you'll be careful crossing the roads. If you go as far as Fortess Road, you might as well go to the dairy and get me a pint of milk – and a quarter pound of butter, too.'

With the money clinking in her pocket, Annie felt she must be the happiest girl in the world as she and Tilly set off down the road pushing the huge wobbly black pram.

'Let's pretend we're the baby's parents,' said Annie solemnly. 'You can be the father.'

Annie took her friend on a tour of the neighbourhood, up Lady Margaret Road, down Countess Road, up through the top of Leverton Street and then out onto Fortess Road. As they walked, Annie pointed out the landmarks to her, and told her about all the people in the area. She told her about Mr Spratt who lived next door, who loved his chickens and who had never been the same since his wife had died, and the Fenton sisters whose fiancés had both been killed in the Great War and who had never recovered. They lived together and squabbled like children even though they were both older than Annie's parents. Once, Annie's father had found them fighting like tomcats in the hallway. They'd been arguing about who should have the wishbone from a chicken, and he had to pull them apart and calm them down before he felt it was safe to leave them alone.

The girls went to the dairy and bought a bottle of milk and a quarter pound of yellow butter cut off the slab. Clutching the few pennies left over, they went into the sweet shop next door. There, under the tolerant gaze of Mrs Barker, the shopkeeper, they stood for many minutes, agonizing over the rows and rows of sweets laid out on the counter and in the large glass jars on the shelf at the back. There were gumdrops and peardrops, bull's eyes and aniseed balls, long black coils of liquorice and stumpy orange sticks of barley sugar. What a difficult decision it was!

After much deliberation, they made their choice and finally emerged satisfied with a quarter pound of sherbet lemons.

'We have to finish them before we get home,' said Annie, popping one into her mouth. 'We're only allowed to have sweets on Saturday.'

The girls wandered slowly round the streets sucking their boiled sweets and relishing the fizzy sherbet seeping slowly out onto their tongues. 'Next time we'll get gob-stoppers,' said Annie.

Everywhere they went, passers-by stopped to coo at baby Bobby and his chubby red cheeks. At first he sat up in his pram and beamed at every one of his admirers, but he had not had much of a nap that day so by the time the girls turned into Falkland Road again, the little fellow was leaning back sleepily against his pillow, his mouth half-open and his eyelids drooping.

'And there's Mrs Garcia,' whispered Annie, nodding towards a middle-aged woman leaning over her front gate just ahead. She looked rather exotic with thick black hair coiled around her head, and a richly patterned shawl around her shoulders. She had a strong beak of a nose and tanned skin as though she had spent all her life standing against the wind.

'Who's Mrs Garcia?' Tilly whispered as she leant towards her friend.

'She's married to Mr Garcia, the rag-and-bone man,' returned Annie. 'You know, the one with the horse.'

Tilly nodded. She knew the horse. She longed to stroke his velvety nose.

'Mrs Garcia's a nice lady,' explained Annie. 'She ran away with the gypsies when she was little, and she's travelled the world.' She decided not to tell Tilly what Clara said, that Mrs Garcia had never travelled further than Streatham, in south London, where she came from in the first place. It was a mean thing for Clara to say, particularly since it was not true.

As the girls approached, Mrs Garcia looked up and smiled. She had large, friendly black eyes. 'Hello, Annie,' she said. 'And this is your little brother . . .' She peered into the pram at Bobby, who was now lying back fast asleep with his mouth half open. 'What a lovely specimen!' Her laugh was a bit like a witch's cackle. 'Now, I've got something you girls will love,' said Mrs Garcia. 'My cat's had kittens, and they're just beginning to play. Come in and see them. You can leave the pram outside. The baby'll be quite safe.'

Feeling privileged to be invited in, Annie parked the pram against the wall of the house and followed Mrs Garcia and Tilly inside.

The Garcias lived in two rooms on the ground floor of the house. They also had the garden at the back, which Annie could see from the kitchen window was full of the rubbish Mr Garcia collected on his daily rounds. There were rusty old bed frames and huge sheets of corrugated iron leaning against the wall. Broken chairs and tables had been flung into one corner while unidentifiable bits of machinery lay piled up in another.

At the far end of the garden there was a large wooden stable with a roof made of corrugated iron. 'That's where Juniper lives,' explained Mrs Garcia.

She led the girls into the front room. It was dark and crowded, with a double bed in the far corner, shelving, and a table covered with an oriental rug. The atmosphere was claustrophobic with the heavy thick drapes hanging over the windows. A pungent musty smell hung in the air.

'Be very quiet,' whispered Mrs Garcia.

She guided the children over to the corner where a small ginger cat lay in a wooden banana crate. Pushing up at her belly as they suckled and mewled in thin little voices were five kittens of assorted colours.

Tilly dropped to her knees and edged towards the cats as Annie peered at them. It was quite hard for her eyes to adjust to the dim light. Along the mantelpiece there were rows and rows of pots with strange plants growing out of them, and from a couple of hooks screwed into the ceiling were hanging thick bundles of dried herbs.

Tilly was stroking the kittens with great care. 'I really want a kitten,' she said quietly.

'Perhaps your mother will let you have one,' said Annie.

'You can have one of these when they're ready to leave their mother,' said Mrs Garcia.

Tilly shook her plaits sadly. 'Even if my mother said yes, I know that Father won't. He hates animals.'

Annie watched the tiny kittens for several minutes. She was suddenly aware of tears pricking her eyes and an almost overwhelming desire to hold Rabbit. How much she missed her friend! Until now she had not realized just how much she, too, longed to have another pet to love as she had loved her rabbit.

Annie did not want to think about it now, and she certainly did not want to cry in front of Mrs Garcia, so she was relieved when Mrs Garcia got to her feet and shuffled out to the kitchen next door.

A couple of minutes later, Mrs Garcia returned with a plate of ginger biscuits and two mugs of milk. 'I expect you're both hungry,' she said quietly, holding out the tray.

The girls munched their biscuits and sipped their milk.

'Is it true you can look into people's futures?' Annie felt daring to ask the question. 'That's what my sister says.'

Mrs Garcia fixed her dark eyes on Annie and nodded. 'Your sister says quite a lot, as far as I can tell,' she said. 'Some of it nonsense, some of it quite accurate.

'Now,' she said, reaching out to take Annie's wrist, 'let's have a look, shall we?'

She gently turned Annie's hand over, and ran her fingertips over Annie's palm. 'Oh,' she said approvingly, 'you've got some good strong lines here . . .'

Annie stared at her pink palm with interest as Mrs Garcia began to talk about life lines and heart lines. Then Annie made the mistake of looking over at Tilly who was back on the floor playing with the kittens. As Tilly rolled her eyes in mockery, Annie started to giggle. She clasped her hand to her mouth. 'Oh, Mrs Garcia,' she gasped, 'I don't mean to be rude but . . .'

Mrs Garcia smiled benignly. 'It's all right, dear, I'm used to people not taking me seriously . . .'

Annie blushed in shame. 'Oh, but I do take you seriously.'

Mrs Garcia shook her head dismissively. 'I don't care about the mockery. You see, I know people's innermost secrets more than they would like to admit.'

Suddenly fearful, Annie stared at her in silence. Was she joking or not? Mrs Garcia continued. 'For instance, I don't need to read Mrs Whelan's hand to know that she worries about something every minute of the day but never about the things she's really worried about.'

Annie frowned. She could not work that out at all.

'And I don't need to touch your mother's hand to know that she has a lot of troubles to think about.'

Annie shook her head. 'No, you're wrong,' she said. 'My mother's very happy. She was sad for a bit, when she lost the babies, but now she's got Bobby she's all happy again.'

Mrs Garcia nodded. 'Yes, dear,' she said tolerantly. 'But feelings are usually much deeper than that . . .

'Now, what about you, dear?' she said to Tilly. 'Shall we see what your future holds?'

Tilly giggled but got to her feet and held out her hand. Annie sat down next to the kittens and stroked them quietly. Half her mind was thinking about how much she would like to try to paint these tiny mewling creatures with their soft ginger or tabby fur, and the other half pondered Mrs Garcia's peculiar remarks. What did she mean about her mother?

Suddenly there was a loud banging and clattering outside, and they heard the front door opening.

'Oh, there's my young man come home for his tea,' smiled Mrs Garcia.

Annie peered into the hall. There was Mr Garcia, leading his horse, Juniper, through the house to the garden at the back. The leather harness which attached the horse to the flat cart was swinging loosely around its flanks and belly. The cart was parked in the road outside.

'Did you get past the pram all right, then, love?' called Mrs Garcia.

Mr Garcia led the horse past the door and down the

passageway and out towards the back door. 'Pram? There ain't no pram there,' he said matter-of-factly.

As the meaning of his words sank in, Annie gasped and ran to the open front door. There was indeed nothing there. The pram had gone.

She gave a cry and ran to the gate to look out into the street. Up and down she looked but apart from a few people walking along on the pavement, there was no sign of a pram.

She was paralysed with shock. What would her mother say? Who could have stolen Bobby? What if he was hurt? Worse, what if he was dead? What if they never saw him again? Terrifying thoughts ran through her head as she stood frozen to the ground, her legs trembling, unable to decide what to do or where to go.

Tilly, who had run after her, decided for her. 'I'll go that way,' she said, pointing towards the church and the way home, 'and you go that way!' She pushed Annie in the other direction.

Annie started to run. There was an awful buzzing in her ears as the frightening thoughts continued to flood her head. Her heart pounded in time with her running feet.

Reaching Leverton Street, she stopped and looked anxiously up and down. To the left, she saw the Challen twins playing in the road. 'Hey!' She waved and called to them. As she approached, she realized that she was whimpering. 'Please let him be all right, please God, let me find him. I'll always be good, I promise, please just let me find him unharmed . . .'

'Have you seen our pram?' she called to Betty and Kitty Challen. The twins stopped their skipping for a moment to consider but then shook their heads and went back to their game.

At least Annie knew that the pram could not have been taken that way.

She ran north, up the hill towards the shop opposite the Pineapple pub. A man was hanging around outside waiting for the doors to open. 'Have you seen someone pushing a big black pram?' she asked.

The man shook his head. Annie ran on up the road, asking the passers-by. But no one had seen the pram and they generally peered curiously at little Annie Turner, her hands twisting anxiously and her lower lip quivering as she spoke.

Then at last someone could help. 'Yes, I saw a pram, Annie,' said Mrs Patty. 'My eyesight's not too good, you know, so I couldn't see who was pushing it. But as I went into the shop, I saw someone pushing it up that way.' She pointed towards the top of Leverton Street where it curved around towards the church in Lupton Street. 'That must've been about ten minutes ago, I'd say.'

Annie dashed up the hill, her sandals slapping loudly on the pavement.

As she came up to the imposing church on the brow of the hill, to her immense relief she saw the pram in the churchyard. And Bobby was sitting up in it. Thank goodness! He wasn't dead.

The pram was pointing away from Annie so Bobby could not see her as she approached. Sitting on a bench, holding the handle of the pram with one hand and rocking it gently, was Maudie Sprackling. She was talking to Bobby quietly in a soft crooning voice. She was smiling at him and nodding her head, as Bobby stared back at her with an uncertain expression on his face.

'Oh, Maudie!' cried Annie. 'How could you do that?

How could you take Bobby? You scared me to death.'

Maudie jumped to her feet, her big moon face confused and red.

Recognizing his sister's voice, Bobby spun his head round. A second later he began to bawl.

Maudie clenched her fists. 'Oh dear, now look what you've done,' she said faintly. 'He was all right until now.'

Annie ran to the pram. Undoing the straps, she lifted Bobby out and hugged him tight. He immediately stopped wailing and beamed at her and Maudie.

'You mustn't do that, Maudie,' Annie scolded. 'You mustn't take other people's babies and not say where you're going . . .'

To Annie's dismay, Maudie's face suddenly seemed to crumple. She sat down heavily on the bench and began to blubber. 'I'm sorry,' she said. 'I knew it wasn't right but I would never have harmed him. I was going to bring him back soon. It's just that when I saw him there in his pram, I just wanted a little go at pushing him up the road. I've never done that before, you see, and I wanted to see what it was like, to have a little baby in his pram. And he's so good. Even when he woke up, he wasn't afraid. I'm so sorry if I frightened you. I just couldn't help it. It was like someone else was doing it and I was just watching . . .' Tears began to trickle down her pasty face. With her eyes all red and bloodshot, poor, unattractive Maudie looked even more of a sight than usual.

Annie tried to smile. She reached out and gave Maudie a kind pat on the shoulder. 'It's all right, Maudie, I understand.' Inside, she felt sad for Maudie and she wanted to stop the next outburst from her.

But Maudie continued. 'Nobody knows what it's like,'

she moaned, 'to be barren, not to be able to have babies. I don't feel like a woman at all. My Fred left me because I couldn't have a baby. Four years we was married and no baby came. It was this very church that we got married in four years ago. All in white I was, with bridesmaids and confetti. I was slim in those days, too.' She looked down over her heavy body, waving her hands in a gesture of despair. 'Look at me now . . .

'No, I walked up the aisle that day and I was imagining having my first baby christened here. When I walked past the font, I couldn't keep my eyes off it. All I could see in my mind was a baby crying as the holy water dropped on its forehead. I wasn't thinking about the wedding at all.'

Her voice dropped to a whisper. 'He was keen, too. A big family, it was all planned. But then nothing happened according to plan. I couldn't have children and then my husband left me because of it. He ran off with that so-and-so Connie Smith.' She spat out those last few words, her voice trembling with fury. 'Connie didn't hesitate to run off with another woman's man. Not content with any of the other men she'd had in her time, she had to have mine, too.'

Tears of sympathy pricked Annie's eyes as Maudie wailed on. But she did not know what to say. 'I'm sorry,' she mumbled, strapping Bobby back into his pram. 'But I must go or my mother will be wondering where we are.'

Maudie waved her arm at her. 'Yes, you go home,' she said bitterly. 'You don't need to worry about me. Nobody cares about me.'

Annie hesitated as she looked at Maudie's hunched, shapeless frame on the bench. She put her hand in her pocket and pulled out the brown paper bag. 'Would you like a sherbet lemon?' she asked, pushing the bag under Maudie's nose. 'They taste good . . .'

Maudie looked up at her. With its down-turned mouth and red, blotchy skin, her face was a picture of pure misery. But she tried to smile as she took one of the sweets. 'Ta,' she whispered. 'And I am sorry, truly I am.'

Annie turned and pushed the heavy pram out of the churchyard and set off for home.

As she walked down Lady Margaret Road, she began to worry that Tilly might have gone home and told her mother that Bobby was lost But to her immense relief, she spotted her about a hundred yards away, coming up the road towards her.

'Everything's all right,' yelled Annie. 'Bobby's safe.'

As she walked back to the house, Annie felt a surge of happiness fill her chest. After all the fear and panic, the relief was exquisite. She was sure that she knew now what a mother would feel. Her responses had been more than just those of a sister – after all, Clara would have behaved differently. No, she was more like a real mother to a real baby. A smile crept over her face. Never before had she felt so much like her mother. It made her feel extraordinarily alive and purposeful.

CHAPTER 4

❦

Local Boys

ANNIE FIRST LEARNED THAT her mother's general health was seriously worsening on the day Grace could not open the chutney jar.

Before then, Annie had noticed that Grace sometimes had difficulty setting up the ironing board in the kitchen, fumbling for some time as she tried to plug the iron into the adaptor in the light fitting. She had been aware also that her mother was slow to get going in the morning, and occasionally complained about being stiff.

'I'm getting old, that's my problem,' she would say as she hobbled around her room getting dressed. Annie sometimes saw that her mother's feet and ankles were slightly puffy and red. Even though Tilly said that her mother – who was older than Grace – did not seem to suffer from stiffness in the mornings, Annie had never thought there was anything unusual.

One evening the family was eating supper – cold mutton and boiled potatoes – and Grace got out a jar of green tomato chutney to accompany the meat. Picking over her food, Annie noticed that her mother was taking an unusually

long time to open the jar. Grace had not said anything but
persisted in trying to twist the metal top, a frown of frustration on her brow. She was clasping the jar with one hand but
the other hand seemed too weak to get the top to turn.

Clara reached up her hand. 'Let me try, Mother. I can
do it.' With hardly any effort, she unscrewed the lid. It
opened with a whoosh of escaping air, and Clara set it
down in front of her mother.

It was a small incident and nothing was said about it at
the time. But Annie was aware of her father looking
intently at her mother, and her mother was unusually
subdued for the rest of the meal.

A few days later, Annie overheard her parents talking
about Grace's health. Annie had just finished painting a
picture – of the baby Moses being found in the bulrushes
by Pharaoh's daughter – and she was anxious to show off
her efforts to her parents, who were upstairs in the sitting
room.

She could hear them talking as she climbed the stairs
from the half-landing. The tone of her father's voice made
her stop short outside the door.

'Well if you can't even sew without pain,' he was saying,
'then you can't go on ignoring your arthritis. It's affecting
your life in an intolerable way. You've got to find out if
someone can help you. You must go and see a specialist,
someone who knows about these things.' Her father's voice
was firm and concerned.

There was a pause and then Annie heard her mother
saying weakly, 'There's no point. It all costs too much . . .'

'But we can afford to see a specialist,' protested Frank.

'Perhaps a specialist, yes, but you don't know about the
treatment afterwards. I don't want this to ruin our finances,

or to jeopardize the children's futures. I can live with it, Frank . . .'

Annie could hear her father pacing around the room. 'That's quite ridiculous. I *know* things can be done to ease the pain. And if it's really the money you're concerned about, then we should use your brooch to raise the money. We can take it to Fish Brothers. It's obviously worth a lot and we'd easily get enough to cover any major expenses. Then I can pay back the loan.'

Grace's voice was low and plaintive. 'No, Frank, I can't let you do that. I just can't.'

Frank rubbed his eyes wearily. 'But we have the brooch,' he sighed, 'and you never wear it. It sits at the back of that shelf doing nothing. I just think we might as well make use of it when it can help us.'

'I'm sorry, Frank, but I can't. Please let's leave it at that.' Grace turned away, twisting her hands tightly together. 'I'm sorry,' she added quietly. 'I just don't want to use that brooch for anything.'

Frank's voice softened. 'Why not, Grace?' he asked gently. 'I've never understood why you're so peculiar about that brooch. It's a fine piece of jewellery, and it saddens me that you don't wear it, even just in the house, for me . . .'

'No, I'll never wear it,' Grace said, shaking her head.

Frank came over to the sofa where Grace sat and settled down beside her. He took her hand and kissed it. 'I love you, Grace, you know that. I want to help you be in less pain but I don't want to do anything that will make you unhappy.' He paused and then added, 'But I would like to know about the brooch. You've never explained why Camilla Pearson gave you that brooch in the first place, though I've always understood that it was a sign of gratitude towards your parents, or perhaps to make up for her thoughtless behaviour when your mother died. But if that's so, why do you hate it?'

Grace was silent. Her lips were pressed together and she leaned against her husband's chest. 'Please, Frank, I'd rather not talk about it, please don't press me.'

As silence fell, Annie decided to creep on upstairs to her room. She could show them the picture in the morning. Her parents' conversation had revealed that her father knew no more about the brooch than Annie did. Why was her mother so odd about it? What was the story behind it?

A few days later Annie went shopping in Holloway with her mother, Marion and Tilly Banham. Avoiding the noisy, smelly traffic roaring up Camden Road, they took the back route to Jones Brothers where Grace wanted to buy some particularly pretty material. She planned to make some new curtains for the sitting room. Although her arthritis made sewing by hand difficult, she used the sewing machine as much as ever.

It was a long walk, but going to Holloway made a change from Kentish Town Road or Camden Town, Grace's usual shopping areas.

After some successful shopping, when Grace and Marion both found what they had set out to buy, they had tea and cakes in the tearoom. It was good to have a sit-down and rest their legs before setting off home again, and the tea was good, with cucumber sandwiches, scones and butter and deliciously light fairy cakes. Annie and Tilly looked after Bobby who, at two years old, was a bit of a tearaway. He kept grabbing the cakes and stuffing them into his mouth before anyone could stop him.

Well rested, the party set off for home. Bobby was strapped safely into his pram, which Grace pushed as she chatted to Marion about domestic matters. Annie and Tilly followed along behind, playing hopscotch on the pavement as they went, or doing cat's cradle with the elastic that Tilly always carried around with her, just in case.

It was a grey overcast day with a sky that threatened a downpour at any moment. By the time they had reached the final stretch home, walking up Leighton Road, they could feel tiny spots of rain falling.

As they approached Torriano Avenue they could see a man on the corner lurching from side to side. He kept stumbling around in circles. Every now and then he fell to the ground and then picked himself up only to fall over backwards the other way.

Marion turned her head and called quietly, 'Come on, girls, we'll cross here and stay out of that man's way. He's had too much to drink,' she added with distaste.

As the party crossed the road, they noticed Mr Garcia and his horse and cart parked over the other side. Mr Garcia was struggling to haul an old stove onto the cart. Juniper the horse was showing the whites of his eyes and was warily watching the drunken man. Grace pushed the pram out into the road just as a small black car came round the corner phut-phutting and backfiring loudly.

Startled by the noise, Juniper leaped into the air with a great snort. Mr Garcia staggered backwards and the old stove crashed onto his leg. With a yell of pain, he fell to the ground, hugging his leg in agony.

Juniper dashed out into the road and headed off straight in the direction of Bobby's pram. The horse swerved as he reached the pram but as he galloped past, the cart caught the handle of the pram, dragging it violently down the road. A terrified Bobby in the pram held out his arms to his mother and screamed.

Annie watched in horror. It only lasted a few seconds but it seemed much longer. She was certain that Bobby was about to die.

Suddenly a small figure jumped out into the road and grabbed the horse's noseband. It was a boy of about eleven. He hung on tightly to the harness, his legs pulled up under him as he was carried down the road for several yards. Gradually his weight forced to horse to slow down. 'Whoa!' he called in a loud, calm voice, 'Whoa!'

Moments later Juniper clattered to a halt. He stomped his feet, his metal shoes throwing up sparks on the road. His flanks were heaving and his nostrils were still blowing excitedly.

The boy stroked the animal's nose. 'Good boy, good boy,' he was saying as the others rushed up. Annie now saw that Bobby's saviour was Tommy Smith, one of the Smiths in Leverton Street. She did not know him well because he went to Torriano school, not hers, but she knew that he was not a member of Roger's gang.

Grace had reached the stricken Bobby and yanked him from his pram. She hugged her baby tight. Tears of relief flowed down her cheeks. 'Thank you, thank you!' she said to Tommy. 'I just thought that was the end.'

'You're such a brave boy!' exclaimed Marion. 'You could have been hurt yourself . . .'

At that moment Mr Garcia hobbled up to take charge

of his horse. His leg was bruised but not broken. It had been a lucky escape all round.

A small crowd had gathered to watch the spectacle of the runaway horse and the baby. Everyone was now singing Tommy's praises.

'How can I repay you?' Grace was overwhelmed with relief and gratitude.

Tommy smiled and shrugged modestly. 'It wasn't nothing,' he said. 'I just did what anyone else would have done.' He smiled, 'And I've always fancied meself as a lion tamer . . .'

Annie stared with admiration at this stocky boy with freckles and straight sandy hair. He had lovely sparkling green eyes, like the sea.

They all walked up the road together, and Annie was pleased when Tommy accepted her mother's invitation to come home for a glass of barley water and a slice of malt bread.

They all sat upstairs in the parlour with Tommy served as the guest of honour and treated as the hero he was. Annie and Tilly sat together in the corner and watched him in wonder. He talked breezily to Grace and Marion with a maturity beyond his eleven years. He was polite and friendly and answered their questions confidently, while at the same time exuding a genuine charm as he complimented them, praising the malt bread which Marion had baked that morning, and admiring Grace's home.

'What a beautiful house,' he said. 'And you have so much room. So many rooms!'

'Well, these houses are bigger than the ones in Leverton Street,' agreed Grace, 'and we certainly have more room than a lot of people might have.'

'You're telling me!' Tommy sniffed at Grace's understatement. 'We don't have no room to sit in like this,' he said. 'All the action goes on in the kitchen, 'cos there are too many people sleeping in the house. All the rooms are bedrooms . . .' He chuckled. 'Of course, there's a bit of to-ing and fro-ing and sometimes there's a bit more space when somebody is away for a bit, but it's never like this . . .' He waved his arm in a wide circle. 'It's wonderful.'

They recounted the events in Leighton Road, and to their surprise Tommy informed them that the drunken man was Roger Knight's father. 'He's down the pub all hours, he is. Roger's always down there to drag him home to make sure he spends the night in his bed and not in the street.'

Annie listened in wonder. Although her father made the occasional trip to the pub, and a bottle of sherry was kept in the cupboard to be offered to visitors, her parents rarely touched alcohol themselves. It really was the demon drink, as she had heard people call it, if it could make someone's father behave like that.

'I'm surprised that Roger can act like a responsible son,' commented Grace. 'He's always struck me as a cruel boy who does not care much for anyone. The way he rampages around with his gang causing trouble for everyone is quite terrible.'

Tommy raised his brows and nodded. 'Yes, he can be very cruel . . .'

'Perhaps someone's been cruel to him,' said Grace, always on a child's side.

'We think he killed my rabbit,' interrupted Annie. 'He broke Rabbit's neck and threw him on the ground.'

'We don't know for certain, Annie,' Grace chided her

gently. 'And we mustn't accuse without any proof. Besides, that was a long time ago now.'

'It was only two years ago, and it must have been Roger,' protested Annie. 'Lots of people saw him hanging around the gardens that day, and Tilly saw him running along our wall . . .'

'That's right,' chimed in Tilly. 'I did.'

Grace raised her finger to her lips. 'Yes, I know, Annie, we all agree that it was likely, but I'm just saying that nobody actually saw Roger kill your rabbit so we can't know for sure.'

Annie frowned. 'Well, I know he did,' she said crossly.

'It wouldn't surprise me,' said Tommy, smiling at Annie. 'I remember Roger being cruel to animals when he was still at my school. He used to pull wings off flies, and once he tried to flush a kitten down the lavatory. He found it in the playground – it was only a few weeks old, and he poured Ajax all over it and pulled the chain. He was sent home for the rest of the week and the whole school had a lecture on being kind to animals.'

'What a horrible story,' said Marion.

'They're all a bit like that, in that family,' added Tommy. 'So if you think my family's bad, you should hear what Roger's family gets up to . . .'

Marion looked at the boy with interest. Relatively new to the area, she was not fully aware of the reputation of the Smith family. 'Is your family bad?' she asked innocently.

Annie glanced at her mother. Then she looked at Tommy. How would he answer?

But Tommy did not seem to be in the slightest bit embarrassed. He grinned, revealing two strong square front teeth. 'The local coppers think so. And I have to admit that my lot don't have much respect for the law, most of 'em. But they're a decent lot, in their way. They'd never hurt no one, even on a job. They've got standards – of a sort. And you'd never find any of them being cruel to animals, not like Roger . . .'

The room was hushed as Tommy spoke. Everyone stared intently at this open, honest boy.

'But your sister hurt Maudie Sprackling when she ran away with Maudie's husband,' Grace said gently.

Tommy thought for a moment. 'That's true,' he said, 'I won't deny that . . . but that was a bit different, I mean, it wasn't just Connie, it takes two, after all . . .'

Grace and Marion nodded.

'That's true,' replied Marion.

'But Connie ain't my sister, anyway,' Tommy continued. 'She's my cousin. My mum died when I was born, so I was adopted by my mum's sister, Jan, who's my aunt. I've always called them Mum and Dad and they've always treated me like they treat the other boys. But I am slightly different,' he added with a touch of pride. 'And I've always felt slightly different, too.'

Tommy Smith was making a big impression on his audience. His politeness and good manners seemed so uncharacteristic of the Smith family they thought they knew. Annie was fascinated by him. He was so confident and so funny. Every now and then he would catch her eye across the room and wink at her, causing her to look away with a blush of embarrassment.

Tommy was still there when Frank came home from work. Annie heard him come in through the front door. He came upstairs and welcomed Marion with genuine pleasure. He was pleased that Grace had Marion as a friend now.

'This is Tommy Smith, Frank.' Grace held out her arm towards Tommy, who had got to his feet and was smiling respectfully at Frank. 'You know the Smiths, from Leverton Street.'

'Good afternoon, sir,' said Tommy.

Frank's reaction was quite strange. The moment the Smiths were mentioned, the smile on Frank's face froze momentarily and then disappeared. He seemed not to hear Grace's account of how Tommy had saved Bobby's life by stopping Mr Garcia's runaway horse. Annie watched her father's face in astonishment. He looked both uncomfortable and angry, with a frown on his brow and his mouth set in a grim straight line.

But he had taken in some of Grace's words. 'I'm extremely grateful to you for saving my son's life,' he said. 'Now, if you'll excuse me, I have some paperwork to do before tea.'

He walked out of the room and shut himself into his study next door.

Annie could not understand her father's reaction any more than Grace could. After Tommy had gone home and they had said their goodbyes to Marion and Tilly, they tackled Frank.

'I was surprised at you, Frank,' Grace chided him, 'being so unfriendly to Tommy Smith. If the children had behaved as you did, they would have been reprimanded.'

Frank had his head buried in the evening paper. He did not look up but he was clearly not reading. 'He's a Smith,' he said flatly. But in spite of his certain tone, he looked uncomfortable.

'So what?' demanded Annie.

'You've never complained about the Smiths before,' said

Grace. 'I thought you liked everyone who lived around here. I thought you all shared a common history, you all went to school together and your parents knew each other, and your grandparents.'

'The Smiths are different,' replied Frank in a low voice. 'I would rather not have anything to do with any of them. They are trouble.'

'But Tommy's different!' exclaimed Annie. 'He's a cousin, he's not a real Smith. His mother died so he was brought up by Mr and Mrs Smith as their son. He calls them Mum and Dad but really they're his uncle and aunt . . .'

'I don't care,' said Frank, folding up his paper. 'It makes no difference to me.'

'But Bobby could have died if Tommy hadn't been there,' said Grace.

'I know, I know,' replied Frank. 'I appreciate his saving Bobby's life – how could I not? But I'd rather not have any dealings with any of that family. It's nothing specific but you can see they're trouble – one of the boys is always in prison for one thing or another. And I decided a long time ago that we shouldn't have much to do with them. I'm happy to be civil to them in the street, but I don't want them in my home.'

'Well, you weren't very civil to Tommy!' shouted Annie.

'That's enough, Annie, don't be rude to your father,' said Grace quietly.

Frank got to his feet. 'I don't want to discuss this any more,' he said. He had to leave the room before anyone noticed how his cheeks were burning with shame.

He climbed the stairs as Grace and Annie shook their heads at Frank's bewildering behaviour.

CHAPTER 5

❧

Sally Brown

CLARA WAS UPSTAIRS IN her room with her best friend Marie Whelan. The girls were supposed to be rehearsing their parts for the school play but they had lost interest in drama and now sat on the bed, swinging their long bare legs, and discussing their friends and life.

Marie was a thin, gangly girl with a narrow face and thin lips. Her thick brown hair had never been cut and it was always tied up in two fat plaits which fell heavily down her back to her waist. They were like snakes. With her large, wide hazel eyes, Marie was not unattractive but she looked quite homely next to Clara.

Clara's looks gave her a presence. Wherever she went people noticed her. She had sparkling gentian-blue eyes and wavy blonde hair which, even when tied back, tumbled down in soft curls. She had strong clean limbs and even features. Her skin was clear and white, her plump lips the colour of mulberries. Although only twelve, it was evident to all that she was going to be a real beauty as an adult.

Marie felt privileged to be Clara Turner's best friend. Easily dominated, she was happy to be with someone who always knew what to do next. Clara's bossiness never vexed her. After all, her mother was always telling her what to do, and Marie sometimes worried that, left alone in the world, she would not know what to do with herself.

'Kevin Jones tried to kiss me yesterday,' boasted Clara.

'Well, you're sweet on him, aren't you?' Marie looked mournful. She did not expect anyone to want to kiss her, ever.

'Yes,' said Clara, 'but I told him he had to wait.' She paused. 'I thought I ought to get more practice first.'

'All right,' said Marie, without much enthusiasm.

'Shall we begin?' Clara leaned forward and placed her puckered lips gently on Marie's. She pulled away with a loud 'Mwah!'

Marie frowned. 'I don't think it's done like that,' she said.

Clara looked annoyed. 'Well, let's try again,' she said quickly. 'But this time we should shut our eyes.'

The girls leaned forward with their eyes shut and giggled as they bumped their noses clumsily. They fell backwards on the bed in peals of laughter.

'This isn't going to work.'

'No,' said Marie with a look of relief.

Clara was already bored. 'Let's go out somewhere,' she said. 'Let's see if we can feed Mr Spratt's chickens. That's always good fun.'

Mr Spratt, the old man who lived on the ground floor next door, was happy to have Clara and her young friend help to feed his hens. He had been widowed for many years. He was probably not as ancient as he looked but he was very wizened and people said that he had never quite recovered from the death of his wife. Others said he had gone dotty after being shell-shocked in the Great War. What everyone agreed was that whatever was wrong with him, he had become even dottier after Mrs Spratt's death. Now the only thing he cared about was his large flock of hens.

He loved the birds and he wanted everyone else to love them, too. He knew each hen by name and, in his high rasping voice, would list her habits and foibles like a mother talking about her child.

'Well, that Sandy, now, she's very shy and always waits to eat her food last. But Blackie is a little too forward and has to be fed separately otherwise she pecks the others quite nastily. And that old lady Specky, now she's very fussy about where she lays her eggs. She always has to lay them in the top box in the henhouse, while Titch, there, will never lay inside but insists on finding a spot outside in the run somewhere. I spend hours searching for her eggs, I do, but she enjoys seeing me suffer, I bet. Yes, Marmaduke is a happy boy. And so he should be, surrounded by beautiful women . . .'

The old man chattered on as Clara watched the birds clucking around in the run, a fixed look of concentration in her eyes.

The girls helped Mr Spratt mix meal into a bucket of food scraps from the kitchen. This included discarded eggshells.

'Ugh! They're just cannibals,' declared Clara, 'eating part of themselves!'

Mr Spratt had a pronounced stoop and a stubbly chin which he rubbed with twisted, arthritic hands. 'That may be so,' he chuckled, 'but the calcium is good for making the next lot of eggs. It don't bother them and it don't bother me.'

Mr Spratt had always lived next door. He had two rooms on the ground floor where he had lived with his wife. He had adored his wife, a noisy, flamboyant woman who loved to dress up in all her finery. She never left the house without being well turned out in smart dresses, layers of jewellery, and bright red varnish on her long nails. Clara's mother did not approve of ladies who painted their nails but she had not minded Mrs Spratt. 'She was on the stage, before she married,' Grace would say, as though that excused her next-door neighbour.

But after his wife died, Mr Spratt really had gone to pieces.

People described how sometimes he stood in the garden at night and howled like a dog at the full moon, or how in the early hours of the morning he walked up and down the street ringing a bell. Clara was always watching out for him to have one of his funny turns but the most she had seen was a distracted Mr Spratt walking down the road talking aloud to himself and looking dishevelled and unwashed. But Clara liked him. He seemed to be in his own world, not dependent on anyone else, and he was always friendly towards the Turner family, as well as generous with his fresh orange-yolked eggs which tasted so pungent on the tongue.

'Now you girls wait here,' said Mr Spratt to Clara and Marie. 'I might be able to get a letter into the last post. It would help me if you would dish this out to my darlings . . .' He held up the bucket of mixed meal and scraps. 'Just pour this into that long trough over in the corner there, and then scatter this grain onto the ground.' He pointed to a small sack of grain in the box just inside his back door. 'They've got enough water, you don't need to worry about that.'

Clara took the bucket. 'If you're not back, we'll just climb back home over the wall.'

Mr Spratt went off on his errand while Clara and Marie let themselves into the chicken run. The hens were hungry and clucked hopefully as they circled around the girls' legs.

'Good,' said Clara as she heard the sound of Mr Spratt closing the front door behind him. 'Now we can try something I've been dying to do for a long time. You can hypnotize chickens, you know,' she said. 'Apparently it's easy. I read about it somewhere.'

Marie giggled.

'So now's our chance to try it,' said Clara.

The chickens were so used to being fondled by Mr Spratt and so eager to be fed that it was easy to catch them. Clara dumped the food into the trough and grabbed a big black bird. She handed it to Marie.

'That's Blackie, I think,' said Marie.

'Put it down and hold its head so that its beak just touches the ground,' Clara instructed Marie.

While Marie held the frightened chicken in position, Clara ran her forefinger backwards and forwards around its beak making a large semicircle each time. 'We do this several times,' she said, 'and then you let go.'

She did it five times. Marie let go. The chicken picked up its head and, after a moment's hesitation, it scuttled off, flapping its wings and squawking loudly.

'We can't have done it right.' Clara frowned. 'Let's do another one.'

They picked on six other chickens but the experiment was not a success. Some of the chickens remained rooted to the spot for a couple of seconds but most leaped up complaining loudly and rushed out of reach. Certainly

Marmaduke the cock stayed well out of the way. There was no chance of trying it out on him.

'Perhaps they're the wrong kind of chicken,' suggested Marie.

Clara shrugged. 'Never mind, let's go. I'm bored with this. Let's get something to eat and then go up to Parliament Hill.'

The girls scrambled over the wall and let themselves into the Turners' house from the garden.

Clara found her mother in the kitchen busy bottling pickled onions, marrows and beetroots. The smell of the pickling vinegar made their nostrils curl and tighten.

Grace did the pickling every year and always filled more jars than the family could use themselves. Her mother-in-law had always done this with the idea of then giving the spare jars out to various people in the neighbourhood. For Grace, who found that making contact with the neighbours did not come naturally, it was an acceptable way to remain friendly.

While Grace spooned out the pickled vegetables, Annie sat at the end of the pine kitchen table painting a large picture. She had been hoping to play with Tommy Smith that afternoon. Since the day Tommy had saved Bobby's life, Tommy had become a friend to both Annie and Tilly. They often met up after school and at weekends to go to the library or play jacks. Tommy's serious nature appealed to both girls. Annie's father seemed to have accepted him, too, but he still seemed uneasy in Tommy's presence.

But when Annie called round at Tommy's house in Leverton Street that morning she was told that he was in bed with mumps. 'Came down with it last night,' said Mrs Smith. 'Looks like a hamster today, he does.' So Tommy was not around to play with and neither was Tilly, for she had gone shopping in the West End with her mother.

So Annie had been left with no one to play with but she was not too bothered. She had been wanting to start a big new painting that had been building up in her head for days.

Now the painting was finished. It was of a jungle, full of lions and tigers and brightly coloured birds with long feathers. Annie was very satisfied with it. She had worked hard at it, using every bit of the paper as she had been taught, and being bold with her coloured paints. She was going to give it to her father when he came home from work. She poured the dirty water into the sink and cleared up her poster paints.

When Clara announced that she and Marie were going up to Parliament Hill, Annie was desperate to join them. Having been inside all afternoon, she felt she wanted to get some fresh air and stretch her legs. 'Can I come, too?' she asked eagerly.

Clara frowned. 'Do you have to?'

'Now, be kind, Clara,' her mother chided her. 'Take Annie with you, now. You know she'll be no trouble and she enjoys it so. Here, take some stale bread for the ducks . . .'

Clara and Marie were not delighted to have Annie along, but they were willing to tolerate her trotting behind just so long as she did not interrupt their conversation. And they did not even try to walk too fast for her this time, in the way they used to. Clara actually quite liked Annie nowadays and was stand-offish only when she was with her friends.

It was a warm, sunny afternoon with a fresh southern breeze, a good day to go to the Heath. And there were many other people about, courting couples, dog-walkers, mothers with children, nannies with prams.

The girls ran to the top of the hill to watch the kites dipping and rising in the wind. As usual it was blustery up there. Their hair whipped around their faces and when they shouted at each other, their words seemed to blow away across the Heath. They sat on the grass and looked south over London. They could see St Paul's Cathedral and, far beyond, some hills in the distance.

Tiring of the view, the girls ran halfway down the hill and rolled down the rest. They landed in a dizzy laughing pile at the bottom.

Then Clara started to do cartwheels and handstands, and walked about on her hands, her skirt tucked into her knickers. She had an extraordinary sense of balance and could stay upside-down for ages, until she could no longer stand the pressure in her head.

Annie watched her older sister with pride. Clara was so athletic, so easy with her body, which seemed to do anything she asked of it. She felt ashamed of her own weak and clumsy little frame. The older she got the more she agonized about not being like Clara. For a long time she had assumed (or hoped) that it was just a matter of time before she too would develop the robust physique that Clara enjoyed But as the years passed, she could see that she was merely becoming more like herself – straight and angular. She had been nursing false hopes.

When Clara grew tired of her gymnastics, they wandered on up to Highgate Pond, where they threw lumps of hard bread into the water for the eager ducks.

Clara took off her shoes and socks and wandered out into the mud at the edge of the water. She squealed as the black mud oozed up between her toes. 'Come on, Marie, this is fun!'

Marie shook her head. 'I don't dare,' she called back. 'My mother would die if I got any dirtier.' She looked down at the green streaks where the grass had stained her shirt and white socks. She was already wondering how she would explain those to her mother, who could not abide dirt of any sort.

They wandered on across the Heath, watching the squirrels hopping across the branches of the beech trees and laughing at the pigeons puffing out their feathers in their mating rituals. 'It makes them look just like Mr Worth,' cried Marie.

'Or Maudie,' added Clara with a laugh.

The older girls had stopped treating Annie as a nuisance and they now took it in turns to give her a piggyback. Clara snorted and whinnied in her imitation of a horse.

Now they were getting hungry and set off back home. They decided to stop off at Mr Gunn's on the way, to pick up the groceries for Mrs Turner. She had asked the girls to get some cocoa powder and a bag of rice.

Suddenly the camaraderie Annie had felt with her sister dropped away. In a loud, imperious voice, Clara told Annie to stay outside while she and Marie went into the shop.

Annie obediently did as she was told, leaning against the wall and scuffing her sandals on the pavement. It was always the same, she thought with irritation. Just when she thought that Clara had accepted her, just as she felt equal with her older sister, Clara had to put her in her place. It wasn't fair. She felt tempted to go back home on her own, but she was afraid that might annoy Clara too much. It wasn't worth it.

When they came out of the shop a few minutes later, the older girls were giggling. Despite Annie's pleading, they refused to tell her why. Once again Annie was excluded. She trailed along behind them feeling dispirited.

Clara and Marie kept on giggling and whispering as they walked home. When they reached the house, they went straight upstairs to the attic room Annie and Clara shared. It was clear to Annie that her company was no longer wanted.

Annie sat on the stairs with her chin in her hands and wondered what to do with herself between now and teatime. Usually she would just start another picture but she felt that all her energy had gone in to the jungle picture she had painted earlier in the day. Her parents were downstairs in the sitting room. Grace was sewing a shirt on the old Singer machine and Frank was reading the paper. Annie did not feel like joining them. She did not even feel like playing with Bobby, who was in the sitting room in his playpen.

Suddenly there was a banging on the front door. Annie heard her father go downstairs and talk to someone on the doorstep. She could not tell who it was. But whoever it was, he was angry.

The door closed with a loud slam. Annie could hear her father coming rapidly up the stairs. He walked straight past Annie without even acknowledging her, and went on up to the girls' bedroom. Annie followed on behind to see what was happening. She had never seen her father so angry. His face was the colour of chalk, his jaw set in a look of fury.

'Clara!' he yelled as he pushed Clara's door open. Standing behind him, Annie could see Clara and Marie sitting cross-legged on the bed holding packs of cards in their hands. They were playing Racing Demon. On the paisley eiderdown lay a brown paper bag. It had spilled its contents of sugar biscuits between their crossed legs.

'You little thief!' Frank yanked Clara by the arm and pulled her out of the room. 'You come with me! I shall not have any child of mine growing up to be a criminal!'

Annie flattened herself against the wall as Frank dragged Clara past her. He pulled Clara all the way downstairs and on out into the garden. Moments later, Annie could hear the sound of her father whacking Clara's backside with his leather belt.

She was horrified. He had only ever done that once before, a long time ago when Jack had told a lie about something. It was alarming in any event but Annie was particularly frightened and shocked to see that her father – her lovely warm father – could also do that to a girl. Even at school, it was only the boys who got caned. The most the girls ever got was detention, however naughty they had been.

Slap! Slap! Slap! It sounded as though Frank was hitting Clara very hard. She could hear him muttering angrily but Annie never heard a squeak from her sister.

Then the door slammed and Annie could hear the sound of Clara coming up the stairs again.

Her sister's face was red. She looked straight ahead as she pushed past Annie.

Annie followed her up the stairs. 'Are you all right?' she whispered.

'I'm perfectly all right,' snapped Clara. But her lips were

pinched and Annie could see that she was fighting back tears.

From the bed, Marie stared at her friend in horror.

'Mr Gunn told him we pinched the biscuits,' Clara stated flatly.

Marie shrank away, staring at her friend in horror. 'Oh dear,' she wailed, biting her thumb-nail, 'will your father tell my mother?'

'I don't know,' said Clara.

'I knew we shouldn't have done it,' said Marie in a panicked sort of voice. 'I told you it was dangerous.'

Clara spun around and glared at Marie's frightened face. 'We did it together,' she said firmly. Her throat was tight and her voice sounded squeaky but controlled. 'We did it together and we are equally guilty.'

'It was wrong,' said Marie. 'We shouldn't have done it.' She had begun to cry, terrified of her mother finding out about the incident. She started to mutter a prayer under her breath.

Annie stared at the brown paper bag on the bed. The biscuits were sprinkled with icing sugar and looked delicious. Annie longed to eat one but she did not dare ask for one then. To her surprise, Clara picked up a biscuit and handed it to her. 'You might as well enjoy these while we still have them,' she said. 'And you,' she said, turning to the white-faced Marie, 'should stop blubbing. What we did wrong was to get caught.' She tossed back her thick hair. 'Next time, we'll just be a lot more careful.'

The next morning Grace scrutinized her elder daughter for signs of distress from the beating the day before.

Although she would not tolerate stealing either, Grace had been shocked by the force of Frank's rage and the violence with which he had punished Clara.

But Clara appeared as good-spirited as ever. Whatever she felt under her cheerful demeanour, she certainly was not going to show it to her family. Grace was secretly impressed by Clara's strength. It was something she must have inherited from Frank's side of the family; it certainly did not come from her. Grace felt there was no greater coward in the world than she.

After breakfast, Grace asked Clara and Annie to distribute some of her pickles to various people in the neighbourhood, including Mrs Horder and Mrs Whelan. She handed each girl a wicker basket containing the jars. 'Be careful how you go,' she said.

As the girls left the house, they saw Mr Spratt standing outside his gateway. He looked extremely distressed. He pressed his lips together and pursed them anxiously as he rocked from side to side, shifting his weight from one leg to another. He kept wiping his brow and muttering. Suddenly he raised his left leg and hugged his knee.

'Whatever's the matter, Mr Spratt?' Clara's voice sounded kind. Annie was proud that her big sister could be thoughtful towards a lonely old man.

'Oh dear, oh dear,' wailed Mr Spratt, 'it's me chickens.' His rheumy eyes were wet with tears. 'They've got some horrible disease. They're all dying.'

'Why, what do you mean?' The edge in Clara's voice made Annie glance at her quickly. A red blush was creeping up Clara's neck. Now, that's odd, she thought. Clara only blushed when she was embarrassed. Why ever should Clara be embarrassed because Mr Spratt's chickens were dying?

Annie stared at her sister with narrowed eyes.

'I found six of them,' explained Mr Spratt, 'including my darlings – Whitey, Blackie and Sandy – all of them dead inside the hen house this morning. I can't understand it at all. I've never known chickens drop dead like that, not without being ill first. They was perfectly all right yesterday, they was very well, really.' He clutched Clara's wrist. 'You saw them yesterday, they was all perfectly all right when you went to feed them, wasn't they? They was the spitting image of health.'

Clara nodded. 'Yes,' she said in a muted voice.

'Now I'm afraid they're all going to get whatever it is what's killed them,' continued Mr Spratt plaintively. 'I don't know what I'm going to do . . .'

Annie and Clara left poor Mr Spratt wailing by his gate. Clara remained noticeably subdued as they walked along the road. Finally she said, more to herself than to Annie, 'I wonder how much chickens cost.'

'Why?' Annie glanced suspiciously at her sister.

'Oh, I was just thinking,' said Clara, 'that it would be nice to buy Mr Spratt some new chickens as a present.'

'Why?' Annie was not convinced by Clara's breezy tone of voice.

Clara flicked back her hair. 'Stop asking "why" all the time,' she snapped. 'It's very irritating.' With a hand on her hip, she turned to look at Annie. 'If you must know why, I just thought I might have enough money in my money box to buy some new chickens for him, to be kind. That's all.'

Annie shrugged. She knew for certain now that Clara was somehow responsible for Mr Spratt's dead chickens.

They had reached the corner of Leverton Street where

the girls split up to make their respective deliveries of pickles. 'I'll do the Whelans and the ones down here,' Clara said, crossing the road. 'You do Mrs Horder and the others.'

As Clara ran off to discuss with Marie Whelan how to limit the damage their experimentation had done, Annie walked up to Mrs Horder's house next to the Pineapple pub. She knocked on the door.

Mrs Horder opened it, her bright beady eyes friendly and welcoming. 'Come in, come in, dear.' She showed Annie into the front room. 'We were just having tea, weren't we, Danny . . . ?'

Danny was sitting on the sofa against the wall facing the door. He sat in a great crumpled pile on the cushions, with a large white napkin tucked under his drooping wet chin.

'Here's little Annie Turner, Danny,' said Mrs Horder in a loud voice. 'She's come to visit us. She's brought some pickles her mother made for us. Isn't that kind?'

Danny raised his head and grunted loudly.

'Take a seat, dear, and I'll make a fresh pot of tea,' said Mrs Horder. 'Now you entertain our guest, Danny, dear, while I'm in the kitchen.'

Annie sat down in the chair opposite Danny. 'Hello, Danny,' she said with a smile.

Danny had been holding a piece of sponge cake in his hand. He nodded his head and smiled back at Annie, revealing ugly black stumps of teeth, and rammed the cake into his open mouth. Crumbs cascaded down his front and onto the floor. He snorted and wiped his mouth roughly with the back of his hand and smiled again at Annie.

Annie looked away in embarrassment, and felt relieved

when Mrs Horder returned. In spite of her years, she was a sprightly woman with plenty of energy. 'I made a batch of brandy snaps today,' she said, holding out a tin of sticky golden biscuits. 'They're Danny's favourites. I hope you'll have one.'

Annie munched her brandy snaps and drank a cup of sweet tea while Mrs Horder chatted to her. She seemed like the happiest of people. Annie was impressed by the way Mrs Horder always included Danny in the conversation even though Danny never said a word. He only snorted or smiled in return.

Trying to watch him without appearing to stare, Annie suddenly realized that Danny did not understand most of what was said to him. Sometimes he beamed a smile and giggled, just like her baby brother Bobby did. Yet he was a huge man, and over twenty years old.

Mrs Horder talked to him as if he were both a grown-up and a little boy, ticking him off for picking his nose and reminding him not to slurp his tea. Annie liked her love and kindness but it made her feel uncomfortable as well, though she didn't know exactly why.

When Annie finally left, she felt that Mrs Horder was probably the kindest woman she had ever met. It would be easy to lose patience with Danny, him being so big and clumsy and unable to do anything for himself. But not once did Mrs Horder get impatient with him. She loved Danny as if he were the most perfect being on earth.

'He's a good boy, my Danny,' Mrs Horder whispered as she showed Annie out. 'And he likes you a lot.' She squeezed Annie's arm. 'He's very sensitive to people, you know. He knows who's genuine, and who is not . . .'

Annie delivered the other jars of pickle to the people on

her mother's list and set off back home. As she came near the corner of Falkland Road and Leverton Street she heard a sobbing coming from behind a hedge. Peering into the front garden of the house, she saw Sally Brown sitting on the doorstep. Her face was red and blotchy and her eyes wet with tears.

'Whatever's the matter?' asked Annie.

For as long as Annie could remember, Sally Brown had fascinated her. Sally was six feet tall with thick ginger hair wrapped around her head. She always wore lipstick and tight-fitting flashy clothes, which Annie thought really daring. Although she had lived in the neighbourhood for years, she did not have any friends. No one seemed to have a good word to say for her. If she was mentioned in conversation, people lowered their voices and talked in a secretive way. When Sally walked into a shop to buy some groceries, the women in the shop queues turned their backs on her. Then they would mutter and sneer when she left.

Annie did not know why but she realized early on that people did not approve of Sally Brown, who lived on her own and seemed to have several different gentlemen visitors. She did have some kind of job in the false-teeth factory in Angler's Lane but Annie had also heard people making reference to a night job Sally had as well. Annie did not like to ask. She sensed that enquiring further about Sally Brown was stepping on dangerous ground.

All she did know about Sally was that she was pretty, with a big, round, well-proportioned face. She had dark brown eyes and lovely white teeth which flashed when she laughed. And her laugh was deep and throaty, a lovely abandoned sound that seemed to come from deep inside her.

But Sally was not laughing today. She looked utterly miserable. Her lustrous ginger hair was messy and she stared with dull eyes at the child hovering by her gate.

'Is there anything I can do?' asked Annie.

'No,' replied Sally in a flat voice.

Annie frowned. She did not know what to do. It seemed wrong to walk off and leave Sally crying on the doorstep like that. She plucked up some courage and spoke again.

'What's the matter?' she asked.

Sally shook her head and sighed. 'Oh, it's nothing,' she said. 'Nothing and everything . . .'

Annie continued to stare. She felt rooted to the spot. 'You look a bit sad,' she said quietly. 'Are you sure there's nothing I can do?'

Sally bit her lip and sighed again. 'You're right, love, I am a bit sad.' She shifted to one side and patted the step she was sitting on. 'Come and keep me company for a few minutes – if you've got the time. You're Annie Turner, aren't you?' She smiled wanly at Annie who came over and sat down beside her.

They sat in silence for a few minutes, Annie clutching her empty wicker basket and Sally flicking the laces of her brown boots.

'You're a lucky girl,' Sally said after a long pause. 'You come from a good family. You have parents who are kind to you and want the best out of life for you . . .'

Annie wriggled self-consciously but was flattered by the grown-up way in which Sally spoke to her.

'What do I have?' Sally continued bitterly. 'No one to love and no one to love me. When I was your age, all I wanted to do was grow up and get married. It seemed so simple . . .'

Annie realized that Sally was not really talking to her at all. She was talking out loud to herself.

'But things didn't happen like that,' Sally went on, 'and now I'm twenty years older and still all I want to do is get married. All I want is a kind man I can be a good wife to. Does that seem so unreasonable?' She turned to look at Annie. 'Tell me, does it seem unreasonable?'

Annie shook her head. 'No,' she whispered. She did not know what to say at all. She wanted to escape but she did not know how to take her leave and go. Poor Sally was suffering terribly in her loneliness. It was a feeling Annie had often had herself, especially before she met Tilly, but she had always thought it was something to do with being a child. She never imagined that a grown-up could feel lonely.

But now looking at Sally, it seemed the bigger you were the greater the pain.

'Men don't really like people like me,' Sally said quietly.

Annie bit her lower lip and gave a nod. She was beginning to feel completely out of her depth. 'But you have gentlemen friends,' she declared, trying to sound bright and optimistic.

Sally looked away. 'Mmmm,' she said. Then she fell silent, fiddling with her laces again.

It was getting late. 'My mother will be wondering where I am,' Annie said, getting to her feet and picking up the basket. She backed away.

Sally looked up and waved her hand. 'Thanks for listening,' she said flatly. 'I'm sorry to burden you with my problems.'

'That's all right,' said Annie, smiling kindly at her. 'It was very . . .' She searched for the right word. 'Interesting.'

As Annie set off down the road again she felt upset. It had always seemed that growing up would solve all the problems you had as a child. Being a grown-up meant that you didn't have anyone bossing you around and telling you what to do all the time. Now the future was beginning to look quite different and a lot more complicated.

Poor Sally, Annie thought as she swung the empty basket in the air. Her problems were a bit like Maudie's. They were both lonely. Perhaps they should move in together. Then they would have each other for company and never feel lonely any more.

CHAPTER 6

❦

The Street Party

THE FALKLAND ROAD PARTY was always held on a Saturday in the middle of August. The first street party had taken place nearly twenty years ago to celebrate the ending of the Great War in 1918. It had taken place every year since then, with generation after generation of Kentish Towners taking part. For many it was the highlight of the year.

The party celebrations were spread out over two of Falkland Road's three blocks. All the residents of Falkland Road were invited but other people were welcomed from the neighbouring cross streets. Thus the party took in a large part of the local population. The atmosphere was always one of neighbourliness and good will. Old feuds were forgotten, enemies danced side by side, warring families sat down and ate sandwiches and cake together, and everyone smiled and laughed throughout the afternoon and late into the night.

There was music all day long, from the fiddlers playing Irish jigs to the big singsong around the piano in the evening. The Turners' piano was carried outside by six strong men and placed in the middle of the street. Throughout the day, Frank, Jack and Clara took it in turns to play. At the first street parties, it had been Frank and his father who played the tunes all day. It was always understood that the piano entertainment was provided by the Turner family, and would probably continue to be for ever after.

All the way down one side of the street trestle tables were set up. They sagged with the weight of the plates piled high with food: sausages and pork pies, egg and tinned salmon sandwiches, and fairy cakes with different coloured icing. Placed between the plates of sandwiches were large enamel jugs full of refreshing barley water and pale yellow lemonade. Barrels of beer were available for all.

A vast copper kettle had been placed at one end of the street. It was here that Dolly Pritchett brewed up enough tea to last the day. Her fat face was flushed and sweaty in the heat of the sun but she remained unfailingly cheerful throughout the festivities. It was clear to all that she loved being in charge.

Mrs Garcia had set up a tent outside her house and pinned a notice to the flap: 'Your fortune or your palm read by Madam Maria. Tuppence a go.' The tent was dark inside and draped within and without in richly coloured shawls with fringed edges. Maria did a brisk trade all day with people going into the tent laughing and coming out with rather grave and sometimes even shocked expressions on their faces. Mrs Garcia looked the part, with her colourful silk shawls draped around her solid shoulders and a scarf over her entire head. She sat at a round table, hunched over the large crystal ball placed in front of her.

There were always plenty of willing helpers to organize
the Falkland Road party but it was Dolly Pritchett and
Frank Turner who masterminded the great event each
year, just as their parents had before them. It was they
who decided how much entertainment was needed, from
the magician, jugglers and clowns for the children, to the
dancing and plate-spinning for the adults. Months before,
Dolly had drawn up a rota of people whose names she
had collected earlier, people who would help beforehand
and on the day itself. The women volunteers were told
how many cakes needed to be baked, how many sausage
rolls had to be made and how many sandwiches had to be
filled with a specified number of fillings. Dolly also had a
list of people she could cajole to cough up a few more
shillings for the kitty. This helped to pay for the little
extras that made it such a memorable day that people
from the area talked about it for the rest of their lives,
their eyes glistening with tears when they thought back to
those great days.

It was Frank's job to organize the men, arranging for
them to collect the long trestle tables and wooden chairs
from the church hall and to set them up in place, and to
string the bunting (carefully stored in Dolly's kitchen cupboard since last year and the year before that) from house
to house to create an open ceiling of fluttering red, white
and blue flags.

The children planned their costumes for the fancy-
dress parade weeks before – milkmaids, pirates and
Robin Hoods – and assembled them from odd bits of
material begged from their mothers and grannies and
aunts, and bullied their mothers into helping to construct
them – the more elaborate, the better. The street party

had become something that parents could use to hold over their children's heads in the run-up to the day, with threats of being made to stay in their rooms and miss the party altogether if they did not do as they were told. Yes, the street party was the highlight of the year for everyone involved.

It was an event people planned for months beforehand and talked about for months afterwards. No other street they knew had such a splendid affair and outsiders would wistfully listen to descriptions of it from those who had been there, and hope that they might be lucky enough to be invited next year.

For people from outside the immediate area were not welcome unless they had some link with the area – close relatives who lived in Falkland Road or the relevant cross streets.

Although Tilly would have been allowed to come, she was not there, for she had gone to visit her grandparents that week. Life without Tilly had been rather boring for Annie, but she had spent a lot of time helping her parents get ready for the party.

Early that morning she had been out in the road, holding a plan of the street in her hand and instructing the helpers as to where to place the tables, the piano, and the rope in preparation for the tug of war. She felt very important and she knew that the other children in the street envied her for the authority she had been given by virtue of her status as a Turner. But she made a point of being friendly to everyone so that nobody would think that it had all gone to her head.

It was a shock to see Roger there. Annie spotted him first, walking jauntily down the road. With his head held high and his hands pushed deep into his pockets, he looked very cocky.

'What's Roger doing here?' she asked in dismay. 'Roger doesn't live here . . .'

Dolly was standing nearby. She had another list in her hand and was peering at it to see what else needed to be done. 'Oh, I expect he's here with his Aunt Jane. She lives in Leverton Street and finds it hard to get around now. She said she was going to ask one of her great-nephews to bring her. She always likes to have a young man to escort her, does Jane,' Dolly sniffed. 'She always was like that, even as a young woman.'

Annie was now staring at Roger through narrowed eyes. 'Well, after all he's done to us, he still shouldn't be allowed to come,' she muttered.

As she watched him, Annie could see Roger paying attention to a white-haired old lady sitting on a chair by the pavement. Her ankles were fat and swollen and a walking stick was leaning against her armchair. Annie recognized her wrinkled face and stooped shoulders. She had seen this lady many times in the street, though she had never known that she was Roger's great-aunt.

Roger handed his aunt a cup of lemonade before sauntering off into the crowd. He had grown a lot since Annie had last seen him. Like her brother Jack, he was now fifteen, tall and heavily built. He had thick black hair and a wide forehead above dark hooded eyes. He looked tense. Every now and then he clenched his jaw muscles unconsciously, which gave him a nervy manner as if he were always on the look-out for trouble. He rarely stood still, moving through the crowd, stopping here and there, always glancing quickly around him as he picked food off

the plates and swallowed it quickly. Then he walked over to
the piano where Clara had just started playing some lively
jazz tunes.

In past years Clara had led the gymnastics display – a
group of girls walking on their hands, doing flips, and
performing beautifully controlled body movements. But
this year the display had gone on without her. Suddenly
self-conscious about her changing body, Clara had backed
out at the last minute. Everyone agreed that this was a
great shame, since Clara Turner was the best gymnast
anyone had ever seen, but they were also sympathetic.
They could understand how the girl felt, now that she was
less of a girl, really, and, at thirteen years of age, develop-
ing into a woman. She was entitled to be a bit more
modest.

Annie watched closely as Roger sidled up to her sister.
Clara glanced up at Roger as he stood next to the piano
and leaned on the top. To Annie's fury, Clara smiled at
him. How could Clara do that? It wasn't even just a polite
smile either. It was warm and friendly. Didn't she know
who Roger was? Annie scowled.

Dolly had seen the look on Annie's face and squeezed
her shoulder. 'Roger has every right to be here, cock. Now
don't you fret about it . . .'

'But he killed my rabbit,' Annie hissed, thrusting out
her lower lip.

Grace was ladling milk from a churn into jugs. Her
arthritis had not been troubling her much recently, so she
had been able to play an active part in the celebrations
this year. She overheard this exchange. 'Annie, dear, that
was three years ago now. You mustn't hang on to grudges
like this. Everyone's grown up a lot since then.'

Annie scowled again and glared in Roger's direction. 'Well, I'm not going to smile at him. And I don't think anyone else should, either. He's a horrid boy, a bully. He always has been and always will be.'

Grace smiled affectionately at her. 'Just try to enjoy the party, Annie, love. We've been blessed with a beautiful day, so take advantage of it now.'

A big, noisy crowd of people had started dancing. Annie tried to switch her mind off Roger and watch the activities. There was old Mrs Horder dancing with Danny. Mother and son held hands, faced each other and swung their arms in unison. Danny was squealing with delighted laughter, a huge slobbery grin on his wide face. His straight black hair flopped over his forehead. Mrs Horder was tiny but astonishingly agile for someone of her age, pointing her toes as she danced from side to side, her head tilted neatly, her eyes sparkling.

'Danny had better not step on his mother or she'll be squashed in one go,' laughed Frank as he walked past, dragging the thick rope for the tug of war. 'Hey, Annie,' he called, dropping his load and holding out his arms. 'Would you like to dance with your old dad?'

Annie joined her father in the middle of the stretch of road that had become the dance floor. Frank held her in his arms, swinging her round and leading her through steps she didn't know. He manipulated her with such skill and ease that she felt she had been dancing all her life. 'Your mother used to be a great dancer,' Frank shouted at her over the loud, jaunty music. 'She's not up to it any more, which is a shame.' He spun Annie round. 'But you have the rhythm. You're your mother's daughter all right!'

Her father's encouragement gave Annie confidence, and before long she was moving freely to Frank's lead with fluid, graceful movements. As she moved, her heart soared under her budding breasts. I am a woman, she thought. I am eleven years old and a young woman at last!

All around them their friends and neighbours danced. They moved deftly sideways to avoid the Fenton sisters, who were holding each other by the waist and bickering about which direction to go in. They steered clear of Mr and Mrs Smith, too. Although Frank had come to like Tommy and seen what a decent fellow he was, he was still not keen on the parents. In any event, the Smiths had to be avoided because they were such clumsy dancers, taking up a lot of space and barging into other couples without any apologies whatsoever. They also complained constantly about the music and made it quite plain that they did not approve of Clara's choice. 'How about a proper knees-up, then?' they called. 'Let's stop this modern dancing and have a bit of the real thing . . .'

Annie laughed and was surprised to see that her father was relaxed and laughing too.

Later she saw Tommy Smith sitting on a wall. As she waved to him, she felt a twinge in her chest which made her realize how much she was missing Tilly at that moment.

Tommy was still a close friend of the girls. They often all went up to Hampstead Heath together after school, or wandered along the canal from Camden Lock to Islington and back. They were a serious-minded threesome and liked to discuss the books they had borrowed from the library that week. And in their intimacy, Annie had even brought Tommy in on the mysterious existence of her mother's brooch, something she had only ever done with Tilly before now. He thought it was a great intrigue. Once, when her mother was out, Annie had taken Tommy up to her parents' room to show him the brooch. 'Cor!' he said, holding the sparkling jewels up to the light to make them sparkle more. He narrowed his eyes. 'Your mother must have done something very important for the person who gave her this as a thank you.'

Annie nodded. 'What could it possibly be? And why does my mother want to hide it away all the time?'

Tommy looked thoughtful. 'We have to work on this one,' he murmured.

Tommy had seen her. 'Hey, Annie,' he called. 'Want to come up here?' He leaned down to hoist her up next to him.

Annie sprang up and settled beside him.

Tommy gave her a gap-toothed grin. 'Want a gob-stopper?' He held out a crumbled white paper bag. 'They last a good long time and have some smashing colours.'

Sucking their gob-stoppers, the children watched the street party from their elevated position. It was now in full swing. The weather was swelteringly hot. Women wore thin summer frocks and hats to ward off the sun. Those men who did not care about appearing respectable at all times had sensibly taken off their shirts to reveal string vests beneath. Those who did, rolled up their sleeves as far as they could. Men downed pints and pints of beer, while everyone else drank glasses of barley water or lemonade to quench their thirst.

Later on Annie saw Sally Brown and waved to her

across the street. Sally was on the arm of a tall man
dressed in an ill-fitting suit. He had a sharp, rat-like face.
From the way Sally leaned heavily towards her companion
and every now and then stumbled over her big feet, Annie
could tell that she had probably also been enjoying a lot of
the free beer. Annie was rather hurt when Sally walked
right by without a flicker of recognition or acknowledge-
ment. It was as if they had never had that private
conversation on Sally's doorstep. Their talk had made a
lasting impression on Annie and she had assumed that
Sally felt the same way. In fact, ever since, she had felt a
special bond with Sally, even though they hardly ever
crossed paths. Now Sally was acting as though they had
never met.

Next, they saw Maudie Sprackling wandering along the
road. Her sad, downcast face stood out in the happy
crowd. She had several sandwiches in her hands. She ate
these methodically, lifting them up to her mouth and taking bites without pause. Her pasty moon face looked more
bloated than usual, and Annie thought she looked even
sadder, too. Perhaps happy people made her sad.

After a while Annie and Tommy jumped down from the
wall and walked down to the far end of the street, near
Annie's house. They passed Jack on the way. Annie could
tell that he had been drinking beer with some of his mates.
He was looking excited. He kept flicking his hair back off
his face, which was flushed and hot. Most telling of all
was his friendly greeting to his little sister: 'Hello there,
Annie! Hello, Tommy!'

'Hmmm,' grunted Annie. 'Usually he ignores me.'

'Well a bit of beer always makes people friendly,' said
Tommy.

'I don't know what my mother will say about Jack drinking beer,' Annie said with a self-important shake of the head.

It was time for the tug of war, always one of the most popular events of the day. It was Falkland Road versus the Cross-streeters, those from Leverton Street and Lady Margaret Road.

The men were lining up by the side of the road. The younger, stronger men showed off their bare chests and flexed their muscles in a display of strength. Those with weedy bodies just rolled up their shirt sleeves and waited, their arms hanging awkwardly by their sides. The two teams began to jeer at each other with mock rivalry.

Frank was in charge. He had marked out the area and drawn a line across the road with chalk. He had also tied his white handkerchief to the thick knotted rope. 'All right, boys,' he called, 'take your positions.'

Roger had taken up a position on the Cross-streeters' team. Annie felt a twinge of dismay as she saw her father talking to him in a friendly way. He too? It was bad enough that Clara was hanging around him.

Clara had stopped her jazz playing and had come to watch the tug of war. Watching Clara closely, Annie began to suspect that in all the cheering and shouting that was going on, Clara was actually rooting for Roger.

On the Falkland Road team, Jack had stripped down to the waist. His body had filled out and broadened in the past year. He looked more like a mature man than a fifteen-year-old. His muscles were sharply defined over his chest and back and along his arms. Annie was proud of her handsome brother, and pleased to see him narrow his eyes at Roger on the other side of the road. At least Jack had not chosen to forget what Roger had done. Annie was grateful for that.

It was an exciting contest, with the white handkerchief hovering over the line and moving slightly over to one side and then back again as the combined strengths of the two teams battled against each other.

Then suddenly it was over. The Falkland Road team faltered as one man lost his footing, with the others caught off guard. The handkerchief shot over the winning line, and the Cross-streeters fell backwards on top of each other as the tension on the rope was suddenly lifted. A great yell of victory went up. People blew whistles and cheered. 'Well done, Cross-streeters! Well done!'

It was a good-humoured contest. The losing side had to buy the victors a round of drinks in the Falkland Arms afterwards. There was not meant to be any bad feeling about it but Annie could see Jack looking quite disgruntled, especially as Clara had run over to Roger and was congratulating him. He was smiling at her and joking as he wiped the dripping sweat off his brow with the back of his forearm.

'Your sister seems to like Roger,' Tommy commented as they moved away.

'Mmm,' muttered Annie.

Much of the party was over, though many people looked set to celebrate until late into the night. Dolly had brewed the last of the tea. 'There's just beer and lemonade from now on,' she said. Annie was helping her clear up her table.

Suddenly she became aware of a loud bell ringing, and all around people were pointing and laughing. Then she saw why. Coming down the road swinging a large bell in his hand was Mr Spratt. His eyes were wide open and wild-looking, focusing on nothing as he approached. Annie stared aghast. From the top of his bald head to the tips of his gnarled toes, Mr Spratt was completely naked. He was yelling at the top of his voice: 'Bring out your dead! Bring out your dead!'

Women clapped their hands over their mouths and shrieked with laughter. Men looked away in embarrassment. Nobody did anything except gawp and laugh, until Dolly, who was not laughing, swept up her skirts and pushed her way through the crowds. 'Come on, now, Mr Spratt,' she said briskly, handing him her apron. 'Cover yerself up and let's take you home.'

'Bring out your dead!' Mr Spratt called. 'Bring out your dead!' He was oblivious to everything around him.

Dolly turned him around by the arm and gently led him back towards his house.

'He's been upset ever since his chickens died,' someone said behind Annie. 'A whole lot of them died for no good reason a few months ago. They just dropped dead. That young Clara Turner – bless her heart – bought him some new chicks to replace the ones he'd lost, but the poor old fellow's gone ever so queer.'

Annie turned her head to see that Clara had been listening to this conversation, too. Clara quickly looked way to avoid her sister's accusing eye.

Late that night when Annie was asleep in bed, exhausted by the events of the day, Jack and Clara were in Jack's room talking. They were in their nightclothes. Jack had been drinking more beer. Unused to alcohol, he felt drowsy. They had been dancing until quite late when their mother had finally told them to go to bed.

Clara fell back on the bed with a loud happy sigh. 'What a day! The best of my life!'

'It was pretty good,' he said.

'I just love to dance. It makes me feel so alive.' Clara stretched her arms above her head.

Jack was feeling peculiar. He felt oddly excited but he did not know why.

Clara lent backwards against Jack's legs, pushing her toes under the soft eiderdown. 'I feel so safe and snug,' she said dreamily.

Jack was aware of his sister's body beneath her white cotton nightdress and the soapy fragrance of her skin. He lay back against the bedstead and stared out of the window. The sky was blue-black. A midsummer evening. It was now late but still not pitch-dark outside. Unconsciously he ran his hand up and down Clara's arm. He could feel the soft hairs on her skin. It was a comforting rhythm. Up and down. He was only vaguely aware of his sister's hand on his thigh. She too seemed to be in a trance as her arm moved along his skin. Up and down, up and down.

Then they were aware and not aware. The pleasure of the sensations they were creating was strong, so strong that it overwhelmed any sense that what they were doing was wrong.

Clara turned to Jack and reached up. As their lips touched, powerful forces surged through their bodies. Turning to each other, they pressed themselves close.

Jack knew that Clara felt the same. They should stop but they could not. They wanted to go beyond the line, they wanted to find out. And nobody would ever know.

Skin on skin. Flesh on flesh. Clara winced and shifted slightly as Jack pressed against her. She did not cry out. She did not tell him to stop. Their breathing quickened, their limbs tensed. Flesh in flesh, warm and enclosed. Once Jack opened his eyes to look. Clara's eyes were firmly closed, a sleepy sweet smile on her pink open lips.

In the middle of the night, Jack woke up with pins and needles in his arm. Clara was still in his bed and lying on his arm. She lay on her back, her mouth open, and her arm flung back above her head on the pillow. Jack pulled his arm away and shook his sister. Muttering in her half-sleep, but aware of the need to move, Clara stumbled next door to her own room and climbed between the cool sheets of her bed.

Annie slept soundly through it all. The sound of the bedroom door opening and Clara tiptoeing to bed were simply incorporated into her dreams.

The next morning as Annie went downstairs, she noticed something strange out of the landing window. There was something odd about Mr Spratt's chickens, and the way they were circling around in their run and making much more of a racket than usual. She ran downstairs and out into the garden to take a look. The fowl were looking quite extraordinary. Every one, including Marmaduke, had long dangling earrings clipped to its coxcomb. The unhappy birds clucked plaintively and shook their heads in a vain attempt to throw off the clinging jewellery – the late Mrs Spratt's best costume pieces in bright red, green, blue and silver – glittering as brightly as the chickens' frightened eyes.

And there was more. Annie caught sight of the chickens'

claws. Mr Spratt must have been up working all through night. Every one of his hens' talons was bright scarlet, beautifully painted with shiny red nail varnish.

Annie shook her head. Clara was going to have to say a lot of prayers in church that day to make up for what she had done to poor Mr Spratt.

CHAPTER 7

❧

Jessie

THE KETTLE HAD BOILED. Taking it off the hob, Maudie Sprackling poured the boiled water onto the tea leaves, gave it a stir and popped the lid on. Covering the teapot with a red knitted tea-cosy, she placed it on a tray next to the jug of milk and bowl of sugar. She put two butter biscuits on a plate and then carried the tray next door to the front room, stepping around the heavy black pram in the hall as she did so.

She lowered the tray onto the small side table and then she sat back heavily into the armchair with a contented sigh.

She smiled gently as she looked around the room. There was the baby's rattle on the sofa, a discarded muslin nappy used only for the possets, the empty bottle on the side. She would have to boil that bottle soon, to sterilize it, she thought, and she must not forget to boil up the pile of nappies lying in the tin bucket in the scullery. If she washed the nappies before lunch, then she could hang them out to dry in the garden. There was a good wind outside so the chances were she could have them clean and dry by the evening.

Emma Dally

Maudie stared at the bits and pieces lying around the room and thought how pleasant it was not to feel the usual urge to tidy up. No, if anything, she wanted to preserve the room as it was, to give her the chance to relish every bit of evidence of that young life sleeping so soundly upstairs.

What a lot of work it was looking after a baby! There was hardly time for anything. Just as she finished one thing, something else needed to be done. It was just as well that the baby slept so much. At least she could get most of her chores done while he was asleep – the chores at home, anyway. Going out shopping with the pram and all the business of getting the baby ready beforehand was still too daunting for her to attempt very often.

She poured herself a cup of tea and sat back in her chair. Sipping the milky drink, she reflected on how dramatically her life had changed over the last few weeks. Why, it had been less than three weeks since she had met Jessie, yet it seemed like an age.

She did not know why she had gone to Regent's Park on that Saturday morning. She did not know then and she was none the wiser now. Perhaps it was because she had been there once in happier days with Fred, when they had walked hand in hand and talked of their future life together, when she thought she knew what happiness was.

She had gone down there to listen to the brass band on the high bandstand and to wander around the ponds and watch the people in the rowing boats – happy people, laughing and splashing with their oars in the water. Happy people, unlike her, with her plodding legs and lumpy body. Life was a misery for poor Maudie. Everything was grey; she felt she had no feelings about anything any more. Even when the sun was shining and the sky blue, it all felt grey. She didn't care if she lived or died, and she only went on existing because she could not be bothered to think of anything else to do.

She worked a little, cleaning for Dr and Mrs Foster up in Highgate for three days a week, but she did not earn much because up until now she had not needed to. First, Fred had been earning enough working on the trams to pay for most things, and then after he left, she had just paid for the rent on the house with the money her father had left her when he died. It had not been much, but it had been a nest egg of a sort, and after Fred had run off with Connie Smith, it had come in handy. The trouble was it had almost run out and now she was becoming worried about what to do. Part of her could not be bothered to do anything. Life was so bad. But deep down she did care enough not to want to be thrown out of her home for not paying the rent. It was the house in which she had grown up. And her love for it had turned into a compulsive urge to clean it all the time she was there. She hated herself for doing it, but she could not stop herself. It made her feel safe, to keep busy that way, down on her knees and scrubbing.

She knew people laughed at her and thought she was going soft, but she still could not help herself. She did not care what any of them thought, not even those people who had been friends of her mum and dad. Maudie did not have friends any more.

As she had left the park she noticed a young woman pushing a large black pram along the pavement. The woman seemed to be struggling. She had two heavy string bags full of shopping so her hands were full already, and pushing the pram was difficult. She had manoeuvred it to the kerb where she was obviously planning to cross the road. But the front wheels suddenly slipped over the edge of the pavement, tipping the back end of the pram right up into the air.

Maudie did not hesitate. She ran up to the pram and pulled it upright. She held her hand out just in time to prevent the tiny infant inside slipping out onto the road with all its bedding on top of it. She pulled the pram back to the safety of the pavement just as a motor car roared past.

'Oh, thank you, thank you,' gasped the woman. 'You probably saved my baby's life.'

Her accent was quite posh, posher than the woman's appearance suggested. Her clothes were old and tatty, and her shoes scuffed and unpolished.

Maudie smiled and shrugged her shoulders. 'That's all right. I could see you were having trouble.'

The two women went into the park and walked along together. The woman, whose name was Jessie, told Maudie her astonishing life story without prompting.

She told her that although she came from a good family and had grown up in a big house in south London, she was now destitute. This sad state of affairs had come about in little over a year. A year before she had been engaged to marry a handsome young man called Larry. He was a lawyer with a bright future ahead of him. Her parents liked him and were pleased with the match. Because they were getting married, they had been more intimate with each other than perhaps they should have been, but tragically, three weeks before the wedding, Larry was knocked down and killed by a motor car. Jessie's grief was complicated by the fact that a few weeks later she realized she was going to have a baby.

While she was pleased to have a child of Larry's, even in such terrible circumstances, her parents were horrified. They told Jessie that she would have to go away immediately before anyone they knew guessed about her condition, and that she could only return home after giving up the child for adoption.

Jessie had left the family home and given birth in a home for young ladies in trouble. 'My baby was born in the early hours of Christmas Day,' she said. 'At two o'clock in the afternoon, just at the time my family always sat down for Christmas dinner, I telephoned them from the hospital to tell them that they had become grandparents. But they would not speak to me. My mother put the telephone back on the hook. She put the telephone down on her own daughter.'

The two women were sitting on a bench in the park. They could hear the sound of the elephants in the zoo nearby bellowing for their tea, the chattering and shrieks of the monkeys and the shrill squawks from the bird house. Maudie listened to Jessie's story in fascination and when Jessie told her that she needed to find a place to live as she was not allowed to stay in the home for unmarried mothers for much longer, she did not hesitate to offer her a room in her house.

That had been a month ago and the arrangement had worked out even better than anyone could have expected. Jessie and her baby William moved in and the two women found that they liked each other. Despite the great differences in their backgrounds, they felt they had a lot in common. Soon they had arranged their lives to suit each

other. Jessie was very keen to get a job and earn some
money. She felt obliged to pay Maudie rent for the room
but she also wanted the independence her own earnings
could bring. However, she could not work unless she had
someone to look after the baby. She explained that
although she loved William, she did not enjoy looking
after him for every minute of the day. On hearing that,
Maudie did not hesitate to offer her services. And so Jessie
found a clerical job in a department store in the West End,
and earned enough to pay Maudie handsomely for the
rent and for looking after her baby. Maudie could give up
her cleaning job and now had a little baby to look after.
Even if she had to share him with Jessie, Maudie was
happy. William was a sweet-natured little boy and took to
being looked after by Maudie without any objections.
Four months old, with fair hair and huge blue eyes, he
laughed and chuckled at everything.

As Maudie was taking her elevenses back to the kitchen,
she heard William's high-pitched cry from upstairs. He
had woken up very hungry by the sound on it.

She removed the bottle of watered-down milk from the
saucepan of hot water on the cooker. Shaking it up, she
shook a drop of milk onto her wrist to test it. The temper-
ature was just right.

By the time Maudie reached William in Jessie's bedroom upstairs, the baby was screaming. But the moment
he was picked up and gathered into Maudie's fleshy arms,
he stopped. Maudie held him gently against her shoulder
and rubbed his back. William smacked his lips together
hungrily and began rooting into her chest.

'Wait, my pet,' Maudie cooed, sitting down on the bed.
She held William in front of her and kissed him gently on

the cheek. Placing him on her lap, she began to unbutton her blouse. William's hunger was growing and he began to wail impatiently.

The bottle was on the side table but Maudie continued to undo her top clothes. She had wanted to do this for several days. Jessie was still nursing William in the mornings before she left for work and in the evenings when she came home. Maudie watched her intently every time, almost feeling the tug of the baby's demanding lips on her own large brown nipple.

Her heavy soft breast fell out of the brassière. William was whimpering and rooting hard against her white skin. Maudie grasped her nipple in the way she had watched Jessie do it, and guided it towards William's open mouth. William's gums sank with greedy relief onto Maudie's flesh. She jumped at the sensation, surprised by the strength of his mouth. For a few seconds, she gazed down at the baby on her breast, imagining the sight of her and William to be like the Madonna and Child. He was a Christmas baby, after all. She smiled, her eyes glistening with tears.

Suddenly William pulled away from the nipple with an angry cry. He plunged back onto it but pulled away again, his face red with frustration.

'Sorry, my darling,' whispered Maudie, reaching for the bottle and quickly pushing the teat into the baby's mouth. William sank into her arms with a sigh of relief, and gulped down the milk so fast that he nearly choked. 'There's nothing there for you,' cooed Maudie, pushing her breast back inside her blouse. 'I just had to know. I just had to know what it was like.' She smiled serenely. 'It was lovely,' she whispered. 'Thank you, love.'

*

The Easter bank holiday was always popular with the Turner family because of the traditional fair on Hampstead Heath. The children had been looking forward to it for weeks. Annie was particularly keen to win a goldfish this year. It was a popular fair with a carousel and rides for grown-ups and children alike, but it also had great side-shows with the Biggest Rat in the World, the Hairy Lady and (Jack's favourite) the Siamese Lambs, a freakish creature with eight legs and two heads. Frank had explained that although it was dead and stuffed, it was real. 'It wouldn't have been able to live for long,' he explained. Annie liked the two-headed duck, which was also stuffed, while Clara liked the twelve stuffed kittens all dressed up in pretty costumes and playing croquet on a pretend lawn. The kittens looked normal and Annie was afraid that there had been nothing wrong with them to make them die, which meant that probably someone had drowned them when they were a few weeks old. Her father probably knew the answer, but Annie did not dare ask.

Annie's mother had not been well that week – her joints had flared up again – so she said that she would stay at home and look after Bobby, who was too young to enjoy the fair properly anyway. So after lunch, Frank took the three older children on the Underground to Hampstead Heath.

The fair was in full swing when they arrived. Annie said she wanted to stay with her father, while Jack and Clara were keen to go off on their own. They had been fooling around a lot that morning, tickling each other and bantering loudly. When they acted like that, Annie always felt excluded, so she did not want to be with them anyway.

'We'll all meet up here by the candy-floss stall,' said Frank. 'At four o'clock sharp.'

Annie stayed with her father. Although excited to be at the fair, she was quite frightened by the jostling crowd of people who pushed and shoved her as though she did not exist.

The ground was getting muddy underfoot and her leather boots kept slipping. Only by holding her father's hand could she keep her balance.

What fun they had! Frank had his turn at the rifle range and hit three bulls'-eyes in a row. He won a rag doll which he handed to Annie. 'Look after my prize, my dear. It's for your mother. I've never once come away from here without some booty for Grace.'

Annie tried her hand with the table-tennis balls and the goldfish bowls but failed to get anything. She had never had an eye for the ball. They visited the Biggest Rat in the World and the Hairy Lady who was immensely fat and had hair sprouting out of her chin and down her cheeks. Oddly enough, she did not have much hair on her head.

Frank bought Annie a toffee apple which she ate with some difficulty but relished every bit of the crunchy crackly caramel sticking to her teeth. Every now and then they spotted Clara or Jack who were wandering around on their own. Annie watched her father hit three coconuts at the coconut shy.

'No more, sir!' called the man in charge. 'Give someone else a chance now.'

'There's one each for you three children,' said Frank.

'What about Bobby?' Annie always liked to be fair.

'Bobby won't know, and you can give him a bit of yours,' laughed Frank. 'How about a ride on the carousel?'

Annie smiled. She was touched that he had asked. She
thought that perhaps at eleven, she was a bit old to want a
go on the carousel but she still loved to ride on those gar-
ishly painted wooden horses, riding up and down, holding
on tight to the reins as the music started up.

Seeing the look of eagerness on his daughter's face,
Frank pulled out a coin and handed it to the operator.
'Next time you're on, Annie,' he called.

Annie rode on the most handsome horse she could find,
holding her head high and pretending to herself that she
was a prince galloping on a real horse across the fields in
the countryside. The horse tossed his head in the air and
snorted through flared nostrils. The earth thundered past
under his hoofs. The music filled her ears. Annie was soon
so entranced that she forgot to wave to her father as she
went past him.

After the carousel, they went on to the Bowling for the
Pig stand. Twelve large heavy skittles were placed at one
end. Competitors had to roll the bowls to knock them all
down. Ladies were allowed to start halfway up the stand.

'Roll up! Roll up!' The man in charge was heavily built
with a crushed-looking face. He had a broken nose and
scarred skin.

'This is your last chance to win the pig!' he bellowed
through his cupped hands, turning from one side to the
other. 'The play-off is in five minutes. This is your last
chance to qualify!'

Annie peered into the banana crate next to the man.
Lying on yellow straw, fast asleep, was a small pink piglet.
Its tail was curled right round in a circle and its small
snout twitched as he slept. Annie looked in wonder at the
sparse white hairs growing out of its back. It was clean.

She knew pigs were really clean animals, that they liked to be clean if they had the opportunity. Her heart swelled with feeling for this baby animal, and her mind began to work out how she could look after it in the back garden. She had read a book once about a girl who had a pig for a pet. She squeezed Frank's hand.

'Oh Daddy, you have a go! You'll knock them all down.'

Frank laughed. He did pride himself on his strength and his accurate eye. 'I don't know what we'll do with a pig, Annie,' he said, 'but let's worry about that later.' He handed the man a penny and took the three bowls.

As Annie expected, Frank knocked down all the skittles with the three bowls. She jumped up and down with excitement. He had won! She had got the pig!

But she was wrong. Frank gently pointed out that three other men had managed to knock all the skittles down (albeit after several tries) and now there had to be a play-off.

A crowd gathered round to see the final of the bowling contest. Annie stayed close to the banana crate. The piglet had woken up now. He did not shift his position but his little eyes blinked sleepily.

Frank was the third to go. The first man was a young fellow with a patch over one eye. His first bowl was a disaster. It wobbled up the grass and missed the skittles completely. The other two bowls knocked down four skittles between them.

The next man managed to knock down six skittles after some bad luck when one bowl scooted between the targets without touching any of them. Then it was Frank's go. The atmosphere was getting tense. Everyone was quiet. Annie crossed her fingers and held her breath as her father bent down to pick up the bowls. With deft graceful movements, he sent the bowls down in speedy straight lines. The skittles went flying in all directions. 'Well done!' a cry went out. But there was one solitary skittle left standing.

'It's been put in a trench!' one wag called out.

The fourth man took up his position. Annie glared at him, willing him to fail, to let her have the pig as her friend. She leant down and stroked the pig's back. It flinched as she touched its thick, hairy skin.

The man bowled slowly and precisely. The first one knocked down six skittles, the other two the rest. A huge cheer went up. Frank laughed and shrugged his shoulders. Then he shook hands and congratulated the winner, completely unaware of the tears welling up in his daughter's eyes.

Annie stared at the pig sadly. It was too late now, there was no chance. He would belong to someone else.

The winner came over to inspect his prize. 'It's not a bad weight,' he said.

'Would have been better in the summer,' someone commented. 'The pigs are always bigger at the August fairs.'

Annie looked at the man who had won. He looked like a rough sort, not the type to love an animal.

'Too bad, Annie,' said Frank, cheerfully picking up his jacket which he had taken off for better freedom of movement. 'Can't win every time. Have to let others have a chance.'

'But, Daddy,' Annie said anxiously, 'what if that man doesn't have a garden? Where will he be able to keep the pig?'

The couple standing nearby heard Annie's remark and nudged each other. 'Oh, I don't think he's going to be keeping the pig in a garden . . .' the lady said with a laugh.

'No, more like an ice box!' They laughed again. Annie blushed. She felt angry and embarrassed. There was only one way a pig could fit into the ice box. It had never occurred to her that anyone would want to kill this sweet creature. She felt angry with her father for not winning the pig and saving it from such a fate. Surely he could have tried harder . . .

'Come on, Annie, it's nearly four o'clock. We've got to go to the candy-floss stand.' Frank picked up his coconuts and started off in the direction of the rendezvous. Annie lagged behind, feeling both sulky and sad. She had no pets, no rabbit, no pig, not even a goldfish.

The place was still crowded and soon Annie realized that she could not see her father who had been striding way ahead of her. She did not even know where the candy-floss stand was. She stopped and looked around, fighting the rising panic inside her. She realized now that she had lost her sense of direction completely. She was too short to be able to see over people's heads and she had no idea of where to go. She turned round and round in one spot. The ground was mushy beneath her feet. A couple of boys ran by chasing each other, knocking her sideways as they went. Annie lost her footing on the slippery grass and fell down heavily on her bottom.

She sat on the ground dazed. Suddenly a strong arm slipped under hers and pulled her to her feet.

'Up you get. Why, it's Clara Turner's kid sister, ain't it?'

Annie peered up at the person who had saved her. She shrank back. It was Roger Knight, looming over her now with a smile on his face. In his other hand he carried two jam jars with a goldfish in each.

'Thank you.' Annie brushed herself off and smiled stiffly. 'I've got to get to the candy-floss stand,' she said with a worried frown. 'I'm meeting my family there at four o'clock. I lost my father in the crowd.'

Roger took her hand. 'I'll take you there myself. Come on, then.'

Annie allowed Roger to lead her through the crowd. Her heart was pounding. She could not believe that she was holding Roger Knight's hand! Roger Knight, who killed Rabbit! She stared ahead, not daring to look at him. Where was he taking her? Could she trust him to help her find her father, as he said he would?

The glass jars hanging from his fingers clinked together. Roger lifted them up and peered at them. 'Here, would you like a goldfish?' he asked.

Annie stared at him as if she did not understand.

'I won them for my kid brother,' continued Roger, 'but he won't mind if he only gets one. He's got about six already.'

Annie's eyes widened. 'Really?' She breathed excitedly, staring at the goldfish darting about in the small jam jar. 'I'd love it,' she whispered.

'It's all yours!' Roger placed the jar in the palm of her hand and grinned. He looked steadily at her for a moment or two. 'Can't say I'd guess you was Clara's sister if I didn't know already. You don't look like her at all.'

Annie stared at her goldfish and pretended not to hear this hurtful remark. 'Thank you,' she whispered. 'It's very kind of you to give it to me.'

Roger waved off her thanks. 'It's nothing. Now, come on, let's go and find that family of yours.' He took her by the hand again and pulled her through the crowd.

As Annie ran along behind, trying to keep up with Roger's long stride, she felt all muddled. She did not know what she thought about Roger Knight any more. He had given her a goldfish. He had given her a pet. He had been kind to her, when he was supposed to be a bad person.

Everyone was by the candy-floss stand when they got there. Frank was surprised to see his younger daughter arriving holding Roger's hand but when he learned what had happened and how Roger had helped Annie when she was lost, he was openly grateful. 'When I realized we'd lost each other I thought it best for me to get to the meeting place and wait rather than try to find her in the crowd.'

Clara smiled coyly at Roger, while Jack eyed him suspiciously.

'It's time to get home now with all our booty,' said Frank. 'Let's walk back.'

'I'll join you, if you don't mind,' said Roger. 'I've had enough for the day.'

They walked back across the Heath. It was a bright afternoon still, and the light on the grass and trees was soft and warm. As they emerged out of one wood, they saw an enchanting sight. A young girl, of no more than fifteen, was sitting under a large beech tree and playing the accordion to a semicircle of people who had gathered around to listen. The Turners went to join them. The girl was a fine player and ran through all the popular songs. Annie watched and listened. Her heart felt uplifted by the sound. It had been a fun day even if she had not got the pig. She hugged the jam jar to her chest. After all these years, she had got her pet. And what a surprise that it came from Roger, of all people.

She glanced over at Roger. He and Clara were standing extremely close together, almost pressing against each other as they swayed to the music. Frank was watching the young musician and he did not seem to have noticed, but Jack had. He kept glancing at the two of them, his fists clenched tightly by his sides.

CHAPTER 8

Danny Horder

GRACE TURNER WAS OUT in the garden carefully picking over her flowers and shrubs. In rare moments of peace and solitude when domestic affairs were under control, she would step outside to survey her fifty-foot patch of garden behind the house. And if her arthritis was not causing her trouble at that moment, she would begin to pull out weeds, prune a branch here, deadhead there.

Today, her joints were calm, the inflammation lying low. Her garden looked wonderful. The roses were showing off their white, red and pink flowers and the hollyhocks and dahlias were in full bloom. Grace loved this time of year when there was a dazzling display of colour amidst the green. The plants were all looking healthy, apart from the hostas. They were a sorry sight. Gazing in sad frustration at their leaves, now reduced to thin lacy skeletons, Grace had to admit that she had lost her battle with the snails. On Marion's advice, she had sprinkled gravel around the bottom of the plants. 'They hate getting anything on their bellies,' Marion had assured her. But the molluscs had still managed to reach the leaves and devastate them. Grace sighed. She could not think what the next step could be. Perhaps she should try growing them in pots. Or give up on hostas altogether.

At the back of the flower-bed was a large putrid jar full of dead snails. This lot had been lured into the trap by the inch of brown ale Grace had poured in. Perhaps she should put some more salt down. She did not approve of Jack's habit of pouring salt directly onto the snails to make them dissolve, but since the soil was dry, it wouldn't harm to sprinkle quite a bit around for the snails to crawl onto themselves. That way she wouldn't feel quite so responsible for their deaths.

The plight of her hostas made Grace profoundly sad. At her parents' cottage in Sussex where she had grown up, there had been magnificent hostas growing three feet high in large vigorous clumps, with leaves of various colours – powdery blue, pale green with creamy centres, grey-blue, dark green. And all producing the proudest racemes of violet or mauve flowers which crowned the foliage in mid-summer. Slugs and snails did not seem to like the sandy soil down there, for they had never been a particular problem, and the plants had always thrived.

As Grace's thoughts drifted to Sussex and the place where she had grown up, her face looked troubled. She picked up her thick canvas gardening gloves and stood up, straight-backed and rigid, a hand pressed against her ribs. Well, there wouldn't be any need to worry about any of her plants and flowers if war broke out. They would all have to go, poor things. The air-raid shelter would take up most of their patch of ground, and every inch of what was left would have to be given over to vegetables to feed the family. With images of cabbages, swedes, Brussels sprouts, onions and carrots, all thoughts of Sussex had faded to the back of her mind. 'Salt!' she said emphatically, picking up yet another snail from under the hostas and dropping it into the alcoholic pool of death. 'Salt it shall be!'

Annie was happy to run out and buy salt for her mother. Tilly had come round to see Annie that morning and they were glad to have an errand as an excuse to run around the neighbourhood, especially since Grace had told them they could keep the pennies left over and spend them in the sweet-shop afterwards.

Up the road, the two girls bumped into Tommy Smith. He was carrying a bag of books. He beamed at the girls when he saw them.

Now aged fourteen, Tommy had the beginnings of a beard on his chin. He had shot up in height recently and his voice had grown deeper. But he was still the same old grinning Tommy. He had never seemed embarrassed about the changes to his body, just taking them in his stride, as he took everything in life.

'Coming to the library, then?'

Annie shook her head. 'No, we've got to get some salt for Mother.' A musky smell emanated from him and curled around her nostrils. Annie liked it. It smelt foreign and grown-up.

'You're always going to that library,' remarked Tilly. 'You must be able to read very fast.'

'Yeah. I like reading.' Tommy grinned. 'I've decided to be a lawyer when I grow up.'

Annie nodded approvingly. 'That's good. You'll be the first in your family, I expect.'

Tommy threw back his head and laughed. 'That's true,'

he chuckled. 'But my family's had a lot of experience of the law, you know, so it's obviously in my blood!' The latest news from the Smith household was that the eldest boy, Keith, had been arrested for breaking and entering a shop in Holloway. He had stolen thirty tins of paint, and been sent to prison.

Tommy walked with them to Mr Nethercott's grocer's shop. As they passed the Horders' house, they heard a terrible sound, a sort of eerie wailing and howling.

'Have they got a dog?' The children stopped by the gate to listen.

'I think that's Danny,' said Annie. 'That's what Danny sounds like when he's upset. It's not usually as bad as that, but it does sound like him.'

Tommy went up to the door. It was locked. He peered in through the downstairs window, cupping his hands around the side of his face to get a clear look. 'I can see Danny,' he said. 'He's in there. He's crouching down on the floor.'

Annie and Tilly ran to the window to look. Sure enough, Danny was on his knees, rocking backwards and forwards, his huge hands covering his face. He howled in time to his rocking movement. There was no sign of Mrs Horder anywhere. Oddest of all, Danny seemed to be dressed in his stripy pyjamas, even though it was the middle of the afternoon.

Tommy tapped on the window. 'Hey, Danny! What's wrong?'

Nothing happened.

'Do it louder!' Annie's heart was pounding. Something was wrong.

Tommy banged hard on the glass with his fist.

Danny momentarily stopped his wailing and looked up.

Seeing Tommy standing by the window, he turned away and started up again, rocking backwards and forwards even more violently than before.

'Something must have happened to Mrs Horder,' whispered Annie.

'Perhaps she's just nipped out and left Danny at home for a few minutes,' suggested Tilly.

Annie shook her head. 'Mrs Horder would never do that. Danny can't do anything on his own. She takes him everywhere with her.'

'What about the people who live upstairs? Aren't they about?'

'The Spencers? No, they've only just gone away on holiday,' said Annie. 'They've gone to Blackpool for a week. Mrs Horder told me that only yesterday. I saw her and Danny coming home from the shops.'

The noise coming from Danny's throat was sounding more and more distressed. It was alarming. Annie banged on the window but Danny would not even look up any more. She felt confident that she could calm him but it was no good if he did not see her.

'I'm going to try to force the door,' said Tommy.

The girls looked on in wonder as Tommy pulled a penknife from his pocket. It was an old one he had had for years. He was always whittling pieces of wood with it or playing dangerous games of splits with other boys on patches of grass. He opened up the knife and pushed the blade between the door and the frame. He wiggled it up and down. Suddenly the door opened with a little click.

'How did you do that?' Annie was impressed.

'Well, since you ask,' Tommy grinned, 'it was me dad who showed me.'

The children stumbled into the dark hallway. Danny was in the front room where they had seen him. As they came in, he looked up at them.

Annie was shocked at the sight of him. His big round face was swollen from crying. His eyes were puffy and red. She noticed too that his cheeks were stubbly as though he had not shaved that day. She had never noticed that before. It had never occurred to her that the childlike Danny even shaved. Presumably Mrs Horder always did it for him.

'What's the matter, Danny?' Annie walked towards him, holding out her hand. 'Where's your mother?'

Danny's face was crumpled up with anguish. But he nodded when he saw Annie's familiar face. The other two children he was not so sure about, and he glanced at them sideways. He then got to his feet and reached out to take Annie's hand. She tried not to wince as he squeezed it tight. He squeezed it again and would not let go.

The house was quiet. It was as neat and tidy as ever. Nothing seemed different.

'Where's your mother, Danny?' Annie repeated the question in as clear a voice as possible.

Danny shook his head and frowned.

'Is she at home? Is she here somewhere?'

Danny stared at her with blank eyes. Then he frowned and looked away.

'I'm going to have a look upstairs,' said Tommy. He slipped out of the room. Seconds later he gave a shout. 'She's up here!' he called. 'She doesn't seem to be breathing. I think she's dead! She's all cold.'

Tilly's eyes widened. 'Oh, what shall we do?'

'You'd better run to Mr Nethercott's and ask him to telephone for the police and to call for a doctor.' Annie's voice was tremulous. Her hands were shaking too but she was only aware of Danny's tight grip on her upper arm now. He was leaning down on her heavily.

Tilly had gone. Annie sat down on the sofa. 'I think we'd better sit down here, Danny,' she said. 'We have to wait for some people to arrive now.'

Suddenly the house was full of people. The police arrived along with the doctor, and a crowd of people gathered outside in the street to see what was going on. People kept running up and down the stairs and nosing around the rooms. Then the police wanted to take statements from the children. They wanted to know exactly what had happened. Annie heard the doctor telling the police that it looked as though the old woman had had a heart attack in her sleep. 'It's the way to go,' he commented.

Annie was disturbed to see how rough the police were with Danny. They wanted to question him alone in the kitchen. But Danny would not let go of Annie's hand. Every time anyone came near him he started squealing like a frightened animal and huddled closer to Annie. 'Leave him alone,' she said. 'He's upset enough already.'

'It's all right, love,' said the policeman. 'We're not going to harm him. We just need to find out what happened.'

'What is there to find out?' Annie was getting cross with the way they frightened Danny. 'Mrs Horder just died in her sleep, didn't she? That's what the doctor said, I heard him. Besides,' she added, 'there's no point asking Danny questions. He can't talk. He's just like a two-year-old, just a baby, really, his mother used to say.'

The adults gathered around in groups and whispered. Tilly and Tommy were allowed to go home.

'Did Mrs Horder have any other relatives?' the police

sergeant asked Annie. 'Is there anyone else who can take charge of Danny now?'

Annie shook her head. 'Mrs Horder used to say there were only the two of them now.'

It was getting late. There was more whispering and talking. The light was failing outside. Annie was not surprised when her mother appeared. Tilly had informed her about what was going on. 'What's going to happen to Danny?' Annie asked. 'Who's going to look after him.'

Grace smiled and sat down beside Annie. Danny stared at her listlessly. He had dark circles under his eyes and he looked exhausted. 'Danny will have to go and stay in a special home where they will know how to look after him.'

'But he'll be frightened there,' Annie protested. 'He won't know anyone.'

'He'll get used to it,' Grace replied quietly.

'But he'll hate it. Surely he can stay. Someone can look after him here. Or perhaps he could come and stay with us. He is very gentle and kind, and he's very easy.'

Grace shook her head. 'Annie, love, we have to be realistic. Danny isn't like a dog we can take in off the street just like that. He's a full-grown man who can't look after himself. His mother devoted herself to him. Every minute of her day was spent looking after him. How do you think we could cope with him? He can't dress himself or', she lowered her voice, 'even wipe his own bottom.'

Annie's throat felt thick and congested. Tears welled up in her eyes as Danny's fate slowly became clear.

A van had drawn up outside. Some big men in white coats came into the house. There was more talking and whispering. One of the men came into the room and started talking to Danny.

'Would you let go of him, miss,' he said to Annie. 'It would be easier if you left the room now.'

Grace got up. 'I'll be waiting for you outside,' she said.

Annie tried to extricate herself from Danny's clasp but he clung on to her in desperation.

'Tell him to let go, if you would, miss,' said the man.

'Danny,' whispered Annie, 'you must let go of me now. These men have come to look after you.' She stroked Danny's arm soothingly.

Another two men had come into the room. They seemed to take up all the space. Danny slowly let go of Annie's arm. 'That's right, Danny,' she said. 'Good boy.'

'Now quietly leave the room, miss,' said the man. As Annie got up, Danny lunged towards her again. 'No, Danny,' she said quietly but firmly. 'You'll be all right.'

She quickly turned and walked out of the room. As she did so, the men pounced. Danny let out a great howl of outrage. Annie was led out of the house and into the street where she fell into her mother's arms.

'Let's go home now,' said Grace, trying to lead her daughter away from the crowd of people gawping on the pavement. The whole neighbourhood seemed to be there – including Maudie and her friend Jessie out pushing Jessie's baby William in the pram, and the Challen twins, and the Fenton sisters were standing on tiptoe trying to see over the heads of people in front. Even Dolly Pritchett had appeared, her large frame quivering with indignation as she glared at the men from the authorities.

There were loud screams coming from the house and the sound of breaking furniture. Men were shouting at each other over the unnatural screams of Danny himself.

'I'm not going home yet, Mother,' said Annie, pulling

away. 'I have to see. I have to see what they're doing to him.'

The noise had stopped. Five minutes later, Danny was led out of the house. Over his pyjamas he was wearing a strange white canvas garment which wrapped his arms around his body. Someone had pulled his boots on but not tied them up. The laces flapped at the sides as he walked. All he could do was waddle. Annie hardly dared look at him as they led him into the waiting van. She was relieved that Danny kept his head dropped down between his shoulders. She did not want him to look her in the eye and tell her that she had betrayed him. But Danny did not look up once. The doors closed behind him and the van drove off.

Danny Horder was never seen again. And it was a long time before Annie was able to walk past the Horders' home without feeling sharp stabs of guilt at the thought of her treacherous behaviour.

Annie's desire to become an artist was as strong as ever. The urge to paint and draw was with her constantly. She had recently become interested in perspective and how she could draw solid objects on a flat surface to make them appear as they actually do when viewed from a particular point. She was rarely seen without a green pencil in one hand and her sketchbooks in another. If she was sitting in the kitchen talking to her mother while Grace prepared the supper, Annie would be drawing everything before her, from the fruit in the bowl on the table, the plates on the dresser, the roast of meat waiting to be placed in the oven, blood oozing out of it, to the pile of knives and forks waiting to be laid. She drew her father at the piano, Jack bent over his school books, Clara combing and plaiting her long hair, her mother kneading dough. She even managed to draw Bobby, but only when he was asleep, for awake he never stayed still long enough for her to capture him on paper. She painted the Admiral butterfly she found dead on her window sill and the woodlice creeping about under the big rock in the garden. She painted the sky at night over Hampstead Heath, she painted the sky in the morning. Nothing escaped her attention, and her sketchbooks mounted up in the cupboard beside her bed. They were visual diaries of her life.

But as her passion for drawing and painting grew, so did her curiosity about her mother's brooch. It would not go away. She often found herself drawing it from memory over and over again, detailing all the diamonds and sapphires and the pretty gold setting. At night she would lie in the dark with her hands behind her head thinking about the mysterious jewel. She wondered why her mother never wore it but instead hid it away in the back of the wardrobe. Why did her mother refuse to talk about it, even with Frank, and why would she not even consider using it when it could help them, like when they were short of money and worried about treatment for her rheumatoid arthritis? Annie did not understand.

Annie had quizzed both Jack and Clara about the brooch, but neither of them seemed interested at all. Gradually it became Annie's obsession. She often crept into her parents' bedroom to look at it when her father was out and her mother busy with her chores downstairs. She would tiptoe across the room, reach up to the high shelf and pull out the box with the christening robe. She would unfold the tissue paper and hold the glistening jewel in her hand. It covered the whole of her palm. She would tilt her head one way and then the other to see the different patterns the light made as it hit the facets on the stones. Annie would pull down the sleeve of her cardigan and rub the diamonds. The brooch was beautiful, and highlighted by what looked like an aura all around it. Annie imagined that it was magic. Perhaps, if she rubbed it the right way, she might be transported away to some enchanted place.

Whenever she heard anyone coming up the stairs, Annie quickly wrapped up the brooch and slipped it back into the box with the silk christening gown. If found in the room, she pretended that she was looking for her sketchbook which she had left in there.

'Who gave Mother that brooch?' Annie looked up at her father hopefully.

'I've told you before,' replied Frank with a tolerant sigh, 'Mrs Pearson, the lady your grandparents worked for in Sussex.'

'But why did Mrs Pearson give Mother the brooch?'

Frank sighed again and put his arm around Annie's shoulder. 'As I have told you every time you ask me that question, I don't know. Your mother helped Mrs Pearson with something so Mrs Pearson gave her the brooch out of gratitude. If you want to know more about that transaction, you'll have to ask your mother. Perhaps you'll have more luck than I do.'

Annie shrugged and frowned. She could not ask her mother again. She did not dare. It would be too cruel. Whenever the subject of the brooch was brought up, however vaguely, Grace always looked distressed and unhappy.

Annie and Frank were walking down the road on their way to visit the National Gallery. Keen to encourage his younger daughter's artistic ambitions, Frank had promised for some time to take her on a trip to look at the nation's pictures. With all the talk of war in the air, he thought it wise to get Annie to see the country's art treasures before they were whisked away to some secret hiding place, as had been suggested in the newspaper the other day. Clara was supposed to have come too, but she was staying behind as a punishment, having been in trouble all week.

First, she was sent home from school after she had been discovered letting bees out in the classroom deliberately to disrupt lessons. Annie had noticed Clara's sudden enthusiasm for capturing bees in jam jars as they buzzed about the buddleia bushes, but she had not thought any more about it. It turned out that Clara had been letting out one every lesson for a fortnight. The school secretary had been searching everywhere in the playground for evidence of the source of these creatures. It had been serious. Two girls had been stung – one seriously, for it turned out that she was allergic to bee stings. She was rushed to hospital and was lucky to be out at the end of the week. Then Clara was found with a jar of bees in her pocket, and was sent home for two weeks. Then, she was supposed to have been studying for her exams at home but she kept slipping out to meet Roger on Hampstead Heath. This had enraged her parents, who only knew about it because Dolly Pritchett had remarked on seeing Clara walking arm in arm with Roger by the ponds one afternoon.

So Clara was in big trouble. No pocket money and no going out until further notice. And certainly no treats. 'I don't care,' Clara had shrugged. 'I like staying in my room.'

So Annie had the rare pleasure of going out on a trip alone with her father. Halfway up the road they met Dolly Pritchett. She was carrying two large string bags full of groceries and was puffing as her heavy frame swung from side to side. Frank greeted her in his usual friendly manner, and then, as Annie shifted her weight from one foot to the other and tried not to look bored because it was rude to do so, there followed the usual exchange about what Mr Hitler was up to in Europe and what the Prime Minister was going to do about it all.

All anyone ever talked about nowadays was war, she thought. She did not understand it much and it seemed rather exciting, with talk of trenches being dug in the parks and air-raid shelters in the gardens and gas masks to be carried at all times. It also seemed far away from Kentish Town, especially as no one seemed frightened. But her parents listened to the BBC news on the wireless every evening and no one was allowed to make a sound, not even a squeak, until it was finished. So perhaps they were more worried than they let on.

Finally Dolly said her goodbyes and Annie and Frank set off once more for the Underground station. They turned down Leverton Street. Annie chattered gaily to her father, passing on stories about her playmates as they passed. They waved to the Challen twins and said good day to the Fenton sisters who were just setting off on a shopping trip to Queen's Crescent market. Annie waved to

Mrs Whelan, who was busy leaning out of the top-floor window and scrubbing the wall just below it. 'She'll fall out if she isn't careful,' she giggled.

But her father did not laugh. He was not even looking at Mrs Whelan. The laughter had gone from his face and he was looking rather stern.

'What's wrong?'

As Annie spoke, she noticed a woman sitting on the doorstep of the Smiths' house. She was about twenty-five. Although rather blowzy, she was attractive, with a neat compact figure. She had dark brown wavy hair, velvety brown eyes and clear white skin. She was looking up at Frank and smiling. 'Well, good morning,' she called in a cocky sort of way. Her voice was unusually husky.

Frank seemed to hesitate and draw back momentarily. For a second Annie thought that her father was going to bolt in the other direction. But a moment later he had collected himself. 'Good morning,' he said politely. Grasping Annie by the arm, he hurried her on. 'Come on. We mustn't dawdle any more.'

'But who's that?' she whispered, looking back at the woman sitting on the doorstep. The woman was watching them go, a smile on her full red lips. 'I've never seen her before.'

'That's Connie Smith.' Frank was striding ahead. 'Tommy's older sister.' He was matter-of-fact and brusque.

Annie had to run to keep up with him. 'Tommy's older sister,' she repeated. 'You mean, the one who ran away with Maudie Sprackling's husband?'

Frank nodded. 'That's right.' He didn't slacken his pace.

Annie was impressed. 'Well,' she mused, 'I wonder what Maudie thinks . . .'

'Not much, I should think,' said Frank. 'Now, come on, Annie, let's hurry . . .'

They spent the whole afternoon in the National Gallery. Annie felt in heaven. Never had she seen such paintings before. Some of them she had seen in books but she had never seen the brushwork on the oil paintings, or the textures or the colours. She was both awed and inspired by seeing the work of some of the greatest artists in history. Her head was spinning with their names – Michelangelo, Rembrandt, Leonardo da Vinci, Gainsborough, Reynolds, Goya – all painting so many different pictures.

'That should give you something to work towards,' said Frank as they had tea and scones in the Lyons tearoom in the Strand. 'Perhaps one day a painting by you will hang on those walls.'

Annie smiled and, with her finger, scooped up a blob of strawberry jam which had dropped down her front. 'If I work hard,' she said, popping her finger into her mouth and withdrawing it slowly as the sweet gooey jam spread out across her tongue. 'I'd like that.'

The early evening crowds were out as they walked back to Leicester Square Underground station. People were coming out from work and making their way home or arriving for an evening out at the cinema or the theatre or just a good meal in Soho. Annie suddenly noticed a face she recognized in the crowd. Across the road, she saw Jessie. 'That's Maudie Sprackling's friend, isn't it?'

Annie pointed and then quickly dropped her arm. She knew it was rude to point.

Frank looked up across the road. 'I'm not sure,' he said

hurriedly, and quickly guided Annie down the steep steps into the Underground station.

Later, as they emerged at Kentish Town station, they bumped into Maudie Sprackling pushing Jessie's baby, William, in the pram. Maudie had a gloomy expression on her face. She looked the way she used to before Jessie and William came into her life. Her face was red and blotchy as though she had been crying.

'Good evening, Maudie. Are you all right?' Frank could never let anyone go by without seeing if he could help.

'Yes, yes,' replied Maudie, looking away as if embarrassed by the giveaway signs on her face. 'It's nothing really.'

'We saw Jessie,' piped up Annie. 'We went to the National Gallery to look at the pictures. We saw her in town.'

Maudie nodded. 'Yes, she works late on Thursdays,' she said. 'The shop stays open until eight o' clock so she's serving customers and doesn't get back until late. It's my night for putting William to bed.' She smiled fondly at the sleeping baby in the pram.

'Well, we must be off,' said Frank. 'We must get home for our tea now.'

As he and Annie set off up Leighton Road, neither one of them said anything about Jessie. They had seen Jessie at five-thirty, when she was supposedly working. And she had looked different from normal. They had both seen her with rouge on her cheeks and bright lipstick on her lips, laughing in the company of a man who had his arm around her in a familiar way. Frank had a good idea of what was going on. For her part, Annie did not. But she sensed that what Maudie had told them about Jessie was

not the real truth, though Maudie herself did not know
that. Annie also knew that what she had seen down there
on the street between Jessie and her gentleman friend was
something to do with being a grown-up, and with what her
parents sometimes did on Sunday mornings. It was not
for discussion or comment.

CHAPTER 9

❧

Connie

IT HAD BEEN A great summer holiday which culminated in the opening of the Lido at Parliament Hill. This was the huge new swimming pool complete with diving boards, chutes and clear blue water built for the pleasure of the local people. Everyone in the neighbourhood was up there to sample the delights of the water, whether they could swim or not. There was a grand opening and the sound of people shouting and splashing could be heard as far as Westminster.

Annie had gone up there several times with Tilly, and on a couple of occasions with Clara, too, when she was not trying to slip off to see Roger. Much to her parents' relief, Clara had claimed to have lost interest in Roger and announced that she was intending to concentrate on her schoolwork. But Annie and Jack knew better. They knew full well that Clara pretended to be going over to Marie's house but in fact was meeting up with Roger at the cinema or some place on the Heath.

Annie thought Clara was wrong to deceive their parents in this way but she never understood why Jack became

quite as angry as he did about what Clara got up to. If
Clara was out when Annie and Jack were playing gin
rummy or racing demon, Jack would keep looking at his
watch and murmuring under his breath about Clara's
behaviour. Once Annie asked him why he was so cross,
and he refused to answer. His face just went white and he
turned away.

If Annie did not understand her brother's feelings about
Clara, neither did Jack himself. As a boy, and the eldest, he
had always felt it his duty to look after his younger sib-
lings. He had enjoyed their need for his protection. Now
Clara was breaking away from him and not wanting him
to look after her at all. He felt hurt and redundant. The
fact that she was attracted to Roger Knight, whom Jack
loathed, complicated matters further. He could not disen-
tangle one lot of feelings from another. And neither could
Clara. She made it plain that she thought Jack simply
hated her seeing anyone.

Clara liked the idea of Jack being jealous. She assumed
that that night after the street party had been important to
Jack. In fact, it had been no more important to him than it
had been to her. What Clara refused to accept was that
Jack simply disliked Roger.

Annie was still too young to understand such matters.
She watched the goings-on with a cool indifference.
Generally, she was enjoying life. She liked school, and her
mother's rheumatoid arthritis was not too bad at the
moment, so she did not have to worry about that, either.
Her friend Tilly was also cheerful nowadays. Her father
had finally found himself a job in a small business in
Islington. It did not pay much but enough for the family to
be able to rent a larger place two blocks away in Countess

Road and afford a few luxuries. They even managed to get away for a short holiday in Wales. Both Annie and Tilly had passed the scholarship exam last term and were set to go on to the grammar school in Parliament Hill.

But once the summer was over, people started to talk more and more about the possibility of war. There was a lot of talk about air-raid precautions and an autumn drive for volunteers to man the services. Volunteers were needed for each road. After the Munich Crisis in September, gas masks were issued to everyone by hundreds of volunteers. It became illegal to go out without one.

People accepted the masks, for the fear of gas attacks was real, but they hated them all the same. They loathed the claustrophobic feel of the clammy rubber and the suffocating condensation that built up on the celluloid eyeshields.

'Ugh!' said Clara, picking her mask with an expression of distaste. 'I'd rather be gassed than wear this.'

She stared at Annie who was peering out at her through the eyeshields. 'I don't want to look like a giant ant.'

Her mother laughed. 'When it comes to it, my guess is that you won't mind what you look like.'

The spectre of war loomed more and more by the week. It had been hanging in the air for so long, its presence was almost unbearably oppressive.

One morning Tommy turned up at Annie's house with some good news. His mouse had had babies and, as arranged, in a few weeks' time, Annie was going to be allowed to have one of them as a pet. Grace and Frank had finally given in to the pressure from their youngest daughter to have another animal.

'She's had six,' Tommy informed Annie. 'Last night.'

He held out his arm. Balancing precariously along Tommy's wrist and forearm, its tail flipping from side to side, was a black-and-white mouse. 'The proud dad.'

Annie jumped up and down with excitement. Ever since Tommy had suggested that she have one of his mouse's babies and her parents had agreed, she had been waiting for this moment. She had chosen the shoe box she would keep the mouse in. She would fill the box with scraps of coloured wool from her mother's knitting, and keep it under her bed. She would clean it out every other day so that it didn't smell and feed it with cabbage and nuts and perhaps some corn borrowed from Mr Spratt.

It had all been a surprise anyway: when Tommy went to the pet shop in Fortess Road and brought back two mice in a shoe box, he had told his mum that they were both male. A few weeks later, however, he realized that the white one with red eyes was getting fatter and fatter.

It was Annie's mother who had suggested that the mouse was about to have babies and was not just eating too much. Overhearing the conversation between Annie and Tommy about the fat mouse made her chuckle.

'I think you're about to have more mice to look after, Tommy,' she said the week before when Tommy had brought his two mice round to the Turners' house. The mice were tame and seemed quite happy to be handled. Grace held the albino mouse up to her face. She liked the way its whiskers never stopped twitching.

'I suppose they make easy pets,' she said thoughtfully.

'Oh, yes,' said Tommy, giving Annie a nudge.

So her parents had agreed. Now the moment had come.

'I couldn't bring the mother mouse along to show you because me mum said she should stay put. And she said to keep this one away from the babies. Mum said he might disturb them, or something. I have to keep him in a separate box for a while.'

'But when can I see them?' Annie asked anxiously. 'When can I see my new pet?' Suddenly she felt like a different person. Now she was someone who was about to be the owner of a mouse. Her ownership of the goldfish Roger gave her at the Easter fair had been short-lived. The fish was found floating on the top of the water after just a few days. Annie had not cried, though. The goldfish had proved to be a boring pet to have.

'Well, you can see it now, if you like. You can come to my house.'

Annie was surprised. Tommy had never suggested that she go to his house before. He had always been so eager to get away from it.

As they set off for Tommy's house, Tommy began to tell Annie about his sister who had returned after being away for a few years. 'She's great,' he said. 'She's always laughing and having fun.'

'But isn't she the one who ran away with Maudie Sprackling's husband?'

'Well, yes, but it looks like they're going to be good friends now.'

Annie glanced at him with surprise. 'But how's that possible after she stole Maudie's husband from her?'

Tommy shrugged. 'Yeah, it seems like that's all water under the bridge now. For the first few days when Connie was back, Maudie looked quite put out but Connie took her some flowers one day and they had it out. I don't know what was said, but now it looks like they're the best of friends.'

Annie was surprised by the state of the Smiths' house inside.

She had only ever been in it once before, when Tommy was ill and she had taken him some biscuits her mother had made for him. The squalor then had shocked her. The air was heavy with the sour odours of old cooking, cigarettes and unwashed bodies. Tommy's dad, as usual, had no work and he was sitting in the front room in his vest and trousers. A cigarette hung from his bottom lip all the time as though stuck to it. Annie had a quick glimpse of the kitchen and just saw piles of dirty plates and pots all over the place, on every surface but also stacked up on the floor. It seemed no wonder that Tommy was always commenting on how nice the Turners' house was.

But this time it was different. It was still cluttered and crowded but it seemed quite clean. There were no piles of dirty clothes or crockery lying around. The windows were open so fresh air circulated freely and there was even a small jam jar with a few marigolds on the table in the front room.

'Since she's been home, Connie's been doing the house cleaning,' Tommy explained. 'When our mum's out at work all day, she don't have much time for it. Now Connie does it instead.'

As he spoke, Connie appeared down the stairs. 'Hello, there, Tommy,' she said. 'Who's this, then?' She peered at Annie in a friendly sort of way.

Annie smiled shyly at her.

'This is Annie Turner,' said Tommy. 'She's come to see the mice.'

Connie nodded. 'So you're Frank Turner's girl, are you?

I remember, now, I saw you in the street with him the other day.'

'Yes,' whispered Annie.

'Nice man, your father,' said Connie. 'Always ready to help people, he is.'

Tommy led Annie out to the garden through the kitchen. At the table Tommy's two middle brothers were playing cards, beer bottles and cigarettes to hand. They did not even look up as the children went by. Annie recognized Eric from his broken nose. He was rather frightening to look at and she knew from Tommy that he had recently come out of prison where he had been for a few months for burglary.

Connie's influence stopped at the kitchen door. The garden really was a mess, filled with old bed springs and rusty cookers. They picked their way to the far corner where a space had been cleared for a large wooden crate. It had an old bike placed on top. 'I have to put this on to stop the cats knocking over the crate and getting at the mice,' he explained. 'Now, sssh . . .'

They crept over and pulled off the bicycle. Tommy slipped off the lid of the crate and peered over the side. 'You can see them all quite clearly now,' he whispered.

Annie looked into the crate. Her eyes opened wide at the sight of the white mouse lying down with six hairless pink creatures next to her. Their eyes were closed over and they moved about helplessly.

Annie was revolted by the sight but she hid her disappointment. She had imagined that they would be tiny replicas of their parents.

'When will they grow fur?'

'In a few days, I think,' replied Tommy. 'Yeah, they're not much to look at now.'

As he spoke, Connie called to him from the house. 'Want some biscuits, Tommy? There's enough here for you and Annie, if you're feeling a bit peckish.'

'Thanks, Connie,' Tommy called back. 'Just a sec . . .'

Annie peered back into the box. For a few seconds she stared at the animals in the box, trying to understand what she was witnessing. Suddenly she clasped her hand over her mouth as she felt the gorge rising in her throat. 'Aaagh! What's she doing? What's she doing?' She pointed into the crate for Tommy to see. 'Stop her!'

Like Annie, Tommy stared in open-mouthed horror at the sight before him. Frightened by the disturbance, the white mouse had started to eat her offspring, holding them in her front paws and chewing the pink and black skin as fast as she could, rushing from one to the next until the crate was littered with the pink and bloodied carcasses of her babies.

'It's too late,' Tommy said quietly. 'We've frightened her too much.'

Jack looked impatiently at his watch and frowned. Clara was late. It was typical. If only she could be on time, just for once.

The queue to the cinema was quite long now. The new film was clearly popular. Well, if Clara didn't come soon, she would miss it . . .

Jack nodded politely at Maudie Sprackling who was standing in the queue a good ten yards back. She seemed to be with Tommy Smith's big sister, Connie. How peculiar. The two women looked like the best of friends, laughing and joking together. Yet he had always grown up with the knowledge that Connie Smith had run away with Maudie's husband. In fact, he could just about remember the commotion when it happened. He could still see the look of excitement on Dolly Pritchett's face and hear the relish in her voice as she told Jack's mother about how Maudie's husband, Fred, had walked out after a row and never come back. And then it turned out that Connie Smith had disappeared that day too. Soon everyone knew that the two had run off and moved in together, without being married. It was quite a scandal at the time.

The queue had started to move. Where was Clara? She had said she just had to pop down to Daniel's, the department store, to buy some material to sew her sports badges on to. She would meet Jack at the cinema, she said, ten minutes before the film was due to start.

Time was passing fast. Jack felt crosser and crosser. He was not sure whether to go on waiting for his sister or just to file in with the crowd and buy one ticket and go in by himself.

But he didn't want to miss the film. He waited until Maudie, Connie and the rest of the queue had filed past and disappeared into the cinema. He looked down the road one more time. There was still no sign of Clara's blonde head bobbing up and down as she dashed in her characteristic way, late to whatever destination.

With a sigh of annoyance and disappointment – it was never as much fun going to the cinema alone – he bought one ticket and went in. Clara will just have to miss the beginning of the film and sit apart from me, he thought. That will serve her right.

Clara did not make it to the film at all. When Jack came out, he hung around to see if he could see her in the

Saturday afternoon crowd but there was no sign of her. She was definitely not there.

Now Jack began to worry that something had happened. Clara was famous for being late, but she always got there in the end. She had never not turned up before. Jack had always been protective of his sisters and now he began to be afraid that some harm had come to Clara and made her unable to meet him at the cinema as planned. After all, they had made the arrangement only thirty minutes before the film was due to start.

Jack hurried home. He feared the worst, though he did not know what that was. In his head he was working out how to tell his mother that Clara had gone missing. He had to do it without making her too worried in the process. He dreaded that look of panic which came over his mother's face whenever she thought one of her children was in danger. He had seen it quite a lot recently, too, particularly since his mother seemed to fret so much over Bobby. Even Jack's father had told Grace to stop worrying so much about the boy. 'Bobby's four years old,' he would say. 'He's quite old enough to climb down the stairs on his own without you holding him. He's got to become independent some day.'

This, of course, was different. Where could Clara be? Jack began to feel quite frantic as he approached the house.

All Jack's fears proved to be unfounded. And it was unnecessary to convey any alarming news to his mother after all. When he walked in through the front door, there was Clara playing the piano in the hall.

Jack was furious. 'Where were you? I waited for you until the last minute.'

Clara looked up, flashed a smile at him and then turned

back to the piano. Her fingers danced over the keys and the lively music filled the house. 'Oh, I decided not to come after all,' she said casually.

Jack stared at her. 'Why not?' He clenched his fists as his rage built up inside him.

'I met someone and we got talking.' Clara talked in a matter-of-fact voice. 'Then it was too late for the film.'

'Who was it? Who did you meet?'

His sister turned to look at him again. Her eyes stared at him defiantly. 'I don't think that's any of your business,' she said airily.

'Yes it is my business,' snapped Jack. He stepped towards the piano. It is my business if you say you're going to meet me somewhere and then leave me hanging around in a queue and nearly make me miss the film.'

'But you didn't miss the film.'

Jack lowered his voice. ' It was Roger you met, wasn't it?'

Clara began to play some brisk music very loudly, banging hard on the keyboard. She did not reply.

'It was Roger, wasn't it?' Jack repeated. 'You met Roger.'

Clara went on playing and ignoring him. Finally, as his throat tightened with fury, Jack reached out and flipped the piano lid shut. 'Didn't you?'

Clara looked up slowly. 'So what if I did?'

'He's no good. He's a bad influence . . .' The words spilled out from Jack's lips from nowhere.

His sister stood up and laughed. 'You sound just like Father.' She tossed back her hair. 'Leave me alone. I can be friends with whoever I want. And I don't need your permission to see my friends. I don't comment on the people you choose to have for friends, do I?' She stared defiantly at him. Then she glanced sideways and raised her eyebrows teasingly. 'I think you're a little jealous,' she said quietly. 'You're jealous of Roger because he's bigger than you and he's got a job, when you're just a little schoolboy doing your School Certificate.'

'Ha, don't be so ridiculous.' Jack sneered. 'Why should I be jealous of a creep like Roger? Unlike Roger, I want to get educated. I want to get proper qualifications to get a good job and not spend my time just being a labourer, which is all Roger's good for.' He squared his shoulders and stuck his hands deep in his pockets. 'I just think you should stay away from him. He's trouble.'

Jack started to climb the stairs to his room. Clara lifted the piano lid and started to play again. 'Thanks for the advice, bro,' she called gaily. 'I'll bear it in mind for the future. I appreciate the concern, if nothing else.'

Jack went upstairs and shut the door to his room. He sat on the edge of his bed and stared out of the window. He could see his mother pottering about in the garden down below while Bobby stayed in the sandpit. Annie was sitting on the grass, sketchbook and charcoal in hand. Suddenly Jack picked up the pillow next to him and punched it hard. He rolled over, punching it again and again. The rage roared through him. He was not jealous, he was angry, but why and at whom he had no idea. It felt as though he were filled with a crackling fireball of energy which was desperately pushing him inside, seeking a release along the path of least resistance.

Breathing hard, he rolled over onto his back. Staring up at the ceiling, he was aware of how tightly his jaw was clenched. His hand moved over his hip. Unbuttoning his flies, he slipped his fingers under his shirt tails.

He could hear his mother calling to Bobby outside, and Bobby's shouts of joy. He thought of his mother, of the nape of her neck as she bent over her sewing. He thought of his sister Clara, laughing, throwing back her hair with a coquettish smile. But in spite of what happened between them, he did not want her now. He thought of Marie Whelan, but did not dwell for long on her long straight limbs and skinny frame. He thought now of a big tall woman with long red hair. Her small white teeth flashed as she smiled at him invitingly, beckoning him, holding her strong arms out to him as he came towards her. He could smell her, feel her. Jack's body arched in response. He let out a quiet groan of ecstasy as he sank into her soft warm flesh.

CHAPTER 10

❧

A Murder

IN MARCH 1939, HITLER'S army invaded Czechoslovakia. As the Führer's attention focused on Poland, the British public was generally agreed that he had to be resisted. Everyone talked about the war and everyone had an opinion about what should be done, but few people had any real idea of how war might affect their lives. Everybody, except those who were either too young or too old to know what was going on, lived in a permanent state of anxious uncertainty.

The combination of the war threat and Grace's health had made the atmosphere in the Turners' house even more tense. Grace's rheumatoid arthritis was unpredictable and would come and go at different times. When the pains were under control she was remarkably cheerful, but when they were strong she withdrew into herself, leaving the family without a focus.

Annie found her mother's volatile state of health disturbing. With all this talk of war, she needed her mother to be certain and consistent. She wanted her to be a solid rock, at the centre of the family at all times, reassuring her children that everything would be all right. Annie craved it. Even though she understood that her mother was not to blame for being ill, she still expected her to be strong. Her mother was failing her. Sometimes Annie felt more like a carer than the one cared for.

Perhaps her older brother was feeling this, too; for much of the current problem at home stemmed from a change in Jack.

Having always been a compliant and easy boy, Jack, now sixteen, had suddenly become bolshy and difficult. He was sulky at mealtimes and he stayed out late at night without giving any explanation.

One morning, after Jack had once again stayed out until after midnight, Frank confronted his elder son. 'If you don't pull your socks up and spend your evenings studying instead of gallivanting around outside, you won't pass your exams.'

With what could be interpreted as insolent nonchalance, Jack slowly spread marmalade on his toast. He said nothing.

'You used to be so good about your studying,' chimed in Grace.

Suddenly Jack pushed the plate of toast across the table and leaped to his feet. 'Leave me alone!' he yelled at his astonished parents from the doorway. 'It's my life to do what I want!'

Grace rose from the table. 'Jack, dear, don't lose your temper . . .'

'Oh leave him be,' snapped Frank, pouring himself some more tea. 'He's got to learn to control that temper of his on his own.'

Jack had collected up his schoolbooks and left, slamming the door so hard that the whole house shuddered.

Upstairs Annie lay in bed listening to the shouting down below. She wanted to slap her hands over her ears to shut out the noise but at the same time she wanted to hear, not to miss anything that was said.

She was so tired of the arguments at the moment. If it wasn't Clara, it was Jack, and it didn't help that they were probably just going through a 'phase' as Dolly Pritchett had cheerfully suggested to Annie's mother that morning. 'They'll grow out of it and turn into lovely people,' she added. 'You'll see.'

In fact, Clara was much better behaved than she used to be. She seemed to have settled down a bit. She had even lost interest in Roger again and had been having fun flirting with other local boys, and not just to make Roger jealous.

No, it was Jack, who had never argued with his parents before, who was being sulky, distant and even rude. In fact, he seemed angry a lot of the time. Annie hardly dared speak to him at all at the moment for fear of being snapped at like everyone else. She just stayed out of his way.

Early one morning Grace and Annie set off down Kentish Town Road. They did their errands one by one. They bought pigs' trotters and a pig's head from the butcher, for Grace was planning to make a whole lot of brawn later that day if her hands weren't too painful, a big cottage loaf and Chelsea buns from the baker, carrots and greens for supper, and some beautiful material at Daniel's, the department store. Grace had promised to make Annie a new dress for the summer and she said that Annie could choose whatever pattern she wanted, and also the material, so long as it wasn't too expensive.

They looked through the pattern books, and Annie chose a pattern for a simple dress with a swing skirt. Next they went to the haberdashery department where they pored over the rolls of coloured cotton. Annie's head began to spin. The more she looked, the harder it was to choose. Finally, she pulled out a roll of blue cotton with a white polka-dot print. 'That's what I want,' she declared with satisfaction.

As the shop assistant measured and cut the material, she chatted to Grace. 'They say there's been something going on up the road,' she said. 'One lady said the police were running all over the place like a lot of chickens with their heads cut off.'

With the precious material in a brown paper bag under her arm, Annie walked with her mother and Bobby to their next port of call. As they moved from shop to shop, they heard more and more gossip about what had happened in Kentish Town that morning.

'I hear someone's been badly hurt,' one lady told the fishmonger.

'Someone's dead,' they heard at the haberdasher's. 'Been dead some time.'

'A young woman,' someone said in the street as they waited to cross the road.

'A woman, a loose woman,' said another.

'Got her come-uppance,' said someone with cruel relish.

'Up Fortess Road.'

'Somewhere in Leverton Street.'

'A terrible shock for the poor fellow what found her.'

Annie listened to the grown-ups passing bits of information backwards and forwards to each other and tried to piece together all the words to create some picture of what was going on. Although no one seemed to know the exact facts, it was clear that something serious had happened.

They walked back up the high street and turned for home. Annie realized that people were running past them towards Leverton Street, and a large crowd of people had gathered at the junction of Leverton Street and Falkland Road.

'Let's go on up Leighton Road.' Grace wanted to avoid the crowd. But Annie was having none of it.

'Oh, no, Mother, we have to find out what's going on. We must find out what's happening.'

When they got to the place where the two streets crossed, they could hardly move. The police had cordoned off Leverton Street between the junction and the oil store on the next corner. People were milling around and trying to see over the heads of the people in front of them, craning their necks and pushing.

They saw Dolly Pritchett standing next to Mrs Garcia.

'Whatever's happened?' asked Grace. Dolly glanced at Annie and lowered her voice. 'It's Sally Brown,' she whispered. 'Someone's done Sally Brown in.'

Annie's eyes widened in horror. 'Sally Brown?' Her words came out as a whisper. 'But we know her.'

Dolly went on to inform them that Sally had been found strangled that morning. The fact that her cat had been left out all night had alerted the neighbours because Sally always let it in at night. The animal had been scratching frantically at Sally's door, so they thought something must be wrong. Sally's door turned out not be locked anyway, and then they found her dead in bed.

'It's definitely foul play. She was a healthy young woman,' she muttered.

'One of her customers, no doubt,' added Mrs Garcia.

Dolly glanced sideways at Annie and frowned.

'What customers?' asked Annie. 'Why should Sally have customers?'

Grace put her arm around Annie's shoulders. 'Come on, Annie, let's get home.'

Annie walked along pushing the pram in a daze. Sally dead! Another person she knew was dead. First it was Mrs Horder, now Sally. But Mrs Horder died of old age, someone had killed Sally – had put a stocking around her neck and strangled her. Someone had choked her until she had stopped breathing. Someone had ended her life before it was supposed to end.

Sally was dead! It did not seem possible. She and Sally had sometimes sat on Sally's doorstep and told each other their secret dreams and hopes. Annie knew how much she wanted to have a fine husband, someone who would love her and look after her as a good husband should. Even though Sally used to ignore her when she had a friend with her – and come to think of it, they were always men – she was always friendly if Annie was walking past her house and Sally was sitting on her doorstep.

But now Sally was dead. Now she would have none of those things she had longed for, no kind husband, no home, no children. Annie's eyes glistened with tears as she thought about Sally's tall strong body stretched out on the bed, her beautiful long red hair spread out on the pillow like a halo. 'I liked Sally,' she murmured, rummaging up her sleeve for a handkerchief to blow her running nose, 'I thought she was nice.'

'Come on, Annie.' Grace urged her daughter on in a quiet voice. 'Let's get home.'

Mother and daughter went on as Mrs Garcia started to relate to anyone who would listen the terrible thing that had been done to her husband's horse the night before. 'It's sick,' she muttered. 'The person what did it was sick in the head. Fancy attacking a dumb animal like that, in its private parts. And in such a disgusting way, too, cutting it up with a knife!'

The others nodded, their eyes open wide in horror at the description of the attack on poor Juniper the horse.

They came for Jack early that same evening. The family had just finished supper. The dishes had been washed, dried and put away in the cupboards, the plates replaced on the dresser. Bobby was asleep in his cot and Jack was upstairs in his bedroom doing his homework. Moody throughout supper, he had barely spoken a word. But since he had been like this a lot recently, everyone else had learned to ignore it.

Now the rest of the family were in the sitting room. Clara and Annie perched on the sofa playing rummy while Grace knelt on the floor with Annie's dress pattern and polka dot material spread out before her. With her large, heavy pinking-shears, she carefully cut around the markings on the thin tissue paper. In the corner, Frank sat in his armchair smoking a pipe and reading the evening paper.

Suddenly there was a loud banging on the front door. It was a rude violent noise, which made them all start and look around at each other.

'Whoever can that be?' Grace frowned and glanced at Frank who had folded his paper and got to his feet.

'I'll see,' he said.

They all waited to hear him going down the stairs, walk along the hall and open the front door. Annie held her breath as she heard the exchange down below.

'Good evening, officer.' Frank's voice was surprised and quiet. There followed a conversation Annie couldn't follow, but she heard the words 'your son Jack Turner', quite clearly. So did Grace.

'Jack?' Grace pulled herself up, wincing at the pain in her knees. 'Someone wants Jack?'

A minute later, they heard Frank coming slowly up the stairs. He stood in the doorway to the sitting room, his face grey and leaden. 'It's the police,' he stated. 'They're waiting downstairs. They want to take Jack down to the station for questioning.'

'Questioning? What sort of questioning?' Grace's voice rose in pitch as she flew at her husband. 'What are you talking about?' Clara and Annie glanced at each other in puzzlement and fear. Annie edged up to her elder sister for comfort.

'I don't know.' Frank's voice cracked. 'But it's obviously serious.' He turned and went on up the stairs to call Jack down from his room.

Moments later Jack appeared, followed by his father. Grace stood staring at him as he walked past them and down to the ground floor. Annie and Clara watched him from behind their mother's skirts. Jack looked straight ahead of him, not glancing at them once.

As the men reached the hall, Grace gasped as she heard one of the policemen say: 'Jack Turner, I am arresting you on suspicion of the murder of Miss Sally Brown of Leverton Street . . .'

The girls heard no more, for they rushed to their

mother's aid as she sank to the floor in a half-faint.

Once they had helped Grace into a chair, Annie moved to the window. Hiding behind the curtain, she looked down at the scene outside. Jack was being led out by two men. A policeman stood by a black car outside. A crowd of people had gathered around the car and were looking to see what was going on. Annie stepped back a bit. Down below she could see Dolly Pritchett, standing right at the front, arms akimbo, peering at Jack as he climbed into the car. There was Mr Spratt, Mrs Whelan, the Fenton sisters and everybody else from the block and beyond, it seemed. Everyone looked angry, shaking her heads and scowling. What did it all mean?

Suddenly Frank ran upstairs and into the room. 'I'm going down to the police station to sort this out,' he said hurriedly to Grace. He walked over to his wife and gave her a quick hug.

Grace clung to him, sobbing.

'Don't worry, sweetheart,' he said. 'It's obviously all some dreadful mistake. It'll be sorted out in no time.' He kissed her head. 'Look after your mother, girls,' he said, glancing quickly at Clara and Annie. With that, he left.

Annie watched out of the window at her father's figure disappearing down the road.

By eleven o'clock, Jack and Frank were still not back. Annie kept falling asleep on the sofa until her mother quietly told her to go to bed. 'I'll be all right,' she said quietly. 'I'm making myself believe that everything will be all right.'

Clara shrugged. 'I hope so,' she said gloomily. 'I just don't believe this is happening.'

Annie fell asleep the moment her head touched the pillow.

But she was woken a few hours later by the sound of excited voices. It was her mother welcoming Jack back home. Annie crept to the doorway of her room. She could hear the relief in her mother's voice, her father explaining that it was all a mistake. She heard Clara telling them that she had known they would be back in no time, and Jack quietly saying that he was exhausted and needed to go to bed.

Annie tiptoed back into her own bed. She could feel the sleep catching up with her as she pulled the sheets back over her. Everything was all right, she thought, snuggling down with a sigh. She would find out what happened in the morning.

But the next morning the atmosphere was not a happy one. When Annie came down for breakfast she found everyone sitting eating their porridge in stony-faced silence. They ate quietly. The only noise came from their spoons scraping the inside of the bowls. It was only afterwards, quizzing Clara, that Annie found out any of the story.

It seemed that Jack had been arrested because someone had reported seeing him coming out of Sally Brown's door on the night that she was murdered. Not only that, but his schoolbooks had been found in her rooms. An overzealous policeman had acted prematurely and pulled Jack in ready to charge him. But it only took a few hours to sort out the fact that although Jack had indeed been at Sally Brown's, he had left her home at 8.45, and been home at 8.50, a fact verified by Frank Turner. Not only that, Sally had been seen by at least two other people after 9.30 – by the tobacconist at the end of the road, who reported that she had popped in to buy a packet of Woodbines, and the ticket clerk at the Underground station who said he had seen her hanging around in Kentish Town Road at ten o'clock when he was coming off duty.

The police had let Jack go with apologies to Frank for their hasty actions, and advice to Jack not to associate with ladies of loose morals in the future.

Annie hung around in the hall trying to catch her parents' conversation while they sat in the dining room. The door was closed but Annie pressed her ear up against the door and could hear their words quite clearly.

'I still don't understand what Jack was doing visiting that woman.' Grace's voice was low and plaintive.

'What do you think, Grace?' Frank sounded tired and impatient. 'Why should any healthy young boy want to visit a woman known to have plenty of men friends?'

'I'm just so unhappy that my son should do such a thing, that he should need to do it. He's much too young.'

'He's nearly seventeen, Grace, he's a man. He was probably curious.'

Grace shook her head. 'He said he's visited her more than once.'

'I think you're focusing on the wrong thing here, Grace. Does it really matter if Jack's sowing a few oats? And better for him to do it with an experienced woman than a local girl he can get into trouble.'

'It's all my fault. If I were healthier I could have made sure this had never happened.'

Frank frowned. 'You can't blame yourself, Grace, it's certainly not your fault. Please don't say that.'

'It doesn't help that we live in Kentish Town,' Grace sighed. 'It's a difficult place for any child to grow up honest if he's in daily contact with prostitutes and criminals.'

'Come, now, Grace, you're exaggerating.'

'I'm not sure that I am. You know I've never much liked Kentish Town. It's a harsh place to live in and I've had to live here all my married life. To tell you the truth, I'm tired of it. But I know you love it and that's why I've put up with it.'

Frank pulled her to him and held her close. 'I'm sorry you still feel so strongly about it. I'm so sorry. When this war finally starts, nowhere is going to be an ideal place to be. But after the war, if we're still here, I promise we can move, if it means so much to you . . .'

Grace smiled up at her husband. 'Yes, Frank,' she whispered, 'I would like that very much.'

As Annie stood in the hall eavesdropping, the postman pushed a letter through the letter-box. It fell on the hall floor with a plop. Annie picked it up.

It was addressed to Mrs Grace Turner, and the hand-writing was unfamiliar. Annie screwed up her eyes to read the postmark: Petworth, Sussex. It must be from the lady who gave her mother the brooch. Why on earth should she be writing now?

Just as Annie placed the letter on the kitchen table so that her mother could not miss it, Tilly turned up at the front door. Under her arm she had a towel rolled up in a tube. She was hoping that Annie would go swimming with her.

As the two girls walked down to the public baths, Annie told Tilly about the terrible events of the night before. She told her how Jack had been taken off to the police station because he had visited Sally Brown on the night of her murder so the police had thought it was Jack who had killed her. 'So silly,' she laughed lightly. 'How could they think such a thing about Jack?' she said.

'But what was Jack doing at Sally Brown's house anyway?' Tilly turned to her quizzically. 'Why should he have been there?'

Annie frowned. 'I don't know,' she said crossly. 'How should I know?'

Annie went quiet. She was cross because she did not know the answer to Tilly's question but she was even crosser to think that Jack had been friends with Sally Brown without Annie knowing it. What right did he have to be friends with Sally? Sally had been Annie's friend, not his. Jack had even been in Sally's house and Sally had never in all their friendship invited Annie in. Her feelings were hurt. But then she felt guilty for being cross about someone who had just died.

Although Jack was in the clear, his reputation in Kentish Town had been tarnished. Having always been a popular, helpful boy, he was now shunned.

'Fancy a boy from a good family like that visiting a woman like that Sally Brown,' Mrs Rose tut-tutted in the grocer's shop as Grace went past. 'It ain't right.'

'I reckon there's more to it than meets the eye,' added Mrs Barnes.

'That's what I say,' chimed in Mrs Clark. 'There's no smoke without fire, and it's not as if they've caught the person what done it.'

While the local women did not make such remarks to Grace's face, she was aware, as she set about her errands, that they were stiff towards her, even cold. Even Dolly, who had been working for the Turner family for years, who had known the children since they were tiny, suddenly became unfriendly. She no longer relayed all the local gossip to Grace while mopping the kitchen floor or dusting the ornaments on the mantelpiece. She simply came in and got on with her job, receiving her money at the end of each stint with a quick nod.

Annie was not aware of these changes. All she cared about was the fact that that letter from Petworth, Sussex had disappeared and her mother had never said a word about it. She had also come to the realization that her father had stopped walking down Leverton Street. In fact, he went out of his way to avoid that particular street. Perhaps it was because of the murder, she thought, but thinking back, she realized that he had been avoiding Leverton Street for a long time now, certainly long before Sally Brown was murdered.

Annie waited for her mother to comment on the letter she had had that morning. In the drama of the day it arrived, it was forgotten. Nothing was said at supper that night, nor at breakfast the next day. Or the next. A few days later, as Annie cleared the breakfast things, she plucked up courage to ask her mother. 'Did you get that letter which came for you the other day? I left it on the kitchen table for you.' She tried to make her voice sound bright and innocent. Now she stared at her mother expectantly.

Grace did not pause as she began stacking the dirty plates by the sink. 'Yes,' she replied breezily. 'I got it.'

Frank looked up from his newspaper. 'A letter? Who wrote you a letter?'

Grace shook her head quickly. 'Nobody,' she replied. 'It was nothing.'

Encouraged by her father's look of interest, Annie's courage grew. 'The postmark was from Sussex,' she said. 'Wasn't that where you grew up?'

Her mother did not turn around. A plate slipped from her hand and fell with a crash into the porcelain sink. 'It was nothing. It was nothing interesting.' She began picking up the broken pieces of china plate but kept dropping them as though she were flustered.

Annie sensed she should stop there. She caught her father's critical eye and fell silent. Frank had decided to support his wife.

'It's rude to talk about other people's letters,' Frank said. 'You should know that, Annie, at your age.'

Feeling hurt and confused, Annie finished clearing the table and went upstairs to her room. What with Sally Brown's death, and all that business with Jack, and her parents being so secretive and excluding her, everything suddenly seemed to overwhelm her. She had a strong urge to creep into bed and stay there.

As she passed her parents' bedroom, she had an idea. She tiptoed over to the wardrobe and pulled a chair over. Standing on that, she reached up to the top shelf. To her disappointment, there was nothing new up there – just the box with the christening gown and the brooch. She jumped down and put the chair back in its place.

As she left the room, she noticed a lot of tiny pieces of paper in the wastepaper basket by the door. There it was, the letter, torn into tiny creamy fragments! Reaching down, Annie scooped up the scraps of paper and ran upstairs with the remains of the letter clutched between her hands.

Grace had torn up the letter into such tiny pieces that it

was impossible to put it back together again. For a good hour, Annie worked on it, trying to approach it like a jig-saw puzzle, matching the shape of the edges to each other. At the end of an hour she had tears of frustration in her eyes, and she had not got far. All she had was an address with S-U-S-S-E- and a few words, such as D-e-a-r, y-o-u, c-h-i-l-d-r-e-n, w-a-r.

Her frustration rose like gorge in her throat as she fought back the tears. What was wrong with her mother? Why wouldn't she tell Annie anything? Why wouldn't she answer Annie's questions about the brooch, about Sussex, about her past, indeed, about anything? What was her secret, or secrets? If her children were so important to her, as she said, then why could she not share everything with them?

Part Two

CHAPTER 11

Wartime

THE DECLARATION OF WAR in early September, 1939, brought with it an intense feeling of relief throughout the land. The build-up to war had been going on for so long that many people now felt a perverse desire for something, anything, to happen.

The news itself, though expected, still came as a shock.

On that Sunday morning of 3 September, the Turners had gone to church. As they sat in the pew and waited for the service to begin, the church was in silence. Everyone knew it was about to happen. Hitler had invaded Poland; the world was about to change. The vicar began the service, but ten minutes into it the verger hurried down the nave with a small piece of paper.

Annie felt all her courage draining out of her body as she watched the vicar look at the paper and climb the steps of the pulpit. She leaned against her mother. To her relief, Grace immediately placed an arm around her and hugged her tight.

'We'll be saved, my darling,' whispered Grace. 'We're going to win, I know we are.'

Her mother felt warm and solid. Annie was instantly less afraid.

The vicar cleared his throat. 'We are now at war with Germany,' he said in a quiet voice. 'We will go to our homes.'

Her mother's reassuring words and gesture remained with Annie for a long time. She clung on to them, even in times when her mother had withdrawn again. They carried her through the anticlimax of the phoney war, that strange period after war had been declared and nothing happened. They carried her through the long hot summer of 1940, with its warm sunshine and cloudless blue skies. But by the time the Blitz began, Annie was feeling very frightened again.

It was in early September of 1940 that the German Luftwaffe launched its savage attack on London. The East End and the docks were the main targets. On the first day, three hundred tons of high explosives and thousands of incendiary bombs were dropped onto the cluttered slums of Cockney London.

After the all-clear in the evening, Annie and Clara climbed out of their bedroom window onto the parapet outside. From here they could see the whole sky to the east was blazing red. The barrage balloons beyond were tinged pink from the reflection of the fires.

Clara shook her head in wonder. 'Half of London must be burning,' she whispered in awe.

Annie suddenly started to cry. She felt terrified.

Clara turned to look at her. Normally she would snap at Annie and tell her to stop blubbing, but this time she did not. This time she put her arms around her little sister and hugged her tight. 'Don't cry, Annie,' Clara whispered, 'you'll be all right. You mustn't be afraid. I'll always look after you.'

Clara's gesture made Annie cry even louder. Her eyes were flooded with tears of love and gratitude. Clara was the strong one. If she could rely on Clara's protection, she would always be all right.

For the next fifty-six nights, London was bombed from dusk to dawn. Vast areas of the city were destroyed. In spite of the devastation, the damage, the injuries and the loss of life, Londoners quickly learned to settle down to their regular routines. The German activities simply became the background to everyday life. Even at the peak of the bombing, in October, when it came very close to home and many bombs were dropped in Kentish Town and Hampstead, and Camden Town Underground station was hit and several people killed, the effect was to strengthen rather than weaken the collective resolve to win. 'We'll beat those buggers!' people would declare.

Extraordinary events can take so little time to appear normal. The sight of enormous bomb craters with fountains of water cascading from the broken mains, the smell of gas, and the burning after the bombing was not unusual anymore. After two and a half years of war, little seemed unusual. Everything was taken for granted. The absence of young men, the blackout, the rationing, the sandbagged buildings and the shop windows smothered with tape and cigarette paper were all as ordinary as the sight of women in trousers, steel-helmeted police and ARP wardens patrolling the streets. Even the Blitz, which had been so terrifying at the time, seemed, with the protection of hindsight, like something they had all taken in their stride.

Annie lay in her narrow bunk one morning thinking back on those terrifying days of the Blitz. It seemed astonishing now that so many people had survived it at all. She stared up at the ceiling above her head. She had stuck lots of her drawings and paintings all over the shelter to cheer it up. She liked to examine them dreamily in the half-light of the morning while her thoughts floated in and out of half-sleep and she conjured up new paintings in her head.

She could hear her father's heavy breathing while he slept just a few feet away. Every now and then the even sound erupted into a snort. She could also hear Bobby's snuffling as he tried to breathe through his summer cold. Looking down, Annie could just make out her mother's face on her pillow on the lower bunk on the other side of the shelter. She looked serene and calm, and out of pain. At least sleep did bring Grace relief from the otherwise constant agony in her joints.

By the door of the shelter Annie could just make out the thermos flask of cocoa, the dried figs, and the thick slab of chocolate her mother always brought in to the shelter every night. By morning what was left of the cocoa was tepid, if not cold, but Annie still enjoyed sharing it with Bobby, pouring the sticky brown liquid into a tin mug and afterwards wiping off the dark moustache from her upper lip.

Looking across at the other top bunk, Annie could see that it was empty. She still could not believe that Clara was refusing to sleep in the shelter. Her sister had not slept there for days now. She had announced two weeks before that she would rather be bombed than go on sleeping in the smelly old shelter, and her father had agreed that now she was sixteen he could not force her to do much, even if he did not approve. So Clara had returned to sleeping in the house, though she had taken the precaution of creeping into a cot bed on the ground floor rather than her bed upstairs. She had made up the cot bed in the dining room, with the windows well taped and heavy dark curtains to prevent any flying glass falling into the room.

Annie was now wide awake. She put her hands behind her head and chewed her lip. Now fourteen, she had suddenly shot up in height and developed 'a bit of a figure', as her father would say, causing Annie to blush coyly. Although she did have curves of a sort, they did not amount to much. Besides, she felt clumsy and gawky most of the time, and she did not remember Clara ever appearing awkward.

Clara was right about this war; it was more than a nuisance. Ordinary the conditions might have seemed, but the war was still an endless bad dream, edging on a nightmare, spoiling their lives when they were supposed to be having fun. How could they possibly have fun with rations and shortages, sudden air-raid warnings and blackouts and bossy air-raid wardens ordering them around all the time? Most of their friends had disappeared from Kentish Town, with the eighteen-year-olds, like Jack and his friends, signing up in 1941 when the call-up age was lowered. And Roger Knight and all the older Smith boys were also conscripted and packed off for active service along with every other young able-bodied man in the country. Even Tommy had signed up and gone off to training camp. At sixteen, he was too young to join up but he lied about his age, and was believed. The powers that be never doubted that this big, fit, enthusiastic youth was a day under the age of eighteen.

So everyone who mattered had gone. Even the little ones at the beginning of the war had been evacuated to the country. It did not take long for huge numbers of them to come back, like William and his mother Jessie. They had left London on a crowded train full of crying children and mothers on Evacuation Day. Maudie had insisted that Jessie go, to get the child to a safer area. Jessie had been gone a week before she returned, disgusted by the way she was treated by the family who took her and William in. She was expected to sleep on a mattress on the floor in a box room and look after the woman's four children for her during the day. 'I'm not a maid,' she sniffed indignantly on her return. 'And even if I were, I still shouldn't be treated in such a way.'

So Jessie and William were back with Maudie in Leverton Street. Although Maudie worried openly about the child's safety, it was clear to all that she was really rather happy to have her family back with her. Maudie herself was always cheerful nowadays. She worked as a telephonist for the London Fire Service. Recently she had become much slimmer and her sweet round face always had a healthy bloom to it.

Annie and Bobby were, along with Tilly, now being educated at the emergency school set up in a big house in Leighton Road. Now that so many evacuees had returned to London, the schools were opening again, though not in their own premises, many of which had been taken over for civil defence purposes. For a short while, after a bizarre incident over the second letter from Mrs Pearson, the children had been educated by their mothers, Grace and Marion.

It must have been in August, 1939, two and a half years

ago and a few weeks before war was declared, that that other thick creamy envelope had plopped onto the hall mat. This time it was addressed to Mr and Mrs Francis Turner. Grace was still upstairs getting Bobby dressed, while Frank and Annie got the breakfast. Frank brought the letter into the kitchen and opened it. It was from Camilla Pearson, inviting Grace and the children to spend the necessary time at her home in Sussex 'while the danger is greatest in London'.

'What does this mean?' Annie was excited.

When Grace came down to find Frank sitting with the letter in his hand, her face went white as she realized what it was. She sat down suddenly as though her legs had given way under her.

Frank looked at her. 'It was addressed to both of us, Grace. Camilla Pearson mentions that you didn't respond to the letter she wrote earlier this year but hopes that this one will get to you now that the situation has become so critical.'

There was no escaping the situation for Grace. She could only sit down and allow the conversation to continue.

'We're invited to be evacuated to Sussex?' repeated Clara when she came down for breakfast five minutes later. 'Well, I'm not going.'

'The schools are all being evacuated anyway,' said Annie. 'Our school's going to Norfolk.'

Frank re-read the letter. 'This is a great opportunity, Grace,' he said. 'It can keep you and the children safe and together in the part of the world you know so well. Your own home, if you please! What could be better?'

Grace stared ahead of her at the butter dish on the table. 'We're not going,' she said quietly. 'Nobody's going.'

'But think of the children,' Frank protested. 'They'll be much safer in the country. The bombs will be coming for the cities and the children will be far from where they might fall.'

Grace shook her head. 'I don't care. You can't leave, Frank, you have to work, and I'm not leaving you. And I'm not leaving the children, either. I'll not be parted from them.'

Frank frowned. 'Shouldn't we put the children's safety first? They'll be safer out of London.'

Grace hesitated. 'Clara and Annie can go if they want . . .' Then she changed her mind again. 'No, they can be evacuated with their schools when it comes to it. We are just not going to Sussex.'

Annie stepped forward. 'But, Mother, I'd like to go and stay in the country. And I'd like to see where you grew up.'

Grace stared at her. There was a look of anguished uncertainty in her eyes.

'Well, I'm not going anywhere,' Clara announced. 'I'm staying put in London . . .'

'But it could become dangerous with the bombs,' Frank replied.

'I don't care,' said Clara. 'I'm a Londoner and I'm staying here. Besides, I can leave school soon and get a job doing something useful . . .'

Frank folded his newspaper and placed it carefully on the table. 'You're not leaving school, Clara,' he said. 'You've got a lot more studying to do before you start working.' Having enjoyed the fruits of his own hard work at night school, Frank was a firm believer in education as the path to progress and betterment. He was anxious that all his children get good qualifications. 'You know how I feel about this. And you'll thank me later in life when you know you can stand on your own two feet, and you've done even better than your mother and I. You can't always expect to be supported by someone else.'

Clara rolled her eyes. 'Studying is boring, Dad. And you can't make me stay at school.'

Frank looked wearily at his elder daughter. 'No, I can't make you stay at school,' he said. 'All I can do is give you some advice, and warn you.'

Clara sniffed. 'Well, thanks for the advice, Dad. I don't need it.' She hesitated and then smiled sweetly at her father. 'Maybe when the war's over, Dad, maybe then I'll go to college.'

Frank gave her a resigned smile. 'All right, Clara, you know what I think.'

And so no one left London in the end. Grace and Marion talked it over and decided to risk it. For Marion, too, felt reluctant to leave her husband, or be separated from her only child, Tilly. Together they could teach the children – meaning Annie, Bobby and Tilly – if there were no schools for them to go to. Both women felt that they did not want to be separated from their husbands who, in their early forties, were fortunately too old to be called up to fight, though were certainly useful for war work in London.

Annie had been bitterly disappointed not to go to Sussex, but the idea of going on her own to a strange home while the rest of her family stayed in London was daunting. It would have been different if her big sister had wanted to go.

And so Grace had replied to Mrs Pearson, thanking her politely for her kind offer but turning it down all the same. Grace then placed Mrs Pearson's letter in her wardrobe next to the brooch.

Frank was puzzled by Grace's decision. 'I'm surprised at you,' he said. 'It seemed such an easy way of making sure the children are safe.'

'As you said, no place is going to be safe, and since that's the case, I'd rather we all stayed together as a family. We'll manage all right in London, even in Kentish Town,' she added with a wry smile.

The bad feeling that had arisen over Jack's involvement with Sally Brown soon died down. After being rather cold for a while, Dolly had warmed up again in gratitude towards Grace for encouraging her to become an air-raid warden.

At first everyone had been astounded. Dolly had always been renowned for her hostility towards anything to do with the 'authorities'. 'No one has a right to tell me what to do,' she would always say. 'Never let anyone from the authorities into your home,' she warned people. 'They'll take over your life in a flash.'

At the beginning of the war Dolly had found herself in big trouble with the authorities in the form of the air-raid wardens. Before the Blitz, these volunteers did not have enough to do and tended to exercise their authority with a heavy-handedness that made them extremely unpopular. Dolly proved to be careless about her blackout curtains and was always being fined for leaving a light showing from her flat window. In no time, the local warden would be knocking on her door and shouting at her to black out the window immediately.

'It's not my fault,' Dolly would grumble to Grace. 'I just keep forgetting.'

'Accidentally on purpose,' Grace would whisper to Marion, rolling her eyes knowingly.

It was Grace who came up with the solution to Dolly's problems. 'I think you'd make a good air-raid warden yourself,' Grace said after Dolly had been complaining about another nosey parker who had ticked her off the night before.

Dolly's stared at her. 'Who, me? You must be joking!' She threw back her wide shoulders and roared with laughter.

'I'm not joking, Dolly,' replied Grace. 'You're very good at organizing things yourself – look at the way you do the street party – and everyone likes you around here. I think you'd be good at it because you know how to talk to people.'

Dolly laughed again. 'I've never heard anything so ridiculous.' But then she paused and thought about it. She shook her head. 'What a daft idea.'

'Why don't you volunteer? You know they need as many volunteers as they can get.'

Dolly was frowning. 'Well, even if I did, they wouldn't let me . . .'

'Why ever not? Of course they'd want you. You just have a bit of training, and that's that.' Grace peered at her. She sensed that something else was bothering Dolly.

Dolly shrugged. 'Na, there's no point . . .' She hesitated.

'What do you mean, there's no point?'

Dolly ran her hand over her hair and adjusted the bun on the back of her head. 'Well, just look at the size of me,' she said. 'They wouldn't have a uniform to fit me, would they!'

Grace had never seen Dolly embarrassed before.

Looking at Dolly's wide frame with her rolls of fat and ham-like forearms, she could see that Dolly was probably right. 'I could make you one,' she said quietly. 'It would be easy to measure you up and do it on the Singer.'

Dolly's face lit up. 'Really?'

'Yes, really,' nodded Grace.

And so Dolly became an air-raid warden and looked splendid in her custom-made blue uniform carefully sewn together by Grace.

That was the last garment Grace made. After that, she found it too difficult to thread the needle and manipulate the sewing machine. She handed over all her sewing things to Clara and Annie.

A large part of the garden was taken up with the Anderson shelter, but the rest of it was dug up and laid out for growing vegetables. Like the rest of the population, the Turners were digging for victory. Every inch of garden was used for growing food. Hampstead Heath and Parliament Field were covered with allotments, as was the moat around the Tower of London. Those people without any land of their own were given permission to use the gardens of empty houses. Next door to the Turners, Mr Spratt had extended his chicken run and reared even more chickens than before. Now that eggs were rationed to one per person per week, his eggs were even more precious and in demand. Many people kept chickens now. The clucking of hens was heard throughout the streets of London.

But Grace seemed to have lost interest in gardening, just as she had lost interest in so much of life. She claimed that now that she could only grow vegetables, she no longer felt joy in seeing plants grow. 'There's nothing unpredictable,' she said wistfully, 'nothing uncertain.' And when she said it Annie felt she was talking about more than simply her garden.

Grace had become sadder and more remote at times. Annie thought it was probably her arthritis but she also thought it might be something else. For although it was true that Grace's condition had worsened, there did seem to be more to her sadness than that. Something else seemed to trouble her as she sat so frequently staring into the distance, her thoughts miles away, in another place, another land, another life. Who knew? All Annie knew was that sometimes she felt that she did not have a mother any more.

Grace was also becoming increasingly religious. She had always been a believer, sending her children to Sunday school, and attending the service every Sunday. Her involvement in the church had seemed normal, no more or less than what other people did.

But recently she had taken to going every day, and sometimes Annie would go out to the church and find her down on her knees in a pew, praying half aloud and staring up at the stained-glass window above. Even at home, when Grace was sitting in a chair, her lips moved quietly as if in prayer. Nobody said anything about it in the family, but Annie could tell that her father was not happy with his wife's growing religious fervour.

As for Frank, although he had never been religious, he had been happy about the children being sent to Sunday school because for years it had meant that there was some peace and quiet for him to have sexual relations with his wife. But now he was growing more concerned about Grace's love of the church. Like everyone else, he felt increasingly excluded from Grace's thoughts and life. He had certainly been excluded from her embrace for a long time. Her body, which had once been so yielding, soft and receptive, was now brittle and rejecting. Now it seemed that the only person whose presence brought Grace to life was Bobby.

Bobby was the apple of his mother's eye; he could do no wrong. An attractive boy with his father's curly brown hair and high forehead, he had twinkling blue eyes under dark eyelashes. His puckish smile and quick tongue made him a popular fellow wherever he went. Sturdy and well co-ordinated, he was athletic as well as clever. But there was a strange naiveté about him. Unlike the other children of his age, Bobby had no common sense, no sense of self-preservation against the world. Frank was sure that Grace was to blame for this; she had overprotected Bobby so much that the child had no idea of how to look after himself.

One Saturday in the autumn, Frank took his daughters to the ARP dance at the St Pancras Town Hall. It was quite an affair. They had been sold tickets by Dolly, who was helping to organize the event, and originally Grace had said she would get Mrs Whelan to look after Bobby so that they could all go. On the day itself, Grace had bowed out. 'My aches are too bad today,' she said. But Annie knew that she had never intended coming, since her mother had never mentioned the occasion to Mrs Whelan in the first place. But she did not care. She would rather go with her father and Clara, who both loved dancing, than her mother who might not want to join in at all.

It was a grand affair. Everyone from the neighbourhood

was there. There were few young men between the ages of seventeen and thirty-five, but it did not seem to matter. Everyone was dolled up in their best clothes determined to have a good time. The music was wonderful. Jimmy Rope crooned to the Alf Rogers band. The large hall was decked out with coloured lights hanging from the four corners of the room, directed at a large revolving glass ball, high up beneath the main chandelier, and a never-ending stream of multi-coloured lights flooded the walls, ceilings and floors. The waltzes in the dark were particularly popular, with the old codgers pressing their prickly cheeks against the soft skin of shy fourteen-year-old maidens, and fresh-faced young boys dancing with their mothers.

Annie was having a wonderful time. She was dressed in a skirt and top Clara had lent her for the evening. Although she did not fill it out well, the soft lawn cotton of the blouse and the full skirt swirling around her legs made her feel alive and full of energy. Many times she danced the Lambeth Walk with her father, clinging on to his strong arms, kicking her legs proudly as she marked out the steps, feeling the heat of his body. At one moment she buried her face in her father's chest and felt a strange pull inside her. It seemed like a deep primitive feeling, a longing for something she did not know. It was as if in that fleeting moment she had crossed the threshold to womanhood and she understood that she was longing for love. Then the feeling was gone.

She waved to Dolly, who was dressed in her uniform and going round trying to persuade more people to volunteer for the ARP. She waved to Marion and her husband, who were dancing close like two love-birds. She waved to Maudie Sprackling who was there with a man

Annie had never seen before. Maudie looked great. She
was a normal size now and really quite pretty. Annie was
pleased to see that Maudie's companion had a kind smiling face. She felt a quick rush of happiness for poor old
Maudie.

Clara was in an exuberant mood, too. She looked lovely,
with her straw-coloured hair pulled back into long tresses
down her back, her lips red and her cheeks flushed with
excitement and the beers she was surreptitiously drinking
in the corner. She hardly stopped for a moment, throwing
her head back, stamping her feet, gliding over the floor
with effortless grace. Her vibrancy was clearly appreciated
by many; often when she stopped dancing there were mur-
murs of appreciation from the onlookers standing around
the edge of the hall.

Across the room, Annie saw Connie Smith. She was
wearing a dress that was a little too tight for her. It accentuated her curves in a slightly disturbing way. Annie kept
glancing at her, but looked away in embarrassment whenever Connie noticed her and waved.

At the end of the evening Frank walked home with his
two daughters. They held each other's arms and guided
themselves by the light of the moon and the white painted
markings on the pavements. Annie felt happy, as did
Clara. It was not so late. People were still up, putting the
cat out or listening to the wireless. A dog barked in the
distance.

'If the bombers come now and we die tonight,' Clara
stated, throwing back her head, 'it won't matter. Nothing
matters. I have lived my life to the full.'

Frank laughed and put his arms around his daughters'
shoulders. 'Well, I hope you'll have a little bit more life

ahead of you,' he said. 'Let's hope Hitler grants you that . . .'

The house was dark when they got home.

'Your mother must have gone to bed already.' Frank yawned. 'Well, I'm knackered, too.' He shook his head sadly. He used to be able to dance until the early hours.

He heated up some cocoa for all of them and went off to bed in the shelter, leaving the two girls sipping their hot drinks in the kitchen.

Annie loved to sit up late talking to her big sister. Recently she had been enjoying Clara's company a lot. True to her word, Clara had ignored her father's wishes, and left school to get herself a job. She had found work in a factory in Leyton making parts for aeroplanes.

Annie could never hear enough about Clara's working day and all her new workmates. They sounded so grown-up and fun, these fast-talking young women who wore their hair tied up with scarves, or used pipe cleaners as hair pins, and shared their lipsticks and any other cosmetics they could get their hands on in wartime. She also liked to hear what Clara said about the soldiers and sailors she and her workmates often met at dances. They were all boys on leave wanting to meet some nice girls in the short time they had before being sent off to fight in some part of the world they had never heard of.

Clara seemed so grown-up and sophisticated as she sat at the table, dragging on a cigarette and then blowing out the smoke slowly through her pursed lips, her eyes half closed.

Watching her sister, Annie felt a great surge of pride rush through her, pride at her sister's beauty, her talent, her charm and, above all, her courage. She seemed not to be afraid of anything. Clara was so uninhibited; Clara was a free spirit.

They talked on into the night. Clara told Annie that she had received a letter from Roger. 'Just a note. It was from somewhere in Africa. It didn't say much but he sounded a bit fed up. He doesn't like being a soldier. I suppose he doesn't like being told what to do.'

Annie was intrigued. 'I thought you weren't friends any more.'

Clara shrugged and laughed. 'I suppose he wanted to write to a girl and he knew my address.'

The girls talked on until Annie's eyelids began to droop. She wanted to stay up forever but her fatigue was taking over. 'I think I might stay in the house tonight,' she said. 'I could sleep on the sofa.' Yes, she could be brave, too.

Clara leaped up. 'Great! I'll get you some sheets and blankets.'

Wrapped up snugly on the sofa, like a chrysalis, Annie listened to Clara's chatter with a delicious exhaustion taking her over. Then just as she was drifting off, the silence of the night was shattered by the loud wail of the air-raid siren starting up.

Annie leaped off the sofa, the bedding dropping to the floor. 'Oh help!' she shrieked. 'We're going to die!'

Clara sniffed. 'There's no need to worry,' she said cheerfully. 'Just stuff some cotton wool into your ears. You'll get used to it.'

But Annie was already collecting up her clothes and putting on her slippers. Picking up her clothes, she bolted out of the room. She was not going to take any chances. It was going to be a long time before she was brave enough to stay indoors.

Annie crept outside and into the Anderson shelter where her parents and Bobby were all sleeping soundly. With a sigh of relief, she climbed into her bunk and snuggled down to sleep.

Within moments, she was asleep and dreaming of her little brother Bobby. He was standing high on a hill and holding his arms out to her and calling out her name into the wind.

CHAPTER 12

Sussex

EVERY NOW AND THEN Annie had an overwhelming urge to touch and look at the mysterious brooch in her mother's wardrobe. It had been several months since she last looked at it, and suddenly, again, the urge was irresistible.

The house was quiet. Her mother was out with Bobby, queuing at the shops in the hope of getting a pig's head from Mr Worth. He had been expecting a supply for some time, and Grace planned to make plenty of brawn as well as serving up the tongue and the ears in some delicious form. It was fortunate that her family loved offal as much as it did, since it was one of the few foods that were not rationed.

Annie crept upstairs to her parents' bedroom and reached up to the shelf in the wardrobe. She had grown taller so she no longer needed to stand on a chair to reach it.

The brooch was looking quite a bit duller. The sheen had gone from the gold and the jewels did not seem so dazzling in the light. It all needed a good polish. Annie rubbed it against her sleeve, then turned it over slowly in her hands.

'Tell me what you mean,' she said. 'What is your secret?'

She stood there motionless, as if she were half-expecting a little whisper in her ear which would explain everything. But there was just silence.

As she put the brooch back, she noticed an envelope on the shelf of the wardrobe, pushed right back into the corner. It was the letter Mrs Pearson had written to her parents at the beginning of the war, the one offering to take the children.

Seeing the letter suddenly gave her an idea. She scribbled down the address, shoved the envelope back in its place, and disappeared up to her room. Later that day she went to the post office, bought a stamp and posted a letter into the letter-box in Fortess Road.

Mrs Pearson's reply came three days later. She was delighted that Annie had written and invited her down to the house near Pulborough on the following Saturday. She included details of the train times, and suggested Annie catch the late morning train which arrived at Pulborough just before lunchtime. 'Please let me know if you are not going to be on that train,' she wrote.

For the next week, Annie could barely sleep. She lay awake in her bunk in the Anderson shelter imagining her meeting with this mysterious woman, and going over and over in her head the conversation she was going to have with her. She could barely contain her excitement. She was certain that this meeting was going to change her life dramatically for ever. At last she was going to find out about the brooch. At last the mystery would be solved.

Annie did not tell anyone about her plans. With foresight she was proud of, she prepared the ground by saying in advance that she and Tilly were planning a picnic with friends that weekend, and were going off together for the day.

Annie felt uncomfortable about deceiving her mother. She tried to avoid spending too much time in her company for fear that she might guess what she was up to. She was convinced that her intentions were written all over her face.

Saturday was a clear, sunny day, with a fresh breeze and just a few wispy clouds floating in the sky. Dressed neatly in a blue cotton skirt and white blouse, Annie scurried along the road to the Tube station with her head down, hoping that no one would notice her. She was wrong.

'Hey there, Annie!'

Annie gasped and spun round, her face hot with a guilty blush. It was Tommy.

The sight of him filled her with a mixture of relief and confusion. She barely took in his words as he explained that he was home on a forty-eight-hour leave from his army training. Seeing him kitted out in his smart uniform, Annie blushed more deeply. She was sure that he would know that she had dreamed about him several times over the past few weeks, and they had not been the innocent dreams of the past. They had been quite embarrassing in their content, with Tommy removing his uniform, and embracing her in his strong arms. These dreams had surprised and shocked Annie for the adult longings they revealed deep within her.

Fortunately, Tommy did not act as though he knew about her dreams. He was his usual friendly self. He had always been a confident boy and now he seemed even more sure of himself than ever. He had always known about Annie's mother's brooch, so she hurriedly told him where she was off to that day.

'Well, I'm coming with you,' he said. 'At last we'll learn what the mystery is all about. I was hoping to see you today, anyway,' he added, 'so it doesn't matter if it's on a train or on Hampstead Heath.'

Annie was touched that he felt like that. She was also pleased to have a companion for her trip, for she was nervous about going down to Sussex on her own. Quite apart from meeting this formidable Mrs Pearson, she was worried about navigating her way there. She was not experienced at travelling on her own and she was terrified of getting on the wrong train.

Tommy had grown up and filled out a lot since she had last seen him. His hair was short, his shoulders broad and solid. His khaki serge uniform made him look big and strong.

He grinned. 'I'll just tell Connie to tell Mum we're off for the day. They're all at work in the day so they won't miss me.'

Annie waited outside the Smiths' house while Tommy ran indoors to tell his sister he would be back that evening to see them all. As she stood there, Annie could see Mrs Whelan peering at her from behind the lace curtains next door.

Tommy reappeared a few minutes later. 'That's all right, then,' he said. 'Connie didn't seem too pleased that I was going off. I suppose she thinks I should be stopping home all day.'

The couple took the Underground to Victoria station, changing at Charing Cross. Once there, Tommy bought some cigarettes at a kiosk.

The train was packed with soldiers. Corridors were full, with men hanging out of the windows, talking and smoking.

One man gave up his seat for Annie. She settled down on
the soft bench seat while Tommy stood beside her, holding
on to the wooden luggage rack above her head.

Watching Tommy's strong body and legs from her position, Annie suddenly felt self-conscious. A part of her was
pleased to see Tommy again, and she realized how much
she had missed his company over the past year, but another
part of her was aware that they had both changed. Before
they had just been pals, children who caught sticklebacks
together in Highgate Woods. Now they were boy and girl,
man and woman. She found herself being conscious of how
she looked – her hair, her clothes, her skin.

For his part, Tommy did not seem to be aware of any
difference. He grinned his gap-toothed smile as he joked
about his family and the neighbours. As the train pulled
out of the station and set off creakily across the Thames,
he told her stories about his training and about some of his
mates at the training camp. He enjoyed the army. 'But I
can't wait to get out there to kill a few Germans,' he said.
'We'll show that Hitler.'

Annie did not really follow or understand much about
what was happening in the war. All she knew was how it
affected everyday living for her and her family, the restric-
tions and the shortages, the making-do and the bravery. It
was a completely different kind of war from the war that
Tommy knew.

Soon they fell silent as the train chugged through south
London and out into the Surrey countryside. Annie stared
out of the window at the backs of the houses, the little
gardens and then the fields passing by. Soon they were in
the country. It all looked so tranquil. Who would know
what horrors were going on abroad? She suddenly had a

mental image of those lush green meadows overrun with Germans. She shivered and looked up at Tommy. She was immediately embarrassed to see that he was looking down at her with a thoughtful expression on his face. He had clearly been looking at her for some time. She smiled shyly and quickly looked away.

One hour later, they arrived at Pulborough Station. Annie and Tommy alighted from the train and walked towards the platform exit. Annie let the other passengers pass her. As the doorway cleared, she could see standing next to the ticket collector a tall, elegant woman dressed in a tailored dark-blue suit and a blue hat. She was peering at all the female passengers as they went past.

'That must be her!' Tommy dropped his voice to a whisper.

'Mrs Pearson?' Annie straightened her back and approached the woman with a nervous smile.

'Yes.' The response was hesitant, almost cold.

But then she responded, leaning forward to grasp Annie's hand. 'Anne, my dear . . .' She paused and looked at Tommy. 'Oh,' she said, 'you have a companion.' She smiled at Tommy who was standing back a few feet away from Annie.

Annie suddenly felt confusion swamp her. As she opened her mouth to explain, Tommy stepped smartly forward and held out his hand. 'Thomas Smith, ma'am,' he said with cool confidence. 'I'm a family friend and I accompanied Anne because her parents were concerned about her travelling on the train alone. I'll just wait here for her now and accompany her back to London when you've all finished your business. I have a book to read.' He patted his pocket.

Mrs Pearson frowned momentarily but then smiled again. 'I won't hear of it, my boy,' she said with the insistence of one who was used to having her own way. 'You must join us for luncheon. It will be most pleasant to entertain a young man for a change.' She flashed another radiant smile at Tommy, who nodded.

'Well, if you're sure, ma'am, I'd like that. It's kind of you to invite me.'

Annie was relieved that Tommy had given in and was coming, too. Confronted with Mrs Pearson, she was suddenly feeling out of her depth. She could not imagine how or why she had initiated this meeting.

'That's settled, then,' said Mrs Pearson with satisfaction. 'Now, come over here. I've brought the pony trap. I tend to use it whenever possible now, what with this tedious petrol rationing.' Mrs Pearson pointed to the station forecourt where a small grey pony stood patiently between the long wooden shafts of a dark green trap.

Perched high up on the seat next to Mrs Pearson, with Tommy squashed into the space at the back, Annie enjoyed the fresh breeze on her face as the pony trotted smartly along the narrow lanes. The hedgerows were thick and high, so it was only when there was a gate or stile that she could get glimpses of the wide green meadows and yellow cornfields beyond.

Above the soft thud-thud of the pony's unshod hoofs on the road, Mrs Pearson conversed. 'I'm living in the mill cottage at the moment. The army has taken over my house for their operations. I couldn't really stop them, though I thought it a bit outrageous. But my husband died several years ago and I live here alone with only a few staff now. I can't say I'm delighted by the arrangement. The house has been in my family for generations and I feel that I'm the caretaker for my descendants, so I'm always worrying about the place.'

'I'm sure the army will recompense you for any damage done,' Tommy said cheerfully.

Mrs Pearson nodded. 'Yes, I'm sure they will, of course. I just don't want them to do any damage in the first place,' she said wistfully.

'No, of course not,' Tommy agreed tactfully.

Annie was hardly listening to their exchange. She had noticed Mrs Pearson's hands. How elegant they were! They had long tapering fingers and long nails. In fact, with her neat hair and smooth white skin, Mrs Pearson was an elegant woman in every respect.

'Did you say you're living in Mill Cottage?' she asked.

'Yes,' replied Mrs Pearson. 'It'll be interesting for you to see the house your mother grew up in. Of course, it looks different inside. I've brought quite a few bits of furniture with me from the house, and various objects I couldn't live without.'

After about ten minutes, they turned into a wide drive with tall plane trees on both sides. They had arrived. An old man dressed in a dark suit immediately emerged from the front porch to help Mrs Pearson and Annie down from the trap. Then he led the pony and trap away while Mrs Pearson took her guests in through the open door of the cottage.

Annie was feeling increasingly nervous. The unexpected venue had made her feel even more anxious about bringing up the subject of the brooch. She found herself wondering why she had ever had the mad idea for making this trip in the first place.

They sat in the small sitting room. The warm sunlight shone through the open window. Mrs Pearson showed them photographs of her son Julian who was away at school.

Annie looked carefully at the photograph. Julian was a tall good-looking youth with floppy wavy hair falling over one eye and a cool gaze as he stood holding a shotgun, a black labrador at his knee.

'He's a very good shot,' commented Mrs Pearson. 'He says he can't wait to go off to fight, which worries me dreadfully. He's only sixteen, after all.'

'Oh, the same age as me,' said Annie.

Mrs Pearson glanced up at her. She hesitated momentarily. 'Yes, indeed, of course you are exactly the same age,' she said with a smile. But it was a strange smile, a secret sort of smile about something she was not going to share.

'I can understand how your son feels,' said Tommy. 'I feel the same.'

The smile had gone. Mrs Pearson sighed heavily. 'I think it's dreadful that you young men idealize war. War is a ghastly business . . .'

She fell silent and stared down at the photograph in her hands. 'I just don't know what I would do if anything happened to Julian.' She seemed to be talking more to herself than anyone else, and neither Annie nor Tommy felt it wise to comment.

They ate a light lunch of cold ham and potato salad. Mrs Pearson was gracious. She showed a genuine interest in Annie's family, and asked about Tommy's with interest. She expressed her condolences when Annie told her that her mother's health was not good.

'I remember your mother so well as a child,' said Mrs

Pearson, offering slices of freshly baked bread.
'Remarkably shy,' she said. 'At least with us, she was . . .

'There was a time when we played together quite a bit –
I think after my brothers had gone off to boarding school
and I needed a companion to play with. I liked her parents, too – your grandfather managed the farm. My father
always thought he was the best employee he'd ever had.
But I liked your grandfather because he always let me see
the calves being born, which my mother didn't approve of
at all. He'd beckon me from behind the stables and lead me
into the barn to see them. He'd let me feed the orphans
and the rejected ones with a bottle. Yes, he was a nice man.
He understood children. He knew what interested them.

'And your grandmother, of course, taught me my first
French words. I remember her standing in front of me – I
can't have been more than about three – and making me
repeat *un, deux, trois* . . .'

She paused and shut her eyes for a moment. 'Goodness,
what a long time ago all that was!' she said, opening her
eyes again and shaking her head. 'And so much has happened since. My dear brothers were both killed in the
Great War. That's how I came to inherit the house.' She
stared out of the window. The light coming in caught the
tears glistening in her eyes.

For a moment Annie thought she was going to cry. She
did not know what she was going to do if she did. 'I'm
sorry,' she murmured.

'Yes, yes.' Mrs Pearson blinked several times. Now there
were no tears. 'People die,' she said with a sudden sharpness. 'It's a fact of life. A sad one, but a fact of life
nevertheless.'

Tommy placed his buttered bread on his plate. 'And

sometimes,' he added, 'people have to die if it's for a good cause . . .'

Mrs Pearson turned and stared at him. 'Well, I'm not sure that either of my brothers died for a good cause. Theirs were stupid, unnecessary deaths which nearly destroyed my parents. I don't believe my mother ever recovered. My father was upset that neither of his sons would inherit the house, which has been passed down from father to son since 1640. But although I wasn't the right sex, at least I could ensure that the house stayed in the family.'

Her voice drifted off again as her thoughts went back to a past age. 'And now Julian will take it on after my death,' she added quietly.

Annie thought it best to change the subject. 'Do you live here all alone?'

'Yes,' replied Mrs Pearson. 'There's just Dobson and his wife now. All the young staff went off when the war started. So it is probably just as well that I'm not in the big house at the moment.'

After lunch, Camilla Pearson offered to show Annie and Tommy around the garden. 'You might like to see the motor cars, Thomas,' she said, waving an arm in the direc- tion of the stables. 'My husband had quite a collection and I've never had the heart to get rid of them. We use just the Riley nowadays but Dobson keeps all the other ones tuned and in good condition. I think it's become his hobby.' She laughed. Annie was pleased to see Mrs Pearson relaxing again. She seemed like a nice woman, even if she was fierce.

Tommy was delighted to be able to examine the old Bentleys and Rolls-Royces in the coach house while Annie walked with Mrs Pearson around the garden. Before Annie went off, Tommy caught her eye and winked. She knew it was meant to give her courage to ask the question.

It's now or never, thought Annie, bracing herself. She took a deep breath. 'The reason I wanted to see you and talk to you,' she said, staring down at her shoes, 'is that I thought you might be able to solve a puzzle for me . . .'

'Oh yes?' Mrs Pearson turned and fixed her gaze on her. Her brilliant blue eyes seemed to pin Annie to the spot.

'My mother has a brooch,' said Annie, 'a valuable brooch, which she told me you gave her.' She paused. Mrs Pearson gave no indication of knowing what she was talking about.

'I wondered if you would be able to throw some light on the brooch – on why you gave it to my mother in the first place. It would help me to know these things, you see . . .'

Her voice tailed off as she felt those blue eyes burning into her. 'I mean . . .' she had started to stammer, '. . . my father would . . .' She swallowed hard as her voice dried up.

Mrs Pearson stopped and turned to face her. 'And has your mother told you about the brooch?'

'Only that you gave it to her.'

Mrs Pearson turned away and walked on. 'Well, it's up to your mother to tell you, child. It's not for me to say.'

Annie ran to catch up. 'I know, but she won't tell me. I just hoped that you would be able to . . .'

'I'm sorry.' Mrs Pearson's voice was suddenly hard and cold. 'It's not for me to tell you anything. If your mother hasn't told you, she has her own reasons for that. Does she know you've come down here?'

'No.' Annie looked down at the ground. 'No, she doesn't.'

'Well, then, it's a bit naughty of you to come here behind her back, don't you think?'

Mrs Pearson's tone of voice changed as she deftly changed the subject. 'Come, now, let's see what I can give you from the kitchen garden. We grow most things here so we don't go without.'

She led Annie through a gateway into a walled garden laid out in neat rows of vegetables – lettuces, runner beans, carrots and sweet green peas.

Mrs Pearson bent down and pulled up a lettuce, shaking the dark crumbly soil off the roots. 'And have some salsify, too.' She pulled up a long black root. 'Oyster plant, some people call it, because it tastes like oysters. A wonderful delicate flavour – divine!'

For a few minutes Camilla Pearson bent and stooped as she pulled and picked a generous armful of vegetables. Handing Annie a wicker basket filled with the freshly harvested vegetables, Camilla Pearson peered at her again. 'You've got a pretty complexion,' she commented, 'and pretty eyes. You've got some potential there. And you've certainly got some brains in your head . . .' She paused. 'Now what about this young man?'

'You mean Tommy?' Annie stared at her. All afternoon she had had the impression that Mrs Pearson had taken to Tommy.

'Yes, Thomas.' Mrs Pearson paused. 'Of course, you're far too young to be thinking of these things but sometimes it's good to be aware . . .'

Annie did not know what she was talking about. 'I'm sorry?' She stared at the older woman in puzzlement. 'Be aware of what?'

Mrs Pearson hesitated but then spoke again. 'Difference,'

she said flatly. 'He's a nice enough young man. In fact, he's a nice young man. But he's not, in my opinion, good enough for you. I'm sure your mother would agree. Why, I find it quite hard to understand what he is saying.' She reached over and touched Annie's arm. 'When the time comes,' she said in a confiding tone, 'you can do better . . .'

Annie drew her arm away. 'But he's my friend,' she said quietly. She was shocked. Until that moment, Mrs Pearson had given the impression that she genuinely liked Tommy.

'Yes, yes, I understand,' said Mrs Pearson, collecting her trowel and secateurs, 'and that's perfectly all right, just so long as it stays that way. Just regard it as advice from an old woman.' With that, she strode out of the garden, leaving Annie staring after her in astonishment.

On the train home, Annie felt gloomy and disappointed. The high expectations with which she had started out were dashed. 'What a wasted journey,' she murmured. The train was not quite as crowded as the earlier one and there were a few empty seats so they were not as cramped.

Tommy laughed. 'In some ways it has been, yes,' he said, 'but in another way it's been very interesting. If Mrs Pearson doesn't want to tell you about the brooch, then she and your mother must have done something too terrible to tell anyone.'

'But that's awful,' said Annie. She was now afraid that what her mother had done was illegal, and she could not bear it if she went to prison. It made her frightened of stirring things up.

'Maybe,' said Tommy, 'but it's all the more intriguing. And I've certainly enjoyed myself. I've always wanted to

look at a Riley at close range. What beauties those cars
are!' He looked at Annie and smiled. 'But the best thing
about the day has been being with you.'

At Horsham two passengers got out, leaving Annie and
Tommy the only people in the compartment. Tommy
moved over and sat closer to Annie, placing his arm
behind her shoulders as he did so. 'I rather liked your Mrs
Pearson,' he said. 'She seems a nice enough person, even if
she didn't solve the mystery for you.'

Annie felt her throat tighten. How could she tell him
about Mrs Pearson's unkind comments? How could she
tell Tommy that he had been taken in by Mrs Pearson's
hypocrisy? She couldn't hurt his feelings or his pride. And
now his hand was on her arm and her skin felt as if it were
burning where he touched it.

She blushed. 'Oh, Tommy.' She looked away in embarrassment, turning to stare out of the window, not daring to
turn back to look at him.

Tommy reached over with his other hand and turned
her face towards him. With a soft sigh, Annie allowed him
to pull her over and kiss her gently on the lips. His chin felt
hard and prickly, his lips dry and firm. 'Oh Tommy!'
Annie buried her head in the rough uniform on his chest as
Tommy folded his arms around her and held her close.

The train chugged along towards London. Annie's head
rolled gently against Tommy's shoulder as she stared out of
the window. Sometimes they kissed again, and she mar-
velled each time at the sweet hard-softness of his lips. Her
head spun, full of confusion from the events of the day. It
was all too much to take in, in too many ways. She did not
want anything to spoil this delicious feeling of closeness.
She wanted it to go on forever. She wanted to hang on to

this feeling rather than think about the bitter disappoint-ment she also felt at failing to learn anything at all from Mrs Pearson about the brooch. No, Mrs Pearson had proved to be as reluctant to talk about it as Annie's own mother had been. She had had such high hopes, such high hopes that were now dashed. Never had Annie felt so helpless and dispirited.

CHAPTER 13

❦

The Visitor

WHEN CLARA FIRST CONFIDED in Annie that she was pregnant by a GI she had met at a dance, Clara's attitude was casual. 'It's all a mistake anyway,' she told her younger sister breezily. 'You're not supposed to get caught if you do it standing up. So I can't really be blamed for it, can I?'

Annie had not seen many of these American soldiers since their arrival in Britain after the Japanese bombed Pearl Harbor, for they did not have much reason to come to north London. But she knew that Clara and her friends spent a lot of time with them when they were not working, enjoying the gifts of Lucky Strike cigarettes, chewing-gum, Hershey bars and nylon stockings. Now it seemed that one of these generous men had given Clara something more.

It was late. The sky was dark outside and the girls' parents had taken themselves off to bed in the shelter some time before. Annie was taken aback by the news, and Clara's offhand attitude did nothing to reduce the effect of her comment on her sister. 'You're going to have a baby?' She stared at Clara with her mouth open.

Clara rolled her eyes. 'No, silly, I'm not going to have a baby.'

'But you just said you were pregnant, that you haven't had the curse for three months.'

'That's right, I did,' replied Clara, staring back at her steadily.

Annie frowned. 'I don't understand,' she said. Clara's contradictory statements were making her feel stupid.

Clara cocked her head to one side. 'Listen, I am pregnant, that's for sure, but people don't have to have babies if they don't want them. There's a way of getting rid of them.'

'There is?' Annie looked at her in puzzlement. 'So what happens to the baby?'

'Oh, nothing, it's just got rid of, that's all.' She frowned back at Annie as if to warn her off asking any more questions.

'The point is, Annie, that I know about someone who can help me. One of the girls at work has given me the name of a man who helps people in trouble. I'll have to go sooner rather than later because it gets more difficult as time goes on. Also, Annie, I don't want Mum and Dad to ever know about this, so I have to trust you to keep this as a secret.'

Annie nodded. 'Of course, Clara, I won't tell anyone. I'll help you in any way I can.'

The next day Annie had accompanied Clara on the bus to a dispensary in a row of shops in a leafy street in Hampstead.

Clara had been cheerful on the bus. She had been laughing and joking and acting as if she did not have a care in the world. Perhaps it really was not something to make a fuss about. Everyone made a big fuss when you had a baby. Perhaps the opposite was true when you did not have one. They got off and walked half a mile up the road until they reached the dispensary.

The shop was closed but Clara rang the bell and the chemist arrived to let them in. He was a tall, middle-aged man with a bald head and a small brown moustache. Annie thought that his clothes were rather shabby. He led the girls through the dark shop to a room at the back. Annie was told to wait there while he led Clara into another room beyond.

As Annie sat on the chair outside, she wondered what the man was doing to Clara on the other side of the door. She stared at the dreary posters on the wall opposite and tried hard not to think about how she might have been an auntie. No, that was really selfish of her. She thought about how Clara could not possibly have a baby when she wasn't even married. But killing a baby! That had to be wrong. Annie's head felt completely blocked with confusion. She could not think clearly at all. What she did know was that if Clara had a baby when she was not married then their mother would be very upset indeed. And their father would not be pleased, either. At least if Clara did something so that there was no baby after all, their parents would never know, and they would never need to know. Annie felt relieved to know that something made sense even if it did not feel right.

The clock on the mantelpiece was ticking loudly. The ticking noise seemed to get louder and louder until it felt as if it were actually striking her each time. What was happening? How much longer was she to wait?

Now she could hear noises next door. There was a clink of metal falling on the floor, a groan and then a sharp cry. Then there was another groan. Annie could hear the man's voice, muffled and incomprehensible.

She watched the door anxiously. Her hands were clutched together tightly in her lap.

It felt like an hour but the clock on the wall informed Annie that the procedure had taken twenty minutes. The door opened at last. The chemist came out first, drying his hands on a blue towel. He was followed by Clara.

Clara looked like a different person from the blasé young woman who had marched into that room twenty minutes before. She hung her head low. Her movements were slow and cautious and her lips, which were usually such a healthy red, looked yellow and waxen.

The moment she saw Annie, Clara's face crumpled up. She reached out towards her. 'Annie . . .'

Annie jumped to her feet and cried out, just as the chemist spun round in time to catch Clara as she collapsed into his arms.

Annie's fears that her sister was dead were soon dispelled. The chemist told Annie that Clara had just fainted. Soon he had Clara on a chair with her head down between her knees. He poured some sharp-smelling liquid onto a cloth and held it briefly under her nose. Clara jerked her head back. For a few moments, her eyes opened and flickered. Then, although her eyeballs seemed to be rolled back, her lips regained their colour.

'You're perfectly all right,' the chemist said gently. 'This sometimes happens. It's nothing to worry about. You're just a bit shocked, that's all.'

Once Clara had recovered enough to go home, the

chemist repeated what he had told her before. 'Go home and take it easy. It will happen within twelve hours or so.'

He squeezed Annie's shoulder in a friendly way. 'You'll look after her, will you? She should have someone with her.'

Annie nodded. He seemed like a kind man. He was clearly concerned about Clara and was trying to help. But Annie did not really understand what was happening. She did not know what had happened behind the closed door and she could not imagine what was going to happen within the next twelve hours. She also did not want to ask.

The chemist took them back through the shop and unlocked the door. 'Good luck,' he said as the girls left. 'And remember, we've never met . . .'

'Yes,' said Clara meekly. Her voice cracked. 'Thank you.'

Going back on the bus, Clara was quiet

'Has it gone?' Annie asked quietly.

'What?' Clara barked at her.

'Well, the baby . . .'

'Of course not, yet!' Clara snarled at her. 'What do you think that man was talking about when he said it would take twelve hours, you idiot?'

After that, Annie did not dare say anything. She kept wondering what the baby would look like, and whether she would get to see it. She also wondered whether she would cry when she saw it.

Back home, Clara told her mother that she wasn't feeling well because of her monthly, and took herself off to her bedroom. As soon as she could after supper, Annie followed

Clara upstairs to look after her, as she had promised the chemist she would.

The pains started at about nine o'clock that evening. At first they felt like the usual cramps but then gradually they grew more powerful. Clara had been pacing around the room. Annie looked in horror as Clara suddenly let out a deep groan and bent over double. A minute later, Annie noticed a crooked line of dark red blood trickling slowly down Clara's bare leg.

Feeling the wetness, Clara looked down. 'Get some towels, Annie!' She sounded quite desperate. 'Oh, goodness, I think there's going to be a bit of a mess . . .'

By the time Annie had returned, Clara was lying on her bed curled up into a ball and hugging her knees. Every now and then she pulled her legs in closer and winced as her face became screwed up with pain. Her hair, damp with sweat, stuck to her forehead in frizzy yellow curls.

'Is it getting any better?'

Annie sat at the end of the bed, one hand resting reassuringly on Clara's leg. This had been going on for over half an hour now. Surely it had to be over sometime soon?

The problem was that Annie did not have a clue about what was to happen. But surely the situation could not get any worse than this? Surely Clara had suffered enough already?

There was a terrible mess. By the time Clara's baby had been expelled from her body, five thick towels had been soaked with dark blood.

Clara endured the ordeal with hardly a sound. When a cramp came, her face went red and then white. She bit her lip and tears welled up in her eyes as sweat beads rose on her forehead. But not once did she cry or scream.

Annie held her hand throughout.

And then it was over. Annie gathered everything up, the blood-soaked towels, the massive clots of blood, and the tiny baby itself. But she did not look at it. She tried not to look at anything so that she would not retch. Everything that needed to be destroyed, she put in a bucket ready to put into the fire of the kitchen boiler later that night.

Once it was over, Clara was calm again. She was exhausted, and lay on the bed, staring at the ceiling. 'Thank you, Annie,' she whispered.

Much later, when the night was still and Annie was certain that her parents had taken themselves and Bobby off to the shelter in the garden, she started to take everything downstairs.

'Thank you,' repeated Clara.

'That's all right,' returned Annie. She closed Clara's bedroom door and carried the bucket and towels downstairs.

She burned the contents of the bucket in the boiler and dumped the bloody towels in the bath. As she scrubbed and rubbed, she thought about Clara's terrible experience that day. It was all a disaster, a terrible, terrible thing. No, that was never going to happen to her. Not in a million years.

It was Saturday morning and the butcher's shop was crowded with people. That morning Mr Worth had in a batch of chickens for the first time in months. Chicken was not rationed but it was an almost forgotten luxury so word about Mr Worth's delivery had spread quickly around Kentish Town.

Annie was quite high up in the queue so she had a good

chance of being one of the lucky ones. As she waited her turn, she thought about how they could make the chicken go as far as possible. If she cut it up into pieces and rolled them in batter, perhaps they could get two meals out of a few ounces.

At the thought of the delicate meat, her mouth began to water. The hundreds of dreary meals of spam or pilchards she had eaten over the past few years had deadened her taste buds, but suddenly she was excited at the thought of food.

The Fenton sisters were standing in front of her in the queue. Annie said good morning to them with a smile. The old women paused for a moment in their conversation to say hello back and then resumed what seemed to be an argument over how many people had been injured by the bomb that had fallen on Peckwater Street two nights back.

As they argued, Mrs Whelan joined the queue behind her. 'Hello there, Annie,' she said. 'And how's your mother?'

'Not too bad today,' replied Annie, 'but her arthritis has been playing up recently.'

Two places up in the queue, Mrs Rose turned and eyed Annie. 'Is your mother taking herself off to church more often or am I imagining it?'

Annie nodded. 'Yes, she has been going up there a bit more than usual. She likes to go there to think.'

The Fenton sisters nodded in unison. 'They say that often happens to people. They get more religious as they get older,' said Ada.

'Mrs Turner's not that old,' replied Emily.

Ada frowned at her sister. 'Maybe not, dear,' she said with a touch of sarcasm, 'but she's older than she was.'

Emily rolled her eyes. 'Well, there's no denying that,' she said. 'But you could say that about all of us.'

The conversation then turned to the latest air raids and the damage caused by the bomb that had fallen on Peckwater Street. It had landed in the middle of a terrace and killed two people.

'It's a wonder no one else was killed,' said Mrs Whelan. As she talked it became clear that she knew most of the details, having spent quite some time standing by the bomb site watching the rescue teams bringing out the dead and wounded. 'One old chap was sitting in his front room. Dead drunk, he was. He didn't know what had hit him. He staggered out but it was the drink what made him stagger, not the shock.'

'Well, that's one way to deal with it,' muttered Mrs Rose.

At that moment, Mrs Whelan stepped towards the window and peered out over the sausages and pork pies. 'Well, will you look at that! There's that Maudie Sprackling, indeed!'

Along with everyone else in the queue, Annie turned her head to look. Walking past was Maudie Sprackling leaning on the arm of a handsome young man. She looked radiant. Now slimmed down, she had a strong shapely figure, and under her blue-and-white hat her face revealed clearly defined features – a well-shaped nose and high cheekbones.

'That's her fiancé,' said Bob Worth, wiping his hands on his apron.

'Why isn't he away fighting, then?' demanded Mrs Whelan. 'He looks fit enough to me.'

'He's got asthma, apparently,' returned Mrs Rose. 'Nice bloke, though. And since you mentioned it, I think it was quite a blow for him not to be able to fight. And they're getting married next month,' she added.

'Well he can't want any children, then,' sniffed Mrs Whelan, who never liked to be filled in on the details of anything, especially when it concerned one of her own neighbours. 'Everyone knows that Maudie is as barren as the Sahara desert.'

'You can't be too sure of that.' The husky voice called across the shop from the doorway. Everyone turned to look. There was Connie Smith standing at the back of the queue with her shopping basket over her forearm. 'It takes two to tango, you know,' she continued, 'and it's not always the woman who's at fault.' She smiled and tossed her head defiantly.

Mrs Whelan drew herself up and pursed her lips. She sniffed sharply through her thin nose. She had never tried to hide her disapproval of Connie Smith for stealing Maudie Sprackling's husband, Fred. 'Well, I suppose you would know more about that than the rest of us,' she said primly, turning her back on Connie, 'but I'm not quite sure how, since you didn't have any children either.' This last remark was uttered in a softer voice but loud enough for everyone to hear.

Connie smiled confidently. 'All I said was that you shouldn't assume it's the woman's fault. No more, no less.' She stepped back. 'I'll return later, Mr Worth,' she called. 'When the shop isn't so crowded.' She stared pointedly at Mrs Whelan, and left.

For a few minutes silence reigned in the shop. All that could be heard was the heavy thump-thump of Mr Worth's cleaver on the wooden chopping table. But then the women started to chat again, the earlier exchanges forgotten.

In spite of being weighed down by the heavy wicker baskets on her arms, Annie decided to go up to Peckwater Street on her way home to have a quick look at the bomb damage.

It was quite a shock to see it. The bomb had devastated the Victorian terrace, blasting the fronts and backs of the houses so that the rooms were pitifully exposed to view like dolls' houses. There were drooping roofs and sagging floors; doors were wrenched off; furniture had been tossed all about, and wallpaper was blasted and tattered. Yet in some houses pictures were still hanging on the walls – slightly askew but otherwise intact. The sight offered poignant snapshots of life seconds before the bomb exploded. Mugs were still on kitchen tables, children's toys were scattered about the floors, clothes were laid out carefully over the back of a chair. And all around these cameos was chaos – shattered wood and bricks and rubble, and dust everywhere. Even houses that were not seriously damaged had had all their windows shattered by the force of the explosion, and were now boarded up with planks of wood.

Long wooden barriers had been placed across the road to keep people away from the rubble and the mess. Wardens were picking through the piles, while the police kept potential looters at bay.

Annie stood by the barriers for some time. This scene was always shocking, no matter how often she had seen it before. People had died and other people's lives were ruined for ever. It made her think about what her house would look like if a bomb were ever to fall on it, too. She imagined a young girl like herself looking in at Annie's house, with Annie's paints and pencils scattered across the floor of the dining room, her paintings lying buried in the dust and bricks.

As she stood wondering and imagining, she heard a small noise behind her. A young ginger cat, no more than a kitten really, came out of the rubble and rubbed its body against her bare leg.

'Hello, cat.' Annie bent down and scratched the cat behind the ears. The kitten pushed itself against her even harder. Then it climbed into Annie's wicker basket which she had put on the ground by her feet.

Annie pushed the animal out and set off for home with the basket on the crook of her arm. Halfway home, she realized that the kitten was following her. 'Go home! You can't come with me!' She waved her arms at the cat who stared at her and opened its mouth in a silent wail.

Annie set off again with the kitten in tow.

When she came to Falkland Road, Annie saw a large, sleek, black car parked outside her house. A chauffeur sat in the front. Small children were circling the vehicle, peering in through the back window and running their sticky fingers over the bodywork. No one in the street owned a car so this was a cause for much excitement and curiosity.

Annie was puzzled at first but then she recognized the face of the driver – the old retainer from Sussex. The car was Mrs Pearson's Riley. Mrs Pearson had come to visit!

With her heart thumping, Annie quickened her pace and ran indoors, unaware of the ginger kitten following close on her heels.

Her father was sitting at the kitchen table reading the paper. Bobby was also sitting at the table trying to push a skewer through a conker. He was concentrating hard, his head tipped over to one side. Holding the shiny brown nut in one hand, he twisted the metal skewer into the flesh. Tiny, damp, pale yellow flakes fell on to the wooden table.

'Your mother has a visitor,' said Frank, looking at Annie over the top of his newspaper.

'It's Mrs Pearson, isn't it?' said Annie. 'Why is she here?' She had never told her parents about her visit to Sussex.

Frank shrugged and looked back down at his paper. 'How would I know why she's here? It's your mother she's come to see.'

Annie unpacked her shopping and put the food and provisions away in the larder. She filled the kettle and put it on the stove to make a pot of tea.

'Who's this, then?' Frank pointed to the ginger cat which was poking its head round the door. 'It seems we've got an open house today.'

Bobby jumped off his chair and crouched down at the cat as Annie scooped it up in her arms.

'Hey, want to hear a good joke, Annie?' Bobby hovered around her excitedly. He smiled at her; the gaps where his milk teeth had been falling out seemed to be growing. Several teeth had all come out in the same month. He had collected quite a few pennies from the tooth fairy recently.

'All right, go on then.' Annie was a resigned and sympathetic listener to Bobby's jokes. She could remember when she was that age and was trying out most of these same jokes on her long-suffering parents.

'Here we go: why did the chicken cross the road?'

Annie rolled her eyes tolerantly. 'Well, I've heard that one before, Bobby, you asked me that only yesterday, and the day before that.'

Bobby chuckled gaily. He was a happy little boy. 'Yes, yes, don't spoil it. There's another part, a new bit . . .'

Annie nodded patiently. 'The answer is, because it wanted to get to the other side.'

Bobby wriggled with pleasure. 'That's right. Now,' he said, 'why did the chewing gum cross the road?'

Frank raised his eyes over the paper. 'I hope Clara hasn't been giving you more gum, Bobby. Your mother won't be pleased, you know.'

Bobby frowned. 'Oh, don't spoil it, Dad.'

Annie laughed. 'I don't know, Bobby, you've got me with that one. Why did the chewing gum cross the road?'

Bobby jumped to his feet and shouted triumphantly: 'Because it was stuck to the chicken's foot!'

Annie and Frank both laughed.

'That's not a bad joke, Bobby,' said Frank, 'not bad at all.'

'Clara taught me that,' the boy said with a satisfied look.

Annie was no longer listening. Her thoughts were now upstairs, in the sitting room where her mother sat with the visitor. If her father had not been there, she would have crept upstairs by now to press her ear against the closed door to hear the voices on the other side.

Inside the sitting room, Grace was on the sofa against the far wall. She had a nervous and pinched expression on her face as she watched the other woman pace across the worn blue carpet. At times, she even looked afraid.

'I must emphasize the importance of keeping everything secret,' Mrs Pearson was saying. 'I was alarmed when Anne came down to see me, but it was evident that she did not know anything. As I said, I am here to make sure that you continue to keep everything under wraps. If anything ever got out about what we did, there could be serious consequences for everyone. I don't have to remind you that what we both did was against the law . . .'

Grace raised her head and a rare flash of emotion showed in her grey eyes. 'Of course it's a secret. It always has been and always will be. Anne is a girl with a lot of curiosity and I'm not surprised that she came to see you like that. Obviously, I'm glad you didn't tell her anything, either.'

Mrs Pearson looked at her fiercely for a moment. 'You should have got rid of the brooch,' she said accusingly. 'Or at least made sure that no one ever had reason to wonder about it.'

'Well, then you shouldn't have given it to me in the first place,' returned Grace. 'I never asked you for it.' She looked away.

'I want to say one more thing before I leave.' Mrs Pearson stood over Grace's form on the sofa. 'There is no point in thinking about the morality of our actions. It all happened a long time ago now, and there must be no regrets. The best thing is to put it out of your mind completely. I think you'll find it never bothers you if you do.'

Ten minutes later, Annie watched from the kitchen doorway as Mrs Pearson swept down the stairs and let herself out of the front door. She could not see clearly but Annie was sure that the expression on Mrs Pearson's face was one of great satisfaction.

Annie was surprised and even a little hurt that Mrs Pearson had left without seeking her out to say hello.

The black limousine drove off, scattering the urchins hanging around it. A few minutes later, Annie heard her mother's slow footsteps on the stairs. 'I'm going out for a while,' Grace called. Her voice was soft.

'Is everything all right?' Frank called back from the kitchen.

'Yes, thank you,' replied Grace. 'I won't be long.'

Annie knew that her mother was taking herself up to the church.

That evening, Grace called Annie in to the sitting room.

'Close the door, Annie and come and sit down here. I have something to tell you. I've thought about this long and hard and feel that I owe you an explanation.'

Annie was amazed. She walked slowly into the room and sat down in the chair facing her mother.

Grace looked down at her hands. Annie noticed that she was unconsciously running the fingertips of one hand up and down the back of the other. 'Annie, dear, I know you saw Mrs Pearson today, and I understand that you went down to visit her a few weeks ago to ask her about the brooch. I won't chastise you for going to Sussex without telling me. Let's just say that I was a little bit hurt. I'll leave it at that. If I'd known that you were so desperate to know about the brooch that you would take yourself off to Sussex like that, I would have told you myself. I certainly think you're old enough to understand now.'

Annie bit her lip. 'Sorry,' she muttered sheepishly.

'But I will tell you about the brooch,' continued her mother. Grace turned her head and stared out of the window as she began to speak.

Annie looked up in surprise. Her mother's words were so unexpected.

'A long time ago,' Grace began, 'when I was still living at home with my parents and before I had met your father, I helped Mrs Pearson. That is why she gave me the brooch. I helped her do a terrible thing.' She turned back towards Annie, her eyes filled with tears.

Annie shifted uncomfortably in her chair. Was she really going to learn the truth she had longed to know for so long? Her heart was racing. Her mother had helped do a terrible thing? She waited for more.

'Camilla was not then married – she was called Camilla Heathcote in those days. She had a liaison with a young man . . .' Grace paused and added, 'I know you're old enough to hear what I have to say . . . In any event, she found herself in trouble, which is a terrible thing for any young woman, but especially in a grand family such as hers. She was panic-stricken and, having no one else to turn to, she confided in me. She did not dare tell anyone else. As it happened, before any decision could be made about anything, she lost the baby. It was a godsend, in a way. Or so it seemed at the time, and I hope God will forgive me for saying that. Camilla was about five months gone and the baby was a fair size.' Grace's voice was getting fainter and fainter. 'She asked me to get rid of the baby for her.' Now her voice sounded choked up. 'I took it out in the night and buried the body in the grounds.' She paused before continuing. 'We never spoke of it again but a few days later Camilla gave me the brooch. It was, she said, a symbol of her gratitude, for being there when there was no one else she could turn to.'

Grace stopped and smiled wanly. There was a terrible sadness in her eyes. 'I'm sorry that it's taken you so long to learn this. I'm sorry that you had to learn of it at all. What we did was a sin. The child was conceived in sin and then buried in unconsecrated ground. I trust you to keep this secret to yourself. I should be grateful if you spoke about it to no one, not Clara, not your father, not Jack, nor Bobby. It's between you and me. I know you will respect that request.'

Annie nodded meekly. She walked over to her mother and kissed her on the forehead. 'I understand,' she murmured. She left the room thinking about how she had tipped Clara's baby into the boiler to burn, as if the poor little thing had been pitched into hell's fires. No consecrated ground for that baby, either. As she climbed downstairs, her face burned with shame.

Later that night, Annie lay in her bunk bed in the shelter. Her mind was racing as she stared up into the darkness. Over and over again she replayed her mother's words in her head. She felt uneasy as she turned them over in her mind, trying to imagine the scenes between the two young women – Camilla in trouble, her mother creeping out in the middle of the night with the dead baby, the unwanted dead baby. They were poignant images which she could picture easily in her mind.

But there was something wrong with it all. Something made her feel uneasy. A cramp was seizing her leg so she shifted position. Something about her mother's account did not ring true. There was a problem. And that problem was that she did not believe that her mother had been telling her the truth. Her sweet, God-fearing and gentle mother had been telling her a bundle of lies.

CHAPTER 14

❧

Annie in Love

IT HAD NOT TAKEN long for Annie to realize that she was falling in love with Tommy. She did not know it at first. It started with her observation that her feelings for Tommy were changing. She noticed that she liked to think about him, to conjure him up in her mind's eye or recall his voice in her ear. She had warm feelings at the thought of him and sometimes even a slight lurch in her belly. She could amuse herself for hours just thinking about him and when she did a smile appeared on her lips and her dreamy eyes would sparkle. Slowly it dawned on her that what she was feeling was love. She was falling in love.

At first she was frightened of the change in their relationship, shifting from a simple friendship to something far more serious, something mysterious and alluring. And these feelings were stronger than any crush she had ever had at school, stronger than anything she had ever felt before. It marked her development from child to woman, as did the physical changes that were still happening to her body.

As an artist, Annie had become very interested in the

human body. At every opportunity, she would draw a hand, a foot, the profile of her mother's head as she read her *Good Housekeeping* magazine, or Bobby's back as he leaned over his Meccano set. Her sketchbooks were filled with anatomical studies. Soon she became fascinated, too, by the way light casts shadows on human flesh, changing the image significantly. Her mother's face could look worn and tired in one kind of light, yet another kind of softer, gentler light could recapture the pretty bloom of youth.

Annie also began to think about her own body and how different it was from Clara's or her mother's. Whereas they both had strong, lean bodies with rounded curves, Annie's frame was slight and angular. Her slender wrists and ankles looked positively fragile against Clara's robust bones, and generally, Annie felt she lacked a womanly shape.

These differences bothered her considerably. Not only did they revive her old fears about being different from the rest of the family but they also made her think that Tommy could not possibly find her attractive.

One day, when Tommy was home on a brief leave, they went for a walk in Highgate Woods. There had been heavy storms the night before and the rain was still dripping off the leaves of the trees and falling on to the brown leaf-mould below. There were few people about – just the occasional woman walking her dog, and apart from the low rumbling of the trains coming into Highgate station, the woods were quiet and still.

Annie and Tommy walked hand in hand. Both were silent and thoughtful that morning.

'I sometimes find it hard to believe you genuinely like me,' Annie ventured.

Tommy gave her a puzzled look. 'Of course I do. What are you talking about?' He squeezed her hand and pulled her to him.

Annie smiled but pulled away. 'I'm being serious,' she said. 'I can't believe that you don't find Clara more attractive than me.'

'Clara?' Tommy looked surprised. He thought for a moment. 'Clara is attractive, of course,' he said, 'but you're the one I like best. And I find you very attractive.'

'But Clara's got curves. All men go after curves. I'm just straight and thin, like a stick insect.'

Tommy laughed. 'Attraction is not just about curves, you know. And besides, do you think I'd court a stick insect? You insult me!'

Annie looked away with embarrassment and he squeezed her tight. 'Annie, love, don't you know, you're very beautiful. You have a gracefulness and elegance that Clara will never have. She is very womanly, yes, but you have something special. I don't know what it is, exactly, but I know I like it. You're like a swan.'

Annie grunted. 'You mean an ugly duckling.'

Tommy placed his hand over her mouth to hush her. 'No, a swan.'

They had come to a clearing. Taking his hand away, Tommy placed his lips on Annie's half-open mouth. He pulled her to him, causing her to stand on tiptoe, and squeezed her tight. One hand ran down her back. Then he pulled up her skirt at the back to allow his hand to continue up her inner thigh.

The feeling of Tommy's rough hand on her sensitive skin sent a tingling between her legs and up to the pit of her belly. Annie felt excited in a way she had never been before.

She leaned towards him, rubbing her own hands up and down his back. She was trembling with new sensations, twinges and deep longing. This poor despised body of hers had suddenly sprung to life.

Tommy kissed her neck. 'You're my swan, Annie,' he whispered, running his lips down her neck. 'Do you believe me now? Just look at this exquisite neck!'

Annie smiled and nodded weakly. 'My father says I take after my great-grandmother,' she whispered.

'Then I'm grateful to your great-grandmother,' Tommy replied.

After that, Annie had no doubts about Tommy's interest in her, and she looked forward to his short furloughs with longing. They spent every minute of his leave together, walking hand in hand across Hampstead Heath and on to Highgate Woods. They rowed on the boating ponds at Alexandra Palace, or swam in the icy cold water of Highgate Pond. They lunched in the British Restaurant in Highgate and went several times to the cinema. They saw a Gracie Fields film at the Hampstead Picture Playhouse, and *Mrs Miniver* at the Court cinema in Malden Road. And at the Kentish Town Forum, they saw Clark Gable and Spencer Tracy in *San Francisco*, which they had first seen years ago, before the war had started.

Sitting next to Tommy in the cinema stalls, Annie often felt she was living a dream. Her head was floating but she remained acutely conscious of Tommy's leg against hers, his fingers interlaced with her own and the musky male smell of his body as he leaned against her.

So many times in the past, Annie had snatched a look at

the courting couples sitting in the back rows of the cinema oblivious to the world as they kissed, or just sitting with blissful expressions on their faces as they enjoyed the simple pleasure of being completely caught up with another person. What heaven it was!

At last Annie had joined the grown-ups, or at least the big girls, with a kind, handsome boy of her own, a decent fellow who treated her with respect and dignity.

On one occasion when Tommy came home it was clearly going to be his last leave for some time.

'I can't talk about it, Annie, you know that, but something big is going to be happening soon,' he said. 'I don't know when myself. No one knows, except the big shots.'

They had gone back to Tommy's home after a walk on Hampstead Heath. At first Annie had not wanted to go to the house in Leverton Street, for she was aware that Connie had had some change of feeling towards her. Tommy's big sister had always been so friendly towards her in the past, but over the last few months she had appeared cold and distant.

However, Tommy assured Annie that no one was at home. It was the middle of the afternoon and his parents and Connie would still be at work.

The house looked neat and tidy. Connie was still keeping it well. Tommy made a pot of tea and they sat in the front room together on the broken-down sofa. It was propped up underneath with some bricks. They talked about their plans for the future, how Annie wanted to apply for art school and Tommy to study law. They talked about the return of Roger to the neighbourhood, after being invalided out of the army. 'He smashed up his leg in a motor-bike accident,' explained Annie. 'He spent a long time in an army hospital but he was sent home a few months ago. His leg was in plaster for ages, and Clara visited him a lot at home.' She sighed. 'I suppose that will all start up again now,' she added wearily. 'He's got a job working for a builder now.'

'There's plenty of that work to be done, that's for sure,' said Tommy.

Then, after a while, Tommy placed his hand on Annie's and they began to kiss, as they had done at every meeting since that first time. Now Annie had got used to the hard prickles of Tommy's chin which had made her own skin sore and red at times. And she no longer felt repelled by the feel of his tongue on hers. Sometimes, she even felt bold enough to move her own tongue against his.

This time, there was an urgency in Tommy's breathing. His hands, rubbing up and down her back and shoulders, seemed stronger, bolder.

'Annie, Annie,' he whispered, taking her hand and placing it against his trousers.

Annie moved her hand away and sat upright. 'No, Tommy,' she said. She straightened her skirt primly.

Tommy placed his hands around her face and stared into her eyes. 'This might be the last time I see you, my darling,' he whispered. 'Let's show our love for each other in the way we are meant to . . .'

Annie swallowed hard. She was feeling excited herself. In fact, she was feeling an almost unendurable urge to let Tommy sweep her up in his arms, pull off her clothes and consummate their love. She longed to be taken over, to give up all control, just like in the films, with all that rich, stirring music in the background. But she did not yield. Because however strong that impulse to surrender herself

to Tommy, there was no escaping the image in her mind of
Clara squatting over the chamber pot and the bloody
remains of that tiny dead baby in the bucket.

She buried her face in Tommy's chest. 'Tommy, Tommy,
I love you,' she whispered. 'But I can't do it yet. Let's just
kiss.'

Tommy shuddered and immediately pulled away. He
looked disappointed and for a few moments was quite
subdued. But he respected Annie and did not want to
push her if she wasn't keen. He knew, too, that he was
partly responsible for feeling so let down. He had fool-
ishly allowed himself to believe his mates back at the
army base when they advised him on how to succeed with
his girl.

'Never mind, then,' he said, adjusting his trousers and
trying to sound cheerful. 'Let's have some more tea.'

As Annie poured out the tea, they heard the front door
open. Then Connie appeared in the doorway. The sight of
Tommy and Annie sitting close together on the sofa did
not seem to please her at all. Annie saw that she was
frowning.

'Oh, it's you, Tommy,' said Connie.

'Well, who did you think it could be?' asked Tommy.
'The seven dwarves?' He laughed.

'Hello, Connie,' Annie said shyly. Connie used to be so
friendly towards her. What could have happened?

Connie left the room and disappeared into the kitchen
to cook some tea. Could it have anything to do with
Tommy and her getting so close? The thought suddenly
seemed to make sense. But why on earth should Connie
mind? Annie was hurt and confused. What was wrong?

Nothing more was said, and Tommy certainly seemed

unaware of any problem. Perhaps it was just in Annie's own head. She tried to persuade herself that it was.

Annie could not have known that Connie's strange reaction stemmed from fear, not disapproval. Connie had just woken up to the fact that Tommy and Annie were extremely serious about each other. They were so serious that Connie could no longer ignore their friendship. Worse than that, she knew that she would have to do something about it.

When Annie left to go home, Tommy kissed her hard, giving her a long, lingering kiss on the mouth. Annie walked backwards up the street waving goodbye to him. Tommy was off early the next morning and she would not be seeing him again before then. Perhaps it would be the last she would ever see of him, but she did not think so. It suddenly struck her that, deep down, she was not afraid for his life. She just knew that he would survive the war, and that they would be together afterwards.

When she reached her own front door, she was surprised to hear someone playing some lively music on the piano. Her spirits rose even higher than before.

Clara was sitting at the piano. She flashed a smile at her sister as Annie came into the hall. Annie had not heard Clara play the piano for a long time and certainly she had not played any music as gay as this for many years.

'Hello, sis!' Clara beamed at her.

Annie nodded. 'You seem happy,' she commented.

Clara's eyes were sparkling. She nodded back, her blonde hair bobbing up and down. Then she stopped playing and held up her left hand with the fingers spread out like a fan. 'Look at this,' she said. 'Roger's asked me to marry him.' She laughed gaily. 'It's an engagement ring. I'm engaged.'

Annie stared at her sister's finger and the ring with its small modest stone. 'Engaged?' She repeated the word slowly. 'To Roger?' She could not hide her disbelief.

Clara leaped to her feet and grabbed Annie's hands. 'Yes, yes, I'm going to get married!' She laughed again, spinning Annie round in a circle. 'I'm about to become a respectable woman!'

Annie's parents seemed resigned to the match.

'He's a nice enough boy,' remarked Grace. 'He's grown up a lot and he's got himself a regular job since he came out of the army.'

'The army was probably good for him,' said Frank. 'Gave him a sense of discipline he never got at home. He said as much to me only the other day.'

'What counts is Clara's happiness,' said Grace. 'She certainly looks happy enough now. And,' she added with a soft smile, 'if they get married in the autumn, we could be grandparents within the year!'

Annie frowned. 'If Clara gets married then she probably won't go to college, will she?'

Frank sighed. 'I've lost that argument, yes. And if marriage is what Clara really wants, then there's no stopping her,' he said. 'Clara's always been one to get what she wants.'

Annie listened to these conversations with interest. She felt her father's disappointment that Clara would not go to college and get some qualifications. And she sensed that beneath her mother's excitement at the idea of a wedding and what it meant, there was a touch of regret that Clara had not done better for herself in her choice of husband. Apart from his charm and good looks, Roger had never given any reason to be considered a catch in any way.

Sometimes, too, Annie felt quite uneasy about Roger. There was an unpredictable side to him that scared her. He could be quite moody, one minute full of laughter and big ideas for having fun, and the next silent and brooding. Annie also noticed that he sometimes spoke sharply to Clara, which never used to happen, and that Clara, to Annie's surprise, tended to take notice without argument. This unpredictable behaviour was disturbing. But generally, she quite liked Roger. She could see through his rough-tough exterior to a softer fellow beneath. He was always kind to her and teased in an affectionate sort of way. Annie liked the way Roger seemed to look up to her father, in the way that Tommy did sometimes, too, as a fatherless boy does. It made her proud of her family, and the way it welcomed outsiders into the fold.

By the time Tommy had returned to camp saying that something big was about to happen, the bulk of Europe, from the Ukraine to the Pyrenees, was an undisputed German fiefdom. D-Day, 6 June 1944, was to change all that.

Ten thousand aircraft took part, each one painted with stripes the night before for recognition. The planes towing gliders and carrying paratroops formed a nose-to-tail stream more than one hundred miles long that morning.

Seven thousand vessels, from midget submarines to the mightiest of battleships, were to head for the Normandy beaches. And so crowded were the British ports that some ships had to sail from as far north as Scotland.

Over a hundred and fifty thousand Allied men set foot on French soil that day, as well as fifteen hundred vehicles.

All were landed on open sandy beaches fortified and protected by wire, mines and steel traps. And all done in
atrocious weather.

Everything had been planned with utmost secrecy. The
whole of south-west England was an army camp, and a
huge armada had gathered.

Annie's first inkling of the importance of that day came
as she was hanging out the washing. High above her, the
sky was almost dark, full of planes, wing to wing, streaming
towards the coast.

Like everyone else in the land, the Turner family gathered round the wireless that evening, listening to the BBC's
accounts of the landings and thinking about Jack, Tommy
and every other boy they knew who was out there that
day.

After D-Day, most people thought that surely the war
was over, but soon afterwards a new kind of German aircraft started terrorizing London: Hitler's revenge bombs.
Unmanned and extremely noisy, they flew at just the
height to avoid both the light and the heavy guns. The
engine would suddenly cut out and then a huge explosion
would follow within seconds. The doodlebugs, as they
came to be known, were then followed in September by an
even more frightening weapon: the flying rockets. These
could be launched from over two hundred miles away and
gave no warning at all. Both weapons represented a sinis-
ter development at this stage in the war when the Allied
troops were supposed to be taking control of Europe. But
still Londoners kept going, making jokes about those cow-
ardly men fighting at the front while those back home were
suffering the worst of it.

*

If marriage had put paid to Clara's plans to go to college, Annie was still determined to make her way to art school. Now seventeen, she was able to apply but she decided to wait until the next year to do so. In spite of the doodlebugs and the rockets, the war had to be in its last stages. There were already signs of peace. In September the blackout gave way to a dim-out, and on Christmas Day, churches could light their stained glass windows for the first time since war had begun. Two days later, car headlights' masks were abolished. It would all be over by next year, and Annie wanted to wait until it was. She wanted the certainty. Until then, she wanted to get out and contribute properly to the war effort like everyone else.

Tilly felt the same way, so the two girls got themselves jobs in a small home factory in Camden. It had been started by a group of women who had got together to set up shop at home, testing screws for aircraft engines. It was monotonous, boring work but the camaraderie and friendly atmosphere in the room where they all worked made up for that. Annie listened to the conversation of the older women with great interest. She listened to the stories of their husbands and fiancés. She heard confessions of infidelity and raucous laughter at the foibles of men. Annie tried not to look too shocked when the women talked bluntly about their men's inadequacies in bed but she liked the way that the women showed a genuine affection for their husbands, even if they did regard them as naughty children. Sometimes the conversation became quite explicit, and Annie would look down and pretend not to listen, or sneak a glance at Tilly, who was always equally embarrassed. But she loved the fact that the women treated her as one of them and did not feel it necessary to clean up their language to protect innocent young ears.

One day, coming home from work on the bus with Tilly, Annie saw a strange sight. Outside the pub on the corner of Islip Street and Kentish Town Road she saw her father deep in conversation with Connie Smith. The bus had been held up by a lorry backing out into the road from a side street, so Annie could watch the scene from her position on the top of the bus. Her father was frowning and shaking his head, while Connie, who looked serious and concerned, was nodding her head vigorously and making the same gestures over and over again.

Annie watched with them with fascination. She could not think what they were talking about but she had a feeling that it was serious. It was most odd. As far as she was aware, they hardly knew each other.

The bus moved on but even as Annie alighted and set off up Falkland Road with Tilly, the image of those two adults in animated conversation lingered in her mind.

Later at supper that evening, Annie thought her father was acting rather strangely. He was uncharacteristically detached and quiet as Clara and Grace discussed the wedding plans. It was decided that the wedding would be in the autumn.

'If the war's properly over by then, perhaps Jack will be home,' said Grace hopefully.

Annie pushed a forkful of mashed potato into her mouth and said nothing. Thinking of how much her brother disliked Roger, she knew he was not going to be pleased at the news of Clara's marriage. She knew how possessive Jack could be about Clara. She did not know why he was, but she had always been aware of it. And she knew that the idea of having Roger in the family would make Jack angry.

Throughout the discussion, Frank was quiet. He stared down at the table and said little. Even when Bobby tried to tell him his latest joke, Frank was hardly able to raise a smile in response.

Annie was to find out why immediately afterwards.

After the washing-up had been done and the plates dried and returned to their positions on the dresser, Frank picked up his hat and announced that he was going out for a stroll. 'Would you like to come, Annie?' he asked.

Given her father's silent mood, Annie was surprised to be asked. But she always enjoyed going for a walk with her father, which she often did. They would walk and talk and discuss whatever was on their minds.

But this time Frank continued to be rather quiet. He rolled a Woodbine cigarette between his fingers and then lit it. 'Have you heard from Tommy lately?' he asked casually.

Annie smiled but shook her head. 'Not since after D-Day,' she said. 'I got that postcard saying he was well – just like the one we got from Jack. I'm sure he's well. Deep down, I know he's safe.' At the thought of Tommy, a warm feeling crept through her.

Frank was quiet again. The he took a deep breath. 'I have to talk to you about Tommy,' he said.

Annie looked quizzically at her father. 'What do you mean?'

'I want to talk to you about Tommy and your friendship with him.' Frank looked ill at ease and uncomfortable.

'We haven't done anything, if that's what you mean.' Annie blurted out the words defensively.

Frank shook his head. 'No, that's not what I mean, not really. Though, of course, I'm glad to hear you say that, too. No, it's more than that . . .'

'What do you mean, it's more?'

Frank turned and faced his daughter, looking her directly in the eyes. 'Annie, Tommy's a nice boy, you know we all like him. You know that. But I don't want your friendship with him to go any further.'

Annie stared at her father, unable to respond.

'You have to go to art school and do great things with your life . . .'

Annie narrowed her eyes suspiciously. 'So . . ?'

'Well, I want to see you do all those things. I don't want you to give up your ambitions for the sake of a boy. I'm sad that Clara has done that herself.'

He paused and shuffled from one foot to another. Then he came out with it. 'I don't think Tommy is good enough for you. That Smith family is trouble and I would hate to see you a part of it.'

Annie stepped backwards, letting out a light gasp. Her face quickly flushed red with indignant rage. 'How dare you suggest that Tommy is trouble! How dare you suggest that he's not good enough for me. I've heard that said before, and it's not fair. Tommy's the best person in the world. He's worked hard and done well in spite of his family. He plans to go on studying when the war's over and he'll get a good job and earn good money. And I still plan to go to art school. You know that. I've never said I wouldn't. I don't understand why you don't like Tommy. It's so unfair when you don't seem to worry about Clara marrying Roger. And you can hardly say that Roger is the most reliable person in the world. He certainly hasn't got a spotless reputation.'

Frank winced. Taking off his hat, he ran a hand over his forehead and rubbed his eyes. He looked tired and drawn. 'You're right, Annie. You're too clever to be fooled.'

As he started to talk, Annie knew that something extraordinary was about to be said to her and she knew that it had something to do with the scene in Kentish Town Road that she had witnessed that evening.

'I have to tell you the truth. I can't order you to keep it a secret or to keep it from your mother but I can hope that you will. I personally think that it would kill her to hear what I am about to tell you.'

'What, Daddy?' Annie gripped Frank's arm in panic. 'What are you talking about?'

'What I'm talking about is Tommy,' said Frank, 'Tommy and you. You cannot have a friendship. You must not take it any further.' The next words felt like a physical blow. 'The fact is, Annie . . .' Frank was sweating. His hand had dropped to one side and the expression on his face was one of extreme anguish. 'The fact is that Tommy is your half-brother.'

Seeing the incomprehension on Annie's face, Frank grabbed her by the shoulders and pulled her round to face him. 'You see, Tommy is my son.' His voice cracked as he pulled her against his chest. Burying his head on her shoulders, he let out a series of loud, choking sobs.

❧

CHAPTER 15

Frank's Secret

ANNIE AND FRANK SAT on the wooden bench in the churchyard. It was a summer evening and the air was still. Two sparrows squabbled over a crust of bread someone had thrown over the brick wall. The sun was disappearing rapidly over Parliament Hill, the sky was streaked with crimson and grey. The light was rapidly fading as Frank Turner began to tell his story.

'I never thought I'd have to tell anyone about this,' he said. 'I thought of it as a mistake twenty years ago and I still do. It never occurred to me that there would be any consequences. You just don't when you're young. I can still hardly believe it myself, though deep down I know that it's true, that Tommy Smith is Connie Smith's son. He is also my son.'

Annie looked vexed, a small frown between her eyes. 'I don't understand,' she said. 'What do you mean he's Connie Smith's son? He told me that he was Connie's cousin. He was just brought up by his Aunt Jan as her son.'

'That's what Tommy believes because that's what he's

always been told. Tommy doesn't know, Annie. It's what everyone's always been told. And it does add up, doesn't it?' replied Frank. 'It all adds up.

'Soon after your mother had Clara, it happened. It just happened once. I can't explain exactly why, Annie, but you must know that what goes on between a man and his wife is an important part of a marriage.' He looked away but Annie could see his face in the descending darkness.

'Once your mother started having children, she became less interested in – how can I say this? – the physical side of marriage. Once we started having a family, she lost interest, except when she wanted another baby. It was hard for me, you understand.'

Frank was looking uncomfortable. His handsome face was contorted into an ugly grimace of pain as he confronted his past sins.

'It's not right for a father to talk to his own daughter about these things but the circumstances mean that I have to.' He paused and cleared his throat with a dry, cautious cough.

'I don't drink much nowadays and I have never been much of a drinking man. But there was a time, before you were born, when I would go for the occasional pint at the Pineapple. I used to meet up with friends or just go in for a gossip and catch up on the news.'

Grace placed the sleeping infant in the cot and stood over her for a few seconds. Frank watched her standing there, her clean profile outlined against the wall in the dim light. As his wife slipped silently into bed and dropped the covers over her body, Frank reached over and placed his hand on her hip. He felt the soft flesh stiffen.

'*Not now Frank, please,*' *said Grace.* '*I must sleep while I can.*'

The baby let out a small cry but then settled back to sleep. Frank pulled his hand back and rolled over on his side, his back to his wife. How much longer was she going to be like this? She had never taken much pleasure in sexual union but she had not objected to his needs. Why, in the early years of their marriage, he had sought comfort in her warm flesh every night. What joy that had been! Every evening as he bicycled home after work, he would look forward to sinking into her arms and abandoning himself to that exquisite pleasure. It had not lasted, of course. His needs were the same but Grace began to resist them more frequently. If he had been a violent man he might have insisted on his rights with a firmness which showed he meant business. He often imagined taking Grace by force but such actions remained in his thoughts only. Frank was essentially a gentle man.

'I'm sure your mother has talked to you about what goes on between a man and a woman.' Frank scratched his ear.

Annie was silent. She could feel a blush creeping up her neck.

'I'm not excusing myself,' he continued. 'What I did was wrong. But sometimes the need is so great . . .'

The pub was quiet that evening. Frank sat and talked to old Jim Horder for a while and shared a joke or two with Mr Garcia. After they had drunk a couple of pints, Mr Garcia fell silent and Jim Horder became maudlin about the tragedy of his idiot son Danny. Frank knew it was time to go. He downed the rest of his pint and pulled on his coat. He felt quite light-headed. He rarely drank so the two pints of bitter had set his body tingling. '*Night all,*' *he muttered as he left the pub.*

Outside, the night air was cool on his face. He set off down the road with his hands in his pockets. The period after Jack's birth had been difficult. He had felt left out, redundant then. But Grace had still allowed him his pleasure. This time round, long before Clara had even been born, Grace had shut him out. She seemed to be completely wrapped up with the baby and her needs. Clara was a colicky baby who cried a lot and often. Frank often spent evenings with hardly any communication between him and Grace that did not concern young Jack or Clara. Frank had not even been able to play the piano as Grace was afraid it would set Clara off again.

Deep down, Frank was sure it would be all right in the end. It was just a period they had to go through. In the meantime, it was tough.

On the corner of the street, he saw young Connie Smith. Connie was a buxom girl of about seventeen. She had a deep husky voice and thick brown hair coiled around her head, and the most compact, neat body he had ever seen. Her tight clothes accentuated her figure. She was always laughing and joking. She was the one member of the Smith family whom Frank liked. He had been to school with her brothers. All three had been ne'er-do-wells then – not incapable of picking the pockets of their teachers – brash and cocky. He had never trusted them, either.

But Connie was different. She had a warm heart. Perhaps being the only girl and the baby of the family had made her different. Everyone knew how helpful she was to her mum and she was frequently helping out the neighbours – always willing to baby-sit or run an errand.

'Hello, Frank,' she called.

Frank nodded and smiled. He pulled out his packet of cigarettes.

'*Have you got one for me?*' Connie asked, sidling up to him coyly.

'*Here.*' Frank held out the packet for her. She reached out to take a cigarette with the tips of her fingers. He could smell her freshly washed hair and the cheap perfume she had dabbed onto her wrists and neck.

She pressed her hand gently on his forearm. '*Got a light then?*' she asked. She stood closer to him, holding the cigarette in her pouting lips.

Frank's heart was beating fast. All he had to do was touch her, and he knew it. His willpower had disappeared. The descending darkness made him feel safe from prying eyes.

'I was wrong,' he said to Annie. 'But I couldn't help myself. I took advantage of her for my own purposes.'

Down a back alley off Falkland Road, Frank pushed Connie against the wall. Hanging on with her arms around his neck she had wrapped her legs around his waist, and was kissing him hard. Her enthusiasm excited him as he had never been excited before.

Frank could not tell his daughter how much he had enjoyed those moments with Connie. Once, fast, against the wall like that, and then again, ten minutes later on the grass. The second time, it had been more gentle and loving, closer to what he longed for from his own wife. Connie had run her fingers through his hair and called him 'love'. And she had groaned in quiet ecstasy when she climaxed. Frank had never known that women could climax like a man, and it thrilled him. But he could never tell anyone how wonderful those moments had been. Many times since then he had gone over the occasion in his head as he lay frustrated beside Grace's sleeping form.

'The moment it was over, I regretted it,' he told Annie. 'I

resolved never to have contact with Connie again. I was disgusted with myself. For the sake of a moment of pleasure, I had failed Grace and the children, my children. After that night, I stayed away from Connie's house and crossed the road whenever I saw her. And I almost stopped drinking altogether as a direct result. I've never gone to the Pineapple on my own since that day.

'Then I heard that Connie had suddenly left the neighbourhood, but she came back again after a few months. A little while later we learned that her mother, Mrs Smith, had adopted her baby nephew. Although Tommy was a cousin, he was brought up as another brother in the family. Some time later, we all heard rumours about Connie carrying on with Maudie Sprackling's husband, and that turned into a scandal when they ran away together.

'Anyway, Annie, Connie has just told me that Tommy is not her aunt's child at all. He is not her cousin. Tommy is her own child, born nine months after that evening with me. She says Tommy is my child. And I believe her.

'When she discovered that Connie was having a baby, Mrs Smith sent her away. No one – not even Connie's mother – knew who the father was. Her mother was disapproving but did not want the baby to be adopted by anyone so she agreed to take him in and pretend that he had been born to another relative. Connie has never breathed a word about Tommy's father to a single soul. She never intended to tell anyone. There was never any reason to. But when she saw that you and Tommy were getting so close, she became concerned. She has told me because she wants me to put a stop to it. She has never told Tommy the truth about his father. And she doesn't plan to, either.'

Annie turned to stare at him.

'How can you be sure that you really are the father? Connie Smith ran away with Maudie Sprackling's husband. How can you trust a woman who is capable of stealing another woman's man?'

Frank shrugged.

'I can't be sure,' he said. 'And you're right to question it. But I do think she's telling the truth. I don't see why she should lie. She's not trying to get anything out of me. She just wants the best for everyone.' He paused for a moment, then said: 'And I do believe that Connie has a good heart.'

Annie sniffed. 'Tell that to Maudie.'

'Oh Annie! That was a long time ago. And Maudie seems set on a happy path now.'

Annie fell silent. Staring at the tombstones in the dark, she felt cut off from everything around her. It was true. All that had been said was true. Tommy was Frank's son, she knew it. She had always known it, in a way. She recalled Connie's words in the butcher's shop about how it's not always the woman who's infertile. Connie had said that because she knew she wasn't infertile. And she knew that because she had given birth to Tommy. But most of all, Annie knew it was true because one of the things she liked most about Tommy was that he reminded her so much of her own father.

A strange noise erupted from her belly and rose to her throat. With a great howl, Annie flung herself against her father's shoulder. Father and daughter clung together in the dark.

After a while, Annie finally spoke. 'Mother mustn't be told,' she said quietly. 'It'd break her heart if she knew.'

Frank nodded. 'Yes. Connie's not prepared to tell Tommy,

either. She doesn't want to upset the apple cart. If Tommy knows the truth, it would cause a lot of trouble in both families . . .' He squeezed her arm.

'I'm sorry, Annie . . .'

Annie stared at the church steeple silhouetted against the night sky. It was up to her. No one wanted to tell Tommy the truth, and she could barely take in the truth herself. They were related. They were half-brother and sister. They could not get engaged and be married. Those would be sins against nature. They could not make love and have children and do all the things they had been planning and hoping to do.

It was Annie who would have to act. She had to break off with Tommy. It had been left for her to deal with, yet she wouldn't be able to tell him why.

Annie bit her lip and fought back the tears. She felt trapped, wanting to escape in every direction, to run away from it all. There was too much to take in – her mother's unhappiness, her father's betrayal, Tommy's ignorance of the truth. There was not room in her head even to think about any one of them. What could she do?

In a way she had no choice about what to do. Too many people stood to lose, to be hurt if the truth came out. But it was the two innocent ones she cared about most – Tommy and her mother. Her responsibility towards both of them made it clear what course of action she had to take.

With her head bowed, she rose to her feet and set off down the road towards home, leaving her father sitting alone on the bench in the dark church graveyard.

CHAPTER 16

Bobby

FOR AS LONG AS he could remember, Bobby Turner had wished that his mother went out to work so that he could have a bit of freedom in the hours after school, like so many of his friends. But she did not, so his mother was always there, every minute of his time at home. And it drove him mad.

Grace Turner fussed over her younger son as if he were still a baby, and every day Bobby hated it more and more. His only consolation in this humiliating situation was that at least he wasn't the only one to think that his mother fussed too much. Recently his dad had been telling his mum to stop pampering him, too.

'Ease up on the boy,' Frank had said only the night before. 'He's got to learn a bit of independence, Grace. There's no danger outside now. The war's practically over, there's no chance of bombs. Bobby's got to learn to look after himself. You're turning him into a sissy.'

Grace frowned slightly, as though put out by the remarks, but she had taken in her husband's words. The Germans had been all but defeated. What with Hitler's suicide in April, she knew it was only a matter of time before Germany surrendered. She had to agree that she no longer had the excuse she had been using for so long. 'Perhaps you're right,' she said, after some thought. She was, in fact, well aware of how much she worried about Bobby. Only she knew the reason why. 'Perhaps I do mollycoddle him too much,' she admitted.

Frank was pleased that his words had had such an immediate effect. 'Let the boy have a friend round and let them go out together after tea. That Davey seems a sensible boy. He'll keep Bobby out of trouble.'

Davey was Bobby's best friend from school. He lived with his mother in Ascham Street, just a few blocks away. His father was away fighting and his mother had a job in a shell factory in Acton from which she did not arrive home until late in the evening. Davey was therefore free to do whatever he wanted after school every day. And Frank was right about him; he was a bright boy who did not look for trouble more than the average eight-year-old boy.

For several weeks now Davey had been telling Bobby about the bomb-sites he had been exploring, and badgering him to come too. Now at last Bobby had been given permission to go out with him. It was great!

Bobby was overjoyed by this sudden chance to be independent. He could hardly believe that it was true. For the whole of that day at school, he and Davey plotted what they were going to do once they were free of adult control. They came home from school together, having agreed to keep their plans top secret.

They ate their Marmite sandwiches and slabs of chocolate, whispering together excitedly. Grace served their food and poured their milk, trying to fight off the tension in her chest. Bobby was so excited that he nearly choked as he bolted down his food.

'Now make sure you're back home by six,' said Grace. 'I don't want you going to bed late, what with school tomorrow.'

'Promise, Mum,' called Bobby, running down the street after Davey. 'Bye!'

The boys ambled along side by side. Bobby shoved his hands into his shorts pockets and kicked stones across the road, scuffing the toes of his leather boots. Davey looked well built and stocky beside Bobby's slight frame. With his skinny limbs and pale skin, Bobby looked like a small plant that lacked enough sun to make it thrive.

Weedy or not, Bobby felt on top of the world. He was feeling exhilarated, but he did not dare tell Davey quite how exciting it all was because he did not want Davey to know that this was his first time out on his own without his mother trailing along a short distance behind him.

'Let's go over to Hilldrop Crescent,' called Davey. 'There's a smashing bomb-site over there, where Crippen's house was – you know, the man what murdered his wife. We might find all sorts of things there.'

'Yeah!' Bobby ran after Davey as fast as he could.

The bomb-site was vast, with huge piles of rubble, bricks, wood and glass in high mounds. Several house walls were still standing but some looked dangerous, leaning outwards, close to collapse. Awaiting proper demolition, they were roped off, with large signs which read: DANGER, KEEP OFF.

The boys ignored the warnings and scrambled up over the bricks and rubble, lifting planks and stones as they went. And they found all sorts of things – a pipe, a leather shoe, a drawer full of knives and forks and serving spoons. Bobby even found a rusty penknife which he stuffed into his pocket. He'd have to remember to take it out and hide it before he got home, or his mother would question him about it if she found it.

Bobby approached one of the standing walls. The stairs ran all the way up one of them, and he started to climb.

'Hey! Look at me!' he called cockily to his friend, stamping his feet hard as he ran up the echoing wooden stairs.

Suddenly a few bricks fell down from above his head, dropping heavily to the ground below.

'Watch out!' Davey called.

Bobby stood still, flattened against the wall. He stayed that way for a few minutes then, feeling quite safe, he started to climb again. He had never felt so free. Next he chased up onto the ledge of a shattered window which he could just reach, pulling himself up with a quick, agile movement.

'Look at me!' he called again, standing up so that he filled the window frame.

Davey was laughing. 'That's great, Bobby!' he called. 'I bet you can't climb along to that window over there . . .' He pointed to the next window. 'I bet you can't . . .'

Bobby looked over to where Davey was pointing. He looked down at the fifteen-foot drop below him.

'Yes I can,' he called to his friend. 'Watch this.'

Bobby edged along the brickwork, scraping his knees as he went. His heart pounded with fear and excitement.

Just as he reached up an arm to grab the side of the other window, a great shout went up. 'Hey! You! Get down from there, you stupid kid!'

Startled, Bobby turned his head to see Dolly Pritchett waving a fat arm at him. She startled him. He looked desperately at Davey and then at Dolly. At that same moment, he lost his footing. In a few split seconds, he scrabbled to get his hold again but the skin and flesh on his fingers were scraped to the bone as he dropped straight down to the ground below.

He never had a chance. His head smashed against a large block of concrete. Bobby Turner died almost instantly.

When news was first brought to the Turners' house of the terrible accident that had taken place on the bomb-site, Grace screamed and ran out into the road. She was hysterical with grief. 'It's all of you!' Her screams carried a long way down the street so that even Mrs Garcia a block away could hear her. She had been tying up herbs for drying, but she put them carefully on the floor in order to go out and see what the fuss was about. 'You've killed my baby!' screamed Grace. 'You've all killed my baby!'

It was Frank who grabbed her and dragged her indoors to make her lie down on the sofa. 'It's your fault,' she started to scream. 'You made me let Bobby go. I knew he shouldn't go, and you made me.'

Frank frowned. Hardly able to take in the news of his child's death, he was shocked to be attacked now. He remained silent. It was not the time to argue.

As her hysteria subsided, Grace sank into a quivering, sobbing heap. She knew that her outburst at her husband and Kentish Town was unjust. She knew only too well that her anger was not at anyone other than herself. It was her weakness and foolishness that had destroyed every bit of happiness she might have had. She had been born with the chance of a good life and it was she, only she, long ago, who had thrown away that chance when she was already grasping it by the hand. It was she who was at fault. And there were no chances left. What she had done had affected many people. She threw herself on her bed and wept. She wept aloud for all her babies, wherever they were. But most of all she wept for her second daughter, the one she had treated worst of all.

After Grace's dramatic display of emotion, she gave up on life altogether. For a few days just before Bobby's funeral she seemed surprisingly strong, though not engaged with the world around her. On the day itself, dressed dramatically in long black clothes and veil, she stood and stared at the small wooden coffin being carried off in the hearse. No emotion showed on her face.

Annie watched it all, unaware that her mother's anguish was for more than the loss of a child. Most of the neighbours were at the funeral but the atmosphere was strange and strained. Annie herself had been shocked by the size of Bobby's coffin. She knew that Bobby had been just a little fellow, but the many funeral cortèges she had seen – during which the strong black horses pulled the heavy black hearse up Lady Margaret Road to the church – had been for old people, adults who had reached the end of their natural lives. She realized that she thought all coffins were the same size. The sight of Bobby's little box, almost completely lost among the flowers and wreaths, caused the salty tears to flood more heavily to her eyes than they had done already.

Afterwards, Clara and Annie sat in their room unable to speak. Annie felt as though she were in a fog, disconnected

from the world around her. She would never see Bobby
again. It was impossible to imagine that he would never
again pester her with his silly jokes, or to play snap or racing demon together. He would never again tease the cat
and then complain that she had scratched him. Never
again would she see his cheeky gap-toothed grin, so like
Tommy's at that age, she could now see. And no one to
talk to about it, either. Everyone was alone in their shock
and bereavement. She dreamed about Bobby every night
and woke up with her cheeks wet with tears.

In the face of such tragedy, how could she even begin to
think about her own problem? It seemed so minor compared with her little brother's death.

Grace's accusation at the neighbourhood did not go
down well with the local people. Although Frank was well
liked, his wife had always been regarded as an outsider
who had been determined not to fit in. Years of resentment
at Grace's aloofness rose to the surface. The less generous
of her neighbours accused her of putting on airs and
graces, but others tried to be kinder.

In the Pineapple pub and the Falkland Arms, people
talked about the situation over their pints of beer.

'Well, we paid our respects for Frank's sake but she's got
a cheek saying it was anything to do with us.'

'Bloody nerve, if you ask me,' said Mrs Rose. 'How dare
she say it was little Davey's fault.'

'I'd say she's more to blame herself, for mollycoddling
that child. She always did, right from the start.'

Dolly Pritchett placed a bowl of pork scratchings on
the table. 'I don't think it's right to go that far,' she said,
settling her bottom onto the wooden bench. 'No one's to
blame for that child's death. It was a tragic accident. We

can't blame Mrs Turner any more than she can blame us folks in Kentish Town. The poor woman's in distress, you have to make allowances.'

The others muttered into their drinks and shrugged.

The day after the funeral, Grace Turner took to her bed. The atmosphere in the house in Falkland Road became heavy and claustrophobic. No one played the piano. No one laughed. Everyone lived their own lives in their own way.

Annie cooked the supper, which they ate in silence with their father. Grace's food was taken up to her on a tray and brought back down half and hour later, barely touched.

Grace started to write in a notebook incessantly, writing with a slow, painful hand, her lips moving as she did so.

Sometimes Annie sat in her mother's room trying to keep her company. Sitting in the chair in the corner she would sometimes suddenly see her mother as others now must see her – as a grey-haired woman with a hunched body and a face pinched with pain.

Grace was cut off from her. She would answer questions if asked but otherwise just stared out of the window, her beautiful grey eyes dull and blank with grief.

Grace's condition threw gloom over the good news from the outside world, too. But even though Grace stayed at home, the other Turners could not fail to join the rest of the country and the whole population of Europe in celebrating the end of the war.

That Tuesday night, thousands of north Londoners made their way to the hills of Hampstead Heath, Parliament Hill and Alexandra Palace. Although it was dark, there seemed to be a special aura around the outlines of the night.

Enormous bonfires had been lit. Fireworks exploded in the sky, competing with the thousands of flickering silvery beams from the searchlights down below. All around, public buildings, flooded with light, loomed eerily.

Gaily coloured bunting and flags hung everywhere – the Union Jack and flags from the Allied nations flew from the flagpoles on Hampstead Town Hall. No building anywhere was without some form of decoration and the British flag hung proudly across every shopping parade in the land.

Women and girls twisted coloured ribbons in their hair. Men and boys stuck red roses in their buttonholes. And while the beer lasted, public houses did a roaring trade.

Frank and his children had joined the gathering crowd on Parliament Hill. What had been a small bonfire had grown into a raging inferno as more wood was added over and over again. The moment was right. As the fire began to burn fiercely and leaped up towards the stars, a lumpy stuffed effigy of Hitler was thrown on top. In the red glow of the flames, crowds set off more fire crackers, waved sparklers in the air and sang and danced to all their favourite tunes. The night throbbed with the sound of 'When the Lights Go On Again All Over the World' and 'When They Sound the All-Clear'.

Down in the streets of Kentish Town fires burned, as they did in almost every street in Britain. Gramophones and pianos had been brought out into the streets, and all around them danced jubilant citizens, free at last from the dreariness of war. In the windows of their houses coloured lights flicked on and off. And while thousands were rejoicing with noisy abandon, many others were quietly praying to God in the churches.

Lying in bed at home, Grace barely noticed it. It all

made so little difference to her now. She did not notice the streets being filled with young men again after so long. She not notice the happy, relaxed faces, the look of hope on people's faces as they looked forward to the new world that the politicians spoke of and newspapers wrote about with such enthusiasm.

Grace had so lost interest in life that she even missed Clara's wedding. Instead of being the festive occasion that had been planned, the ceremony ended up being a quiet affair in the registry office in St Pancras town hall with Frank and Annie as witnesses. No one from Roger's family came. His father had died of cirrhosis of the liver a couple of years before, and his brothers were still away in the forces. Annie felt rather sorry for Roger. It was sad not to have any family at all at your wedding, she thought. But Roger did not seem to care. Or if he did, he did not show it. He looked happy to have acquired a father as well as a wife.

Annie guessed from the slight swelling of Clara's belly under her smart blue suit that their first baby was already on the way. Afterwards, Frank took them out for a meal in an Italian restaurant in Charlotte Street where they celebrated over plates of spaghetti bolognese and a bottle of Chianti in a wicker basket.

Watching her big sister so happy with her new husband, leaning up against him and touching him at every opportunity, made Annie happy for her but very sad for herself. Every tender gesture between the newly-weds reminded her of the task that still lay ahead for her. Tommy had not come home but he had sent a letter telling her to expect him any day now.

The happiness of the young married couple did not last for long. Clara and Roger had set up house together in two rooms in Camden. Roger had regular work as a labourer, for there was much work to be done rebuilding London. For a while Clara seemed happy and settled in her new role as homemaker and wife. She would proudly show Annie some new curtains she had made on the old Singer which her mother had given her, or press on her a slice of cherry cake she had just baked that morning. But every now and then Annie would sense that under the show of domestic bliss there lurked something not so good. Sometimes she sensed that Clara was holding back some information about her new life as an adult, as if there was something too painful to talk about. Sometimes when Annie saw Clara and Roger together, she felt something unspoken and fierce hovering between them. At other times Annie simply did not like the sharpness with which Roger spoke to his new wife.

Back home, every evening, with Grace upstairs in bed, Annie and Frank ate their suppers in near-silence. There was nothing to be said.

Marion Banham was proving to be a good friend to Grace. She came almost every day to sit with her and talk to her. At first it was a monologue, but over the weeks there were sounds of a conversation taking place between the two women. It soon became clear that Marion was the only person Grace really talked to, but what the two women talked about, nobody knew. What did it matter? Annie agreed with her father that it was simply a good thing that Grace was talking to anyone.

With the war over at last, the men were returning home – the local boys Annie had been at school with were now coming back as men, hardened and brutalized by the grimness of warfare. Not a game, not fun, but a place where people died or were hurt and maimed. Brother Jack came home, too, a decorated hero. Apparently he had shown particular bravery and saved the lives of several of his fellow soldiers.

Jack had grown a lot since they had last seen him, now broad and strong, with lines on his face and a hard expression which Annie had never seen before, and it frightened her.

For his part, Jack was shocked to find his mother in such a state. He had been informed by letter of Bobby's death but having lost so many friends in the fighting, he had not really absorbed the tragedy of the news at the time. He was upset about his mother's condition but was equally upset to learn of Clara's marriage to Roger. 'She might have waited until I was home,' he grumbled. And when Annie suggested that there had been a certain urgency at the time (Clara was indeed to have a baby soon), Jack's gaunt face twitched. He said nothing.

The day after Jack's return, Clara came round to the house. Now heavily pregnant, she looked tired and drawn. She kissed her brother warmly on the mouth.

'Congratulations, Clara.' Jack was stiff but not cold with her.

Clara laughed, her lovely, deep, throaty laugh. 'Well, you know I only married Roger to annoy you,' she teased. And Jack had to smile. Then he hugged her tight.

'You'll come to like him, Jack,' said Clara. 'He's a lovely man, you'll see. He's got a lot of troubles, that's all, and it's not surprising after the way he was brought up in that family.' Then she smiled sweetly at her brother. Rather too sweetly, and for a second too long, thought Annie, as though Clara was having trouble convincing herself that her husband was a lovely man.

With the family gathered round Grace's bed, Jack unpacked his heavy backpack, pulling out all sorts of gifts from all over the world. He had beautiful silk jackets from Singapore which he had swapped with a mate in the navy for a German pistol he had captured. He held out a brilliant turquoise jacket for Clara. 'This was made for you,' he said.

Clara laughed and snatched the jacket from her brother's hands. 'It's hardly going to fit me while I'm in this condition but I'll try it on to see if the back fits!'

She pulled off her woolly cardigan and tried on the jacket. As Clara pulled on the silk sleeves, Annie noticed black and brown bruises all along Clara's upper arm. She was tempted to say something immediately but she did not. If anyone else noticed, they chose not to comment either.

Later that evening Annie sat on a stool in the sitting room, balancing a sketchbook on her knee as she did quick portraits of Jack as he sat talking to his father about his life over the past four years. Jack's descriptions of his experiences barely entered her consciousness as Annie sketched and shaded with rapid speed. Her thoughts were not on Jack or the war at all. They were on Clara and those bruises on her arms. It puzzled her that Clara did not comment on them, did not mention them at all. It puzzled her that Clara never complained about Roger hurting her. In fact, she seemed to go out of her way to boast about how kind Roger was to her, bringing her flowers and little presents when he came home from work. Perhaps she was wrong about how those bruises got there. Perhaps Clara had just had an accident, banged herself against the door, for instance. Annie reassured herself that nothing was wrong after all.

While Jack Turner thought about what he was going to do now that he had been demobbed, he hung around at home doing very little. There was plenty of female interest in him. Jack had always been popular with the girls. Even Tilly Banham confided to Annie one day that she found her brother 'irresistible'. 'He's so brave,' she rhapsodized, 'and so attractively aloof!'

Annie rolled her eyes at such comments. She felt uncomfortable about Tilly's interest in her brother. It seemed to change their friendship. Seeing Tilly's look of puzzlement, Annie smiled, but she felt a little sad. Whenever anyone alluded to love in any way, it just reminded her of the terrible task ahead of her when Tommy returned.

It was another six months and spring before Tommy did eventually return. He had been in North Africa and then stayed on in the army to fight in Palestine where his part in capturing some terrorists had won him a medal. All this meant that it would take much longer for him to return home. Tommy had written to say he was definitely on his way. 'I can't wait to look at your sunny face,' he wrote. Annie had felt pained by the innocent excitement in his letter.

Annie was out in the garden pruning the summer clematis which her father had planted for her three years before. It was a healthy, vigorous plant which produced a profusion of pale blue flowers each summer. Each spring, Annie cut back the plant right down to the roots, just as her mother had taught her in the days before Grace had lost

all interest in gardening and given it up, along with
everything else.

Annie was bending down over the flower-bed when she
heard a shout. Turning round, she saw Tommy standing by
the back door. Dressed in his khaki uniform, he had a
broad smile on his tanned face.

'Annie,' he said. 'Here I am. Home at last!'

Annie jumped. She had been expecting and dreading
this moment for so long. She thought she was prepared for
it, having rehearsed it in her head many times over the
past year. She was supposed to stand still and say nothing.
The look in her eyes would be enough to tell Tommy that
it was over between them. He would hesitate and then bow
his head and leave in silence. The scene would be enacted
without a word, like a silent film.

The reality, of course, was different. Tommy bounded
across the garden with his arms stretched out towards her.
'Annie, my darling Annie!'

She could not help herself. Instead of standing firm, she
gave in to her instincts. Letting out a little cry, she ran
towards him and flung her arms around his neck. Their
lips met in a long lingering kiss.

'Annie, Annie,' murmured Tommy. 'I've dreamed of this
moment a thousand times.'

Annie shivered and buried her face in Tommy's chest.
What a fool she was. A reprimanding voice started to
order her around. She had to act now to save them both.
She longed to prolong the kissing and the feel and smell of
Tommy's strong body against her own. How easy it would
be to have it that way, for just one more time. The voice
began to order her to act and act soon. This was not
supposed to have happened. Now she had messed up

everything and made it all more difficult for both of them.

Her body longed to continue to lean against Tommy but her head suddenly cleared. She pushed herself away and smoothed down her hair.

'Oh, Tommy,' she said quickly, 'I do love you, I really do.'

Tommy laughed and tried to grab her wrists again. But Annie twisted her body round, away from his reach.

Now Tommy looked startled by her unexpected movement. Annie took another step back and looked him straight in the eye. The anguish in her face could not be missed.

'I do love you, Tommy,' she repeated, 'and this has nothing to do with you or anything you've done . . .' She twisted her hands together like a worried child. 'But it's finished between us, it has to be over.' Her voice cracked as she spoke these last words.

She stared at Tommy. He had to believe her. He had to know she was being serious.

At first Tommy laughed again, but the smile on his lips faded when she did not smile back. A muscle in his cheek twitched as his quick mind assessed the situation. Then he knew. 'It's over, isn't it.'

Annie dropped her head and nodded shamefully.

'But why? Tell me why.' Tommy suddenly looked angry. He shifted his weight from one foot to the other and placed his hands on his hips. 'Is there someone else?' he demanded. 'You'd better tell me about it now, if there is.'

Annie stared at him, still unable to respond. Now her head was racing with thoughts, with possible lies she could tell him to soften the blow. It would be easier for him if there were another person. She opened her mouth to speak but no words came out. She turned away.

For a few loaded seconds, Tommy stood facing her, his face twisted with confusion and disappointment. Then his expression suddenly changed, and he looked calm.

'Well, I'll go,' he said quietly. 'I'll go. This has happened to plenty of men before me.' He turned on his heels and began to walk back to the house.

As Annie lifted her head to watch him go, tears began to stream down her cheeks. Part of her wanted to shout to him, to tell him to come back and sweep her up into his arms. But that bullying voice in her head prevented her from doing it. She watched Tommy's back as he went, walking out of her life forever.

She picked up the garden fork and smashed it hard into the roots of the clematis, striking it again and again. The green shoots splintered and fell onto the earth.

'Damn you, Father!' she hissed, attacking the earth around the plant's roots and hacking at it relentlessly with the heavy garden fork. 'Damn you, damn you, damn you!'

CHAPTER 17

❧

Jack's Revenge

TO ANNIE'S RELIEF, TOMMY did not make any attempt to get her to change her mind. This did not surprise her for she knew how proud he was. In any case, too many of his army mates had been betrayed by their girls back home and he did not think he was any different. Obligingly, he stayed away from Annie and her family. Annie never even saw him in the street, though she purposefully avoided Leverton Street for several weeks.

Annie settled into a quiet way of life, going out to work and looking after the home for her parents. Grace needed a lot of caring now and was unable to do much in the house. Annie's spare time was taken up with housework and laundry. Occasionally she managed to get out to the cinema with Tilly, if there was a new film on at the local. She rarely had time for her painting now, though the truth was that she had lost much of her enthusiasm for it. That in itself made her feel deadened inside.

At some point Dolly informed Annie that Tommy had gone off to study law at university.

'Always was a clever boy, that Tommy,' Dolly remarked.

She peered at Annie. 'You used to quite fancy him, didn't you? You don't seem to be interested in him any more.'

Annie turned away. 'No, we've gone our separate ways,' she said, swallowing a hard lump in her throat.

Annie tried her best not to think about Tommy at all. She felt she had no right to be concerned about her own sorrow anyway. Clara was giving her far too much cause for worry now. In fact, over the months, Annie had become extremely concerned about Clara.

Clara had given birth to a baby boy earlier in the year. When the little fellow was born, Annie felt strange. Sitting next to her sister's bed in the hospital ward and holding the tiny baby in her arms, she was swept right back to the day of Bobby's birth when she had clutched Rabbit in her arms like this. Poor little Bobby, who had had such a short life.

Within two months Clara had declared that there was another baby on the way. It was difficult nowadays for Annie to get a chance to talk to Clara on her own and it was hard to know what was going on between her sister and Roger. Annie had the distinct feeling that Roger did not want Clara to spend much time with her family. He wanted her all to himself, away from the Turners. He even seemed to have lost his admiration and respect for Frank as a surrogate father. Indeed, Clara and Roger rarely came round to the house at Falkland Road and never invited people back to their flat in Camden, so Annie did not see them often. But when she did, she noticed that Clara frequently had bruises on her arms now, and once she even had one on her cheek.

This time Annie asked about it. 'I fell against the door,' Clara replied hastily.

One day Annie decided spontaneously to drop in on Clara on her way home from work. There she found her sister in a desperate state. It was only a few weeks before the next baby was due and Clara was enormous. Her clothes barely stretched across her huge belly. Ten-month-old Anthony had just gone down for a nap in his cot so the place was quiet.

It was also in a terrible mess. Clothes and toys were strewn all over the floor and dirty plates and dishes were piled up in the deep porcelain sink and on the sideboard. It looked as if Clara had neither the energy nor the inclination to do anything about her squalid surroundings. Annie was shocked.

Clara looked exhausted. Her face was puffy and her features seemed heavy and coarse.

'What's happened?' Annie looked around the room. 'Is everything all right?' she asked warily. Even as she spoke, Clara's face suddenly crumpled.

'Oh, Annie, I'm so unhappy.' Clara slumped into a chair and covered her tearful face with her hands.

Annie moved across the room to her and gently put her arms around Clara's shoulders. 'Why? Tell me, what's the matter?' she asked quietly.

It was several minutes before Clara was able to control her crying enough to speak. 'It's Roger,' she finally said into the palms of her hands. Her words were muffled. 'I just don't think I can take any more . . .'

For the first time, Clara began to talk about Roger. She told Annie that she thought she had made a mistake in marrying him. She revealed that Roger could never control his temper. He hit her whenever he was angry about anything, and humiliated her whenever he chose. He made her do things to him that she hated, and did things to her that made her feel degraded. She feared for the safety of this new baby inside her.

Annie listened in horror and growing rage at her brother-in-law. She did not know for sure what Clara was talking about at times, for she was not explicit, but she knew that they were intimate matters she need not enquire too closely about. It enraged her all the more. How dare Roger treat her sister in this way, and turn her from that brave laughing creature into this frightened person who did not know what to do! Her wonderful big sister, who had once wanted to grow up to be a mermaid. The exuberant Clara, who once pushed drawing pins into the soles of her shoes and tap-danced all the way down Kentish Town Road. All that spirit gone! Clara had always known what to do! What monstrous things had Roger done to her to make her so cowed?

Clara sat with her head in her hands. 'The worst of it, Annie, is that I still love him, even after all this. There is a soft side to him, a soft, almost frightened side to him, which no one knows about. I love him when he's like that, he's almost like a child. But it's been a long time now . . . he hasn't been like that for a long time.' Her voice tailed off. 'It's just as if sometimes something seems to snap inside him . . . It feels disloyal talking about him like this, but I have to tell somebody. And I know I can trust you not to tell anyone else about it.' Clara looked at her with a pleading expression.

Annie waited, dreading some new revelation even more shocking than the last.

Clara continued in a faltering voice. 'There are particular times when he's bad . . .' She coughed. Her words were drying up. Clara took a deep breath and started again. 'There are particular times – just sometimes – when Roger can't do it – you know – in bed.' Clara was blushing more than Annie as she blurted out the words as quickly as she could. She looked down at her knees; her fists were clenched tight. 'He is very demanding about it but he often can't do it. That's when he gets angry, so angry that . . . that's when he hits me . . .' Her voice was suddenly drowned by sobbing as she finally broke down. 'I know it's not really me he's angry at . . .'

Annie hugged Clara tighter as she sobbed into her hands. The two sisters clung to each other in silence for some minutes.

Then Clara began to speak again. 'Do you remember years ago when Mr Garcia's horse was hurt?'

Annie nodded. She remembered the combination of thrill and horror when they heard that someone had cut Juniper's private parts with a knife.

'Roger did that,' Clara said quietly. 'He told me just the other day that he did it.' She started to tremble, her voice breaking again. 'And he said he'd do the same to me too if I wasn't careful.'

Annie left Clara's house feeling shocked and churned up inside. Clara had sworn her to secrecy over what she had just told her. 'You mustn't tell anyone else. You see, I still love him, and I think he loves me too,' she added pathetically.

Clara did understand her husband but she overestimated her ability to help him. She knew that no one had loved him as a child and she had tried to make up for that loss. But Roger was too damaged to be helped. He had never seen how a loved one might be treated. In a home where the only physical contact was a belt around the head, he learned that any frustration was dealt with by violence. It was only when he was in the very best of moods that he could ever meet love with love.

The promise to keep Clara's words a secret left Annie feeling hopeless. She longed to help her sister, to make her life better, but she did not have the faintest idea of where to begin. Everything seemed so grim. Here was her sister so unhappy and trapped in a marriage with a cruel and dangerous husband. Annie's own unhappiness about Tommy seemed minor by comparison. Besides, that was all in the past now. Tommy had long ago gone off to law school, his fees met by the army in payment for his contribution to the war effort. He had climbed onto a train and gone out of her life forever. There was no other young man in Annie's busy life but at night in her dreams she was back in Tommy's arms, loving and kissing, laughing and cuddling. Many mornings she awoke with her cheeks wet with tears at the bitter-sweet memories she had shored up inside her.

Although he was by all accounts a cruel man, Roger did love Clara as much as she believed he did. He loved her as much as she loved him. But sometimes she made him angry, and when she made him angry he could not help hurting her, hurting somebody, or something. He could not stop himself lunging out at her, wanting to strike, to stamp her out, to show her that he was the boss. He did not like to sense that she was defying him, or that she was stronger than he. It was a rage that took him over, causing his jaw to lock and his eyes to become blurred. Ignoring Clara's cries that he would hurt the baby, he would go on, wanting to penetrate and overpower her. But then often, too often, his flesh would fail him. He could sense the sudden softness rising up through his otherwise rigid body. The rage burned even hotter inside him. He had to keep it burning.

When this happened, he pulled Clara roughly by the shoulders and rolled her over onto her belly. Knowing that it was pointless to struggle, Clara let her body go limp as he manoeuvred her into the position he wanted. Her eyes squeezed back tears as she bit into her fist, fighting the urge to scream.

Roger pushed into her. Now she could not stop herself crying out. He was in. There was no softness now; the weakness had vanished. This was the only way, the only way to release the rage that burned in his gut.

Then he was a boy again, lying on his stomach, his head pushed up at an angle against the wall. He was Clara, she was he. It was his whimpering he could hear in his ears as a heavy dark shape pushed into him from behind. Deep inside. He could feel the fumbling hands on his skin and smell the sour odour of beer as it crept around his neck.

His brothers slept in the next room. His father, the brother of the man who took over Roger's body, lay in a drunken stupor on the kitchen floor. His father did not stop what was happening. He could not, he did not. He did not care. And no one heard Roger's stiff cry for his mother – the only person in the world who might have protected him. For she lay buried in the grassy graveyard up the hill.

Roger did not want to hurt Clara and he could not bear to hear her cry. He was always sorry after it was over. But he could not help it. He had been the chosen one, picked out by his uncle as special. He was special. It was his fault. It was Clara's fault.

After her conversation with her big sister, Annie felt very anxious and upset. She felt she ought to be doing something to help Clara, to protect her just as Clara used to protect her when they were little. But what could she do? And since Clara had sworn her to secrecy she could not ask anyone's advice about what to do, either. She felt powerless.

One day she decided to make a batch of mince pies for Christmas. Spending the morning in the kitchen in the comfortable company of Tilly lifted her mood. By midday, they were ready to go out and distribute the pies around the neighbourhood. This was something Grace Turner had done for years until her arthritis and the war had made it too difficult to continue. It had been Annie's idea to start doing it again, and this was the first Christmas they had done it since the war had ended.

The mince pies were still warm as Annie and Tilly gently packed them up, nestled six at a time into brown paper bags. The girls enjoyed making them, measuring out the flour and fat, mixing the greasy crumbs between their fingers and into the bowl, kneading the dough and then cutting out the pastry in small precise circles to fit into the pie dish. They did not talk much as they worked, both preoccupied with their own thoughts. Tilly indulged herself with fantasies about Jack, while Annie worried about her sister.

Wrapped up against the cold, Annie and Tilly set off from home to visit the old people, handing them a branch of holly and a bag full of warm mince pies.

One of the recipients was old Mrs Anderson who lived in Leverton Street opposite the house where Sally Brown had once lived. As they passed Sally's house, Annie had a quick wistful memory of her talks with Sally on the doorstep so many years ago. How simple life had seemed to her then!

Mrs Anderson had been widow for many years. A short barrel of a woman, she was well into her eighties and now toothless and fairly deaf.

'Come on in, my dears,' she said, shuffling ahead of them into her front room. The air was heavy and airless. A musty smell curled around the nostrils. A small coal fire burned in the grate.

'I don't get many visitors nowadays so I hope you'll have a cup of tea and keep an old lady company for a short while.'

The old lady was dressed in a green woollen dress under a floral pinafore. She wore thick brown stockings and slippers which revealed the outline of her misshapen feet. Dark food stains ran down her lumpy front. Long grey hairs grew out of her chin and her fingers were swollen and crooked from arthritis. Annie noticed them straight away. They were worse than her mother's.

Mrs Anderson let herself down in an armchair with a deep sigh. 'Oh, my rheumatism is playing me up right terrible today. Don't get old, darlings, it's no fun.'

Annie and Tilly politely sat on the sofa, sipping tea from greasy cups and nibbling seed cake. Delighted to have willing ears, Mrs Anderson talked to them. In a rasping voice she talked and talked about the old days.

Each time Annie or Tilly said something, she would peer at her through her spectacles. 'Eh, what's that?' She screwed up her wrinkled face and cupped a hand over her ear. 'You'll have to speak up,' she said. 'My hearing's not what it used to be.'

Tilly explained that they had made a batch of mince pies for her, for Christmas. 'We've made them for several people around here,' she added.

They stayed for a while talking to the old lady. Her memory was quite good but occasionally she lapsed into confusion and was not as lucid as she first appeared. At one time she started talking about her friend Amy Horder. 'Had a cup of tea with her the day before she died, I did,' she said. 'Terrible shock, that was.' She leaned forward conspiratorially. 'Her son Danny's not quite right in the head, you know, but you mustn't tell Amy. She won't have any of it. Thinks he's perfect, she does.'

Annie and Tilly exchanged glances.

'What did you say your names were?' Mrs Anderson slurped her tea and nibbled her biscuit, dropping crumbs down her bulky breasts.

'Anne Turner and Matilda Banham,' replied Tilly.

'Turner, eh? Are you related to that Ada Turner what used to live in Falkland Road . . .'

Annie was about to say that Ada Turner was her grandmother when Mrs Anderson interrupted again.

'She really was a one, that Ada,' continued Mrs Anderson, her thoughts drifting. 'She stole my young man from me, she did, and I never forgave her for that . . .'

She was warming to her theme. 'Well, she was a right one, that Ada. No shame, that's what I said at the time and what I say now.'

She sucked her toothless gums. Her watery eyes sparkled with the memory. She looked animated. 'Well, of course, it came back to her. You can't behave like that and get away with it . . . I got my own back, I did.' She chuckled quietly. Then she paused and narrowed her eyes. 'Well, you're too young to remember any of this, you must have been little kids when it happened . . . I've seen a lot in my time, all the comings and goings in this street. I always knew what was going on.' She tapped the side of her head. 'Nothing misses me, I can tell you. Like there was a young woman over there, see.' She indicated a house across the road. 'A low-class sort of girl, if you know what I mean . . .' She leaned forward and whispered, 'A prostitute, she was.' She spat out the words primly.

It slowly dawned on Annie that she was talking about Sally Brown.

'Well, the young lads in the neighbourhood used to visit her, creeping in at all times of the day or night. She used to entertain them all, she did. Disgusting, it was.

'Well, that young woman got her come-uppance, too. Murdered, she was. Strangled one night.'

Annie sat on the edge of her chair waiting for the old lady to say more. Then she prompted her. 'What boys? Do you remember what boys?'

Mrs Anderson was well into her stride. 'Well, I told the police about seeing Ada Turner's grandson there – I can't remember his name. But he used to go in there a lot. He got into big trouble.' She smiled in quiet satisfaction to herself.

'Were there other boys that night, too, then?' Annie was trembling with excitement and afraid that her interest would be obvious.

'Well, yes, come to think of it, there were . . .'

Mrs Anderson hesitated. 'Well, I suppose it can't do any harm now, it was all so long ago. Just water under the bridge now. Yes, me own great-nephew was there that night.' She paused and then added, 'But I didn't tell the police about him. You wouldn't, you see, because blood is thicker than water. Not that he would have done what they said was done to that girl. He was a naughty boy but not bad. No, he was kind, always kind to his old aunt, he was. He used to take me to the street parties what they used to have round here each year.

'Now, I know that you two nice girls wouldn't say anything to cause me any trouble, would you? Not that it matters. I know Roger would never hurt anyone. He used to be a good boy to me, not that I've seen him for a long time, not since before the war started. I heard he was back and got married, but I don't keep in touch with his family, you know – troublesome lot, they are, a bunch of no-goods, they are.'

Finishing their tea, Annie and Tilly escaped into the street. After the hot clingy atmosphere in the old lady's room, the air outside felt deliciously fresh as it hit their faces.

Annie gripped Tilly's arm. 'Did you hear what she said?'

Tilly shook her head. 'It doesn't mean anything,' she said. 'The old lady is so senile, she's probably got her memories all mixed up.'

'No, she definitely said she chose not to tell the police about her great-nephew. She wasn't mistaken.'

Annie felt both excited and frightened. It was terrifying to be plunged back into that nightmarish time just after Sally was murdered when everyone was convinced that Jack had done it.

The girls delivered the last batch of mince pies to Maudie Sprackling.

Maudie opened the door. She looked radiant. Her eyes

sparkled and there was a fresh bloom to her face. Maudie had been married three months now. The married state clearly agreed with her.

She thanked the girls for the pies and hesitated in the doorway. 'I have to tell you something . . .' She glanced left and right. 'I just have to let you know, because you've always been good to me, that Arthur and I, well, we're going to hear the patter of tiny feet . . .' She smiled at them coyly, waiting for a response.

Annie threw her arms around Maudie and hugged her. 'Oh, Maudie, how wonderful!'

Maudie hugged her back. 'I've got more news, too, about Jessie. Jessie's found herself a nice young man and she too is to be married. She's made up with her family, too. Her mum approves of Ken and thinks he'll make a good son-in-law.'

'So Jessie and William will be moving out?'

Maudie nodded. 'Yes, they're going to rent a nice little house in Islington. There'll be plenty of room for William, and any other little ones that happen to come along . . .'

Afterwards, they set off for home. 'I always thought Maudie couldn't have children,' said Tilly.

Annie shook her head. 'That's what everyone used to say. Now it seems that it must have been Mr Sprackling who couldn't have the babies.'

Tilly nodded. 'You know, Connie Smith was always hinting that it could be him who was to blame. I could never work out how she knew that. After all, she didn't have any children with him, either. How would she know it wasn't her?'

Annie was silent. Loyalty to her father prevented her from telling Tilly, her best friend, the truth about Tommy.

She had lied to Tilly about her reasons for breaking off with him. 'I've just gone off him,' she had said; she did not feel it right to reveal the family secrets to anyone.

Her mood fell and she found herself thinking of Jessie and the day she and her father had seen Jessie in town on the arm of a disreputable-looking man. She had guessed for some time that Jessie had been on the game, before she got her job at Daniel's and became more respectable.

But now Jessie was going to get what she wanted – a nice husband to take care of her and William. Annie thought sadly of her conversation with Sally Brown all those years ago. Poor Sally, who longed for a home and a husband and ended up strangled. How different life might have been for her if she had met a nice young man at the right time. Both Maudie and Jessie were getting what they wanted in the end. Yet she, Annie, could never have what she wanted. Connie's conversation with her father had seen to that.

Tilly sensed her friend's gloom. She had no idea that it could be connected to Connie in any way. 'Well, the big question now is are you going to tell Jack what you learned today from Mrs Anderson?'

Annie shrugged, a look of despair on her face. 'Am I going to stir things up? Things that are better left undisturbed? I don't know if my family can take any more.'

'Yes, but just think, if Jack's name can be cleared once and for all – and some people around here still like to believe that he was guilty . . .' Tilly sounded urgent. Her passion for Jack was evident.

'Yes,' said Annie, 'but you have to remember that Roger is part of the family now. He's married to my sister. He's the father of her children. It's not simple at all . . .'

*

Jack was not at all pleased to hear the news.

'I wish you'd never even told me,' he said to Annie. He had been brooding on the information all morning ever since his sister had quietly told him what the old woman had said. They were out in the garden dismantling the Anderson shelter with their father. Frank had gone off to buy a rake for the new lawn he was proposing to sow. As usual, Grace was sitting in a sad state in her bedroom upstairs.

'I've put all that behind me,' said Jack. 'It was a mistake. The police saw that straight away. There was no harm done and I don't want to think about it any more.'

Annie stared fiercely at him. 'How can you say there was no harm done? Sally Brown was murdered. You call that no harm done? She was killed and the person who did it was never caught. Now it looks as if your own sister could be married to the murderer. Don't you care?'

Jack shook his head. 'Of course I care, Annie. But you don't know if what Mrs Anderson said is true. And even if it is true, there's no evidence that Roger killed Sally Brown. Roger could simply have been leaving the house, just as I was.'

'Yes, but the police still ought to know, don't you think?'

Jack shrugged. 'I don't know,' he said wearily. 'I don't know if I want any of that business stirred up again. It was bad enough at the time – there was a lot of bad feeling which still exists, I think. I often think that people think of me as someone who got away with it, from remarks and looks I get sometimes.'

'That's not true!' exclaimed Annie. 'Nobody thinks that. They know you were innocent.'

'Maybe,' said Jack flatly.

'But if Roger is the one who killed Sally Brown, then we should care that he's married to Clara. He might hurt her . . .' She hesitated as she remembered her last conversation with Clara. She was tempted to tell Jack about how badly Roger did in fact hurt their sister. But she had been sworn to secrecy.

'Of course I care about Clara,' Jack said sharply. 'But it's precisely because they're married that I'm reluctant to do anything. Do you want Clara to be a grass widow? Do you want her children to be without a father?'

Annie felt as if all her energy was draining out of her. 'I see,' she said quietly, hanging her head.

Jack could see that he had disappointed Annie. 'I'll sleep on it,' he said. 'Let me have a think about it. It's hard to know what to do, especially since the only thing that's actually happened is that a senile old lady has said something about an event that took place years ago. It's hard to act on hearsay.'

Jack did sleep on the information and he did not do anything. In fact, he did not mention it at all until the day Clara came round to Falkland Road with Anthony, a swollen face and a black eye. In a choking voice, and with tears flooding her blue eyes, she blurted out to both Jack and Frank that she could not take it any more. She was afraid for her and Anthony's safety and had had to run away.

As Annie and Frank comforted Clara and tried to clean up her face, Jack took himself down to Clara's home in Camden. He found Roger asleep on the sofa, in a drunken stupor after a visit to the pub.

Jack lunged at Roger's sleeping body and yanked him to his feet. He pulled his arm round in a half-nelson and charged him towards the wall where he banged his head again and again. 'I'll teach you to hit my sister!'

Momentarily stunned and confused, Roger staggered and stumbled. But then he woke up, suddenly alert as he realized what was happening. All his instincts as a street fighter, sometime leader of the Torriano gang, were unleashed. He let out a great roar and spun round, locking himself into a tight hold around Jack's body.

The men tussled and fought for several minutes, falling about the flat, smashing furniture. Roger was bigger and heavier than Jack and at first seemed to have the advantage. But Jack was nimbler and more agile, and concentrated on trying to get a firm grip to pin Roger down.

As they fought, the people who lived in the other flats in the building slowly emerged from their doors to see what the noise was about. Someone ran for the police. Others gathered in the doorway to watch the spectacle of the two men fighting.

Jack and Roger were unaware of the spectators who were crowding around the door. Over and over they rolled, punching and kicking when they could. Finally Jack got the upper hand. He managed to manoeuvre himself into a position sitting on Roger's back with his arms in a full nelson. Roger's head was wedged against the wall and every now and then Jack pushed him up against it hard, squashing his face with brutal strength.

'Leave my sister alone,' Jack hissed into Roger's ear. 'You touch her again and I'll kill you.'

'That silly bitch deserved what she got.' Roger was defiant.

Jack rammed Roger's face up against the wall. Roger cried out in pain. 'I don't want to hear you say that!'

'She should watch her tongue,' Roger blurted out. 'It was her own fault. She asked for it. She's just like the rest of them, all bitches, all castrating bitches.'

'You mean like Sally Brown?' Jack threw it in.

'Yeah, just like Sally Brown, the stupid bitch. Well, she really got what she deserved. I got her.'

As he spoke, they could hear the sound of heavy boots on the stairs. Two constables appeared, pushing their way through the small group of onlookers at the door.

They pulled the men apart and took them both down to the police station to sort them out. When Jack told the police sergeant that he had new evidence that could solve the Sally Brown case, the sergeant sniffed. But when one of the men who had witnessed the fight from the door confirmed that Roger had indicated that he had hurt someone, or worse, the policeman took more notice. They decided to take up Jack's suggestion to question old Mrs Anderson again after all these years.

CHAPTER 18

❦

Grace

THE AMBITIOUS YOUNG DETECTIVE at Kentish Town Police Station was excited by this unexpected new lead in the Sally Brown murder case. Although it had happened over eight years before, the case had never been closed. And while his more cynical colleagues warned him that it was more than likely to be a groundless accusation motivated by a family feud, as was usually the case in Kentish Town, he felt that Jack's suggestion was worth taking up.

Although old Mrs Anderson did indeed have a failing memory, the detective suspected that she was pretending to be more senile than she was. After some clever friendly questioning, the young man – who had considerable charm when he needed it – got her to admit that she had indeed seen someone else leave Sally Brown's house on the night of her murder, and that that person was in fact her great-nephew Roger.

This information was enough for the detective to arrest Roger and pull him in to the police station again for

questioning. He had grave doubts about whether the case
would hold since he had good reason to believe that the
old lady's memory would conveniently fail once she realized what trouble her great-nephew was in. But he need
not have worried. To his astonishment, after a night in the
cell and half a day of heavy grilling, Roger broke down and
confessed to Sally Brown's murder. He told them that he
had done it because she had laughed at him and humiliated him when he found himself unable to make love to
her. He remained without remorse for what he had done.
No man would put up with a woman laughing at his sexual prowess. 'Would you?' he asked of the young detective,
confident that he would win himself some sympathy. He
was wrong.

Roger continued to confess his guilt. He was a broken
man. He had no fight left in him. Every night while awaiting
trial he cried for his mother.

Six months later he was sent to prison for twenty years
for the murder of Sally Brown. Each night the pubs of
Kentish Town were packed with people discussing the mer-
its of the case and the morality of Jack's actions. A
surprising number thought that he had done wrong.

'He could have let sleeping dogs lie, that's what I say. She
was only a prostitute, after all.'

'Well he's gone and made a grass widow of his own sister and made those kids fatherless. I wonder if he thought
of those consequences beforehand.'

'Yes, it's not really done, not round here, it's not. Roger's
own family is right done in. There weren't no need for it,
really, not after all this time.'

'And it sounds as if the woman did deserve it, if she
really did what he said she did.'

'What I can't believe is that young Jack ratting on his own family.'

'Yeah, you'd think he could have just kept quiet about it.'

'Well, you know that family always have been a bit hoity-toity, always thought they were a cut above the rest of us.'

'Yeah, just because they had a bit more money than most.'

'To be fair, you have to admit that Frank is a good man . . .' Someone felt he had to put in a good word.

'Well, it was that wife of his. She always did think she was better than the rest of us.'

At Falkland Road, the atmosphere in the house was even heavier than usual. Grace had found strength with which to castigate herself.

'It's all my fault that this has happened,' she sighed from her bed. 'Perhaps if we had moved away to a better neighbourhood, our children would never have got themselves mixed up with ne'er-do-wells like this. Bobby wouldn't have died and Clara wouldn't have a husband in jail, our grandchildren wouldn't be fatherless. It's all my fault. I should have insisted that we move away.'

'Don't say that,' said Frank. 'It's too easy to blame Kentish Town. Nobody could have helped any of them. Nobody could have stopped Bobby dying and we certainly couldn't have stopped Clara marrying Roger. You know the girl's got a mind of her own. And you certainly mustn't blame yourself. You have enough of a burden to carry on your shoulders without adding to it. Please don't castigate yourself.' He grasped her by the shoulders. 'I'll tell you what,' he said urgently, 'I'm going to start looking for another house for us to move to, like I said we would. We can get away from Kentish Town, up the hill, to Highgate or Muswell Hill, if you like. What do you think of that? That'll make you happy, won't it, my darling?'

Frank had tears in his eyes as he tried to sound bright and enthusiastic. But he knew his offer was too late.

Grace shut her eyes and sank back with a sigh. 'It doesn't matter any more, Frank. I just don't care any longer.'

In spite of her husband's reassurances, Grace chose to add to her burden of sorrows. The weight quickly proved too much for her. She really did seem to give up on life. She stayed in her bed and for much of the day lay motionless, facing the wall. She would spend perhaps an hour a day writing in her journal, and Marion Banham would come in to visit her in the evenings. Her strength seemed to be seeping from her. She ate little and was listless. She grew thinner and thinner. Everyone understood why: she had nothing left to live for.

Annie was desperately worried about her mother's health and hurt that she could do nothing to cheer her up. Nothing she said or did could bring even a flicker of a smile to her face. It was as if she did not matter to her mother at all. Annie would lie in her bed and cry herself to sleep like a little child. She felt so lonely, meaning nothing to her mother and cut off from Tommy, the one person she loved without reservation.

Jack had had enough. One day he announced that he was heading off for Australia, to make a new life there. His parents were shocked and saddened and Frank pleaded with him to change his mind. 'It'll break your mother's heart,' he said.

But Jack was adamant. 'Mother's heart is broken already,' he replied. He had bought his ticket and was sailing in a fortnight.

The night before he left, Jack knocked on Annie's bedroom door. She was in bed reading.

'I hope you understand why I have to go away,' he said. Even in the soft flattering light cast by the bedside lamp, his face looked tired and drawn.

Annie put down her book and smiled. 'I think I do,' she said. 'Things are difficult here.'

Jack sat down on the bed and took her hand. 'I don't want you to think I'm abandoning you all.'

Annie shrugged. 'But you are . . .' Her voice tailed off. She fiddled with the edge of her eiderdown where some threads had become loose. She could feel tears trying to spill into her eyes but she concentrated hard on the fraying material and pushed the tears back.

Leaning forward, Jack lifted her chin with his forefinger. 'I want you to understand that I have to leave this place. If I'm to make a proper life for myself I have to go some-where completely new, somewhere I'm not known, somewhere I can't be reached.'

'But Australia's so far away.'

Jack nodded. 'Yes, but there are more opportunities out there, as well as lots of space.'

Annie lifted her head and looked straight at him. 'Don't you care about us, Jack? Is that why you're going?'

Her brother looked away. His voice cracked as he spoke. 'Of course I care, Annie. I care about you all very much. I worry about Mother. I feel guilty as hell about Roger, and I can hardly bear to see Clara in the state she's in. I keep thinking it's all my fault. And it is. I just have to get right away for a while. It may only be for a couple of years, it may be more. I feel I have to get away to sort out exactly what I do feel about myself and the family. Once I know, I'll be able to come back and not feel swamped by it all, as I do now.'

Annie could not hold her tears back any longer. 'Just keep in touch, please,' she sniffed.

'I promise,' replied Jack. 'And perhaps you'll come and visit one day.'

When Annie kissed her big brother goodbye the next day, she had a feeling that she would not be seeing him again for a long time, if ever. She did not cry. She was beginning to feel a hard, bitter core inside her that had no room for tears of any sort.

Tilly Banham cried for a whole day for her unrequited love. But then a few weeks later she met an amorous GI who in no time had helped her forget about Jack Turner.

Hank Jackson was a handsome, stocky fellow with a crew-cut and a loud laugh. He met Tilly at a tea dance in Bloomsbury where she and Annie had gone one Saturday afternoon. The dance hall had been packed with GIs returning home from the war and Annie had hated every minute of it. She had not wanted to go anyway and she had a headache brought on by the hot smoky atmosphere. But Tilly was having the time of her life, and was being unusually exuberant. It was almost as if something had been released in her to allow her to be suddenly vivacious and outgoing. Whatever it was, she caught Hank's eye and won his heart. He quickly set out to win hers.

After that tea dance, Annie hardly saw Tilly at all, for they had both stopped working and Tilly now chose to spend her free time with Hank rather than Annie. Annie was happy for Tilly but it seemed that she was losing everyone who had ever been close to her. She began to feel sorry for herself.

Living is always a kind of battle in which there are only so many blows a person can take before they lose the will to fight on. Then the body takes over, dropping all the defences that have protected it until then. Perhaps Jack's leaving was the final blow for Grace Turner. A few months after her eldest child had gone, Grace developed bad pains in her belly. But she ignored them and endured them without a word until they were too excruciating to bear any longer. Frank took her to the doctor who informed him flatly that his wife had an advanced cancer and that there was little that could be done. 'It probably wouldn't have made any difference if you had brought your wife in earlier,' he said. Then he added that Grace probably had a few weeks left. In fact, Grace was dead within the week.

Annie did not cry. It was for the best. Grace had had no life to speak of for years. And now she would be out of her suffering. It could only be a good thing.

Her father was distraught at the loss of his wife. He shut himself up in his study for three days, drinking himself silly with a large supply of whisky.

The funeral was held at St Benet's Church up the road. There was not a huge turnout. The bad feeling that had been created by Roger's arrest and imprisonment was stronger than any goodwill felt towards Frank. Grace had never been one of them, and no one was grieving for her apart from her family and her good friend, Marion

Banham. Jack was not there either. Frank had sent him a telegram at the address he had given in Sydney. But they never heard from him so they did not know if he got the message or not. But most of the closest neighbours did come, even if they did not make a big show of it. Annie saw Mrs Garcia and Mrs Whelan standing at the back of the church. But they did look as if they were there out of obligation more than feeling. There were not many tears.

Afterwards, Clara and Annie had prepared the house for sherry and sandwiches. More people dropped in then, more, it seemed, for Frank's sake than to pay their respects to Grace. No one said anything but Annie could sense the coolness these people felt towards her mother. She felt it in the way they looked around the house, peering in the rooms and scrutinizing the furniture and decorations. Well, Grace had rarely invited people in, so they were in their rights to have a good look now. It was not surprising. Grace had made little effort with them and she had hurt their feelings.

Dolly Pritchett popped in for a brief time. She looked tense and uneasy as she settled her bulky frame on the edge of a chair and knocked back a glass of sherry without pausing. 'You all right, then, Frank?' was all she said.

Mr Spratt came in from next door, too. He looked much the same as he always had, perhaps a little thinner. However, he was almost completely senile now. He wandered around the rooms talking to himself. 'My wife's come home, you know,' he repeated over and over again. 'She's just gone up the road to visit some friends. I can't think why she ever left me.' He shook his head plaintively.

'Don't know why she left. I cooked her some dinner and
she never came home to eat it. My wife's come home, you
know . . .'

Marion Banham was there, warm and smiling as she
helped pass food around. 'You're lucky to have such
lovely daughters, Frank,' she said. Clara was there with
Anthony and Lizzie, now aged two. And Tilly was there,
too, now full of excited talk of Hank Jackson who wanted
her to cross the ocean and marry him in the United States
of America. She did not know what to do, and Annie
certainly couldn't advise her.

It was a heavy, tense day. After the last visitor had
finally gone, and Clara and Annie had cleared up the front
room, Frank began to drink hard. Tumbler after tumbler
he filled with whisky which he then gulped down with
scarcely a moment's hesitation. Then he became maudlin
and talked at length about the old days when he and Grace
had been a courting couple.

The night wore on. Clara's babies had been put to bed
hours before, and now Clara decided to turn in. She had
moved into the house the week before, just after Grace
had died. 'To keep you all company,' she said, but it was
clear that she did not want to go back to her dismal flat in
Camden which still smelled of Roger in every corner. Clara
put her children to bed and retired upstairs herself.

Frank sat slumped in the armchair staring into his lap.
He was motionless.

Clearing up the glasses and plates, Annie glanced at
him. 'Are you all right, Dad?' Her voice was soft. She
walked over to him and knelt down. Then she placed her
arms around his neck just as she used to when she was a
little girl.

Frank burst into tears. He tried to cover his face with his hands as he sobbed uncontrollably.

Annie did not move. She stayed still and quiet, her arms around her father while he wept.

'Annie, my darling, I'm so sorry,' he cried.

'Shh . . .' Annie whispered.

'I'm so sorry for all this mess, and all these terrible things . . .'

'Don't say that, Daddy,' Annie reassured him. 'It's not your fault that anything has happened.'

'Yes, it is, you just don't know . . .' Frank's words were drowned by his crying.

Annie was horrified to see her big, strong father in tears. It frightened her to see him showing such emotion. She had to get him to stop. She ran her fingers over his face and hugged him. 'Please don't,' she whispered, 'I can't bear it . . .'

As she spoke, she began to cry herself. She couldn't help herself. Everything had welled up inside her at once.

Frank was hugging her back. 'Don't you start,' he said, smiling at her through his watery eyes. He kissed her temple and Annie buried her head in his shoulder.

Suddenly she was aware of her father's hands on her arms, then on her chest, running over her breasts. He was holding her firmly.

She pulled away, astonishment on her face. 'Dad!'

As she spoke, Frank pulled her face down towards his and kissed her hard on the mouth. Then he rubbed his rough face against her cheeks.

Annie recoiled. 'Daddy, stop! What are you doing?' She pulled herself away and jumped to her feet. 'What are you doing?'

From her greater height she looked down at the pathetic broken face of her father looking up at her, his tearful blue eyes now full of shame.

'How can you do this to your own daughter?'

Frank could barely speak. He mumbled something and more tears flooded his bleary eyes. 'Oh, I'm sorry, Annie. I'm sorry, so sorry. I didn't mean it. Jesus Christ, you must hate me!' He covered his face in his hands and started to sob again, loud racking sobs which made his whole body shudder.

Annie stared at him. 'What is the matter with you? What are you doing?'

Frank lifted his head once more. He swallowed hard and composed himself as much as the alcohol in his body would allow. 'I'm sorry, I shouldn't have done that in any circumstances.' He said nothing more for a moment or two and then he said it: 'But I have to tell you something more. I have to tell you that you are not my daughter . . .'

Annie frowned at him. 'What are you talking about?'

'I'm not your father,' repeated Frank. 'Your mother left a note for me to open after her death. She says I'm not your father. No more, no less.'

'I don't believe you.' Annie stared at him, waiting for him to tell her it was a joke.

But he did not. 'It's true, Annie. I wouldn't make up such a thing. In other circumstances I might not have said anything about it at all. It wouldn't really have mattered, not at this stage in anyone's life. I've brought you up as my daughter, and you are in my eyes my daughter and always will be. But I have already done you an injustice by destroying your friendship with Tommy.'

Annie turned away. 'Why are you bringing up Tommy?

He's got nothing to do with anything,' she said bitterly.

'Well, he does, Annie.' Frank spoke softly, grabbing her wrist. 'Because if you're not my daughter, then you are free to marry Tommy. If that's what you'd like to do.'

Annie was silent. 'It's all a bit late for that,' she said angrily. 'You destroyed whatever chance I had for that a long time ago.'

Frank winced. 'It's not my fault, Annie,' he said quietly, 'but I am sorry.'

'So who is my father then, if you're not?' Annie glared at him angrily.

Frank shook his head. 'I don't know,' he said. 'Your mother wrote the briefest note just stating that fact. It didn't say anything more.'

Annie thought about her mother sitting in bed or reclining on the sofa writing in a journal. 'Mother's journal!' she exclaimed. 'Where's her journal? She was always writing in it. There must be a clue in there . . .'

'I don't know where she kept it,' replied Frank. I only ever saw it when she was writing in it.'

Annie opened the door. 'I think I know.' She closed the door and quickly ran upstairs.

Moments later she was reaching up into the wardrobe and the top shelf. As she did so, it brought back flashes of the past, of the many times she had snooped in this room over the years. But since her mother had become an invalid and remained in her room, she had not had the opportunity to have a look.

There was nothing there. Annie had been so convinced that the journal would be there next to the other secret thing in her mother's life that she was shocked when it was not. And disappointed.

But it was worse. Not only was there no sign of the journal but the brooch was not there either. Annie tore off the tissue paper wrapped around the christening gown, and rummaged all around the box and the rest of the shelf. But the shelf was empty. Both journal and brooch had vanished.

CHAPTER 19

❦

The Confession

IT WAS MARION BANHAM who produced both the brown diary and the brooch the next day.

She arrived on the doorstep at Falkland Road and handed Annie a bag. 'Your mother gave these to me when she knew she had no time left. She told me to give them to you in person, the day after her burial. She wanted me to make sure you got them.'

Marion's expression was grave and sympathetic. 'Your mother loved you very much, you know. She wanted you to know that.' She reached over and touched Annie's arm with her hand. Giving a quick smile, she turned and left.

Annie was shaking as she carried the bag upstairs to her room. She shut the door and sat on the bed. For a few minutes she did not move. Then she opened up the bag. Inside was a small red box and the large brown notebook.

Annie quickly looked inside the red box. There, settled on the nest of tissue paper, were the familiar diamonds and sapphires of the brooch. She felt a strange rush of old feelings go through her.

With trembling hands, Annie opened the notebook.

It was three quarters used, filled with writing in her mother's hand – thin and delicate but sometimes suddenly uncontrolled in patches when the writing went spindly and untidy. Grace had struggled to write in the diary even on days when her arthritis had been bad and made writing painful.

Annie riffled through the pages, forwards and backwards. Her heart was racing and her mouth was dry. She hesitated. Could she take any more secrets now? Her father's revelation the night before had caused her to have a wakeful night, turning over confused and muddled thoughts in her head at an exhausting speed. Her sensibilities had been knocked so many times recently that she felt almost too numb to care about anything. Nothing could surprise her now. She was powerless to do anything about the truth anyway. What had happened, had happened and nothing she could do would change the facts. What more could she possibly learn that would make any difference?

She swallowed. There was more to learn, of course, and it might make a difference. If Frank's outburst the night before was based on a truth, then perhaps this journal would reveal who her real father was.

Whatever misgivings she had, Annie knew that she had to read the journal. Swallowing back a deep feeling of dread, she curled up on the soft eiderdown, opened the notebook, and began to read:

My darling Annie,
I want you to know from the start, before you begin to read this journal, that I love you very much and always have. What you are about to read will no doubt change

your view of me forever but I hope it won't make you hate me. I hope that by the time you have finished reading, you will understand what happened and why it happened. And I hope that having that understanding will enable you to forgive me.

I know that I am going to die soon. I don't know if I am doing the right thing in telling you the truth but I hope you will be strong enough to allow me to release my conscience before I die.

This is the truth, Annie. I am ashamed to say that I have lied to you in the past – perhaps you guessed that at the time. But whenever you have questioned me about why I am in possession of a valuable brooch that I never wear or use for my own purposes, I have been too stricken with panic to be truthful. I was afraid of saying the wrong thing which would be wrongly interpreted before I could explain. This way, at least, I can get it all down. You can read this account or explanation as many times as you want, and then you can think about it in your own time.

In my worst moments (and I have many of them), I think that you have every reason to hate me and to curse me for the rest of your days. But when I'm feeling strong, I believe that our lives together and my love for you will have made an impression on you enough to withstand the blow I am about to inflict on you. I know you are a sensitive girl with the ability to imagine what I was like twenty-two years ago and not so much older than you are now.

You have always been interested in the diamond and sapphire brooch ever since that day it fell out of the wardrobe when you were reaching for Bobby's christening gown. I still remember that moment with the same horror I felt then! I evaded your questions about it then, and more recently I did worse. In the hope of satisfying your curiosity and stopping your questions, I lied to you about why Camilla Pearson had given me the brooch. I don't know if you believed me then but I know I didn't feel convincing at the time. You haven't mentioned it since or asked me anything else but I don't know what that means.

Now I am going to tell you the truth, dear Annie. I can't face telling you in person. I shall be gone when you read this and I'm sorry if there are any more questions left unanswered. I shall try to cover everything – I owe you that, at least.

As you know, my parents were employed by Camilla's parents, Colonel and Mrs Heathcote. The Heathcotes were kind people who took seriously their responsibilities towards the community they lived in. They paid for new labourers' cottages in the village, for instance, to house young married couples who could not otherwise afford accommodation of their own. They also donated land for a sports field and paid for the building of the pavilion on it. And they were always exceptionally kind to the people they employed.

My parents lived in a tied cottage on the Heathcote estate. My father managed the farm for them while my mother, who was a quite well-educated woman and half-French, taught French to the three Heathcote children when they were small. There were twin boys, Piers and Hugh, and one girl two years younger, Camilla. She was my age.

As small children, we often played together in the

grounds, but when Piers and Hugh were sent off to boarding school at the age of eight, Camilla was particularly glad to have me as a playmate and we spent quite a lot of time together. As I said, I always liked the Heathcote parents. They were unfailingly friendly and generous. But their children were different. They knew they were privileged and they thought they were better people because of it. Now I'm afraid that it was a failing in the parents that must have made their children think this way, though I did not see it at the time. In spite of their superior attitudes, I quite liked Piers and Hugh. There was a good side to them. By contrast, I always found Camilla bossy and sometimes unkind. But since I was an only child, I was also happy to have someone to play with, so I went along with what she wanted. She could be overbearing and mean, even as a little girl. Once she made me eat a worm we had found under a stone. She ordered me to eat it, saying that my parents would be thrown out of the cottage if I did not do everything she said. It was pathetic, but I believed her. I can still taste that worm in my mouth to this day.

As we grew older, we saw less of each other. Camilla soon developed a crowd of riding friends and then she, too, went off to boarding school when she was twelve. After a time, we had nothing in common at all. Tragically, both the boys were killed in the Great War. I remember the terrible heavy air of tragic loss hanging in the house for months on end. Camilla was the only one left.

After going to finishing school, Camilla married a lawyer several years older than herself. She had a huge reception in the grounds of the house with three hundred guests. Soon afterwards, I married your father, whom I had met through a family friend. We had a more modest party. How lucky I felt to be with Frank!

I was very much in love with Frank but I was sad to leave Sussex and move to London. I have never got used to the dirty air in London and it was also so far away from my parents. My father was not at all well with a bad heart, and not so long afterwards he died – just before Jack was born. The Heathcotes were exceptionally kind to my mother. They paid for my father's funeral and assured her that she could stay in the cottage for as long as she wanted. They had sold off the farm soon after the war and the cottage wasn't needed by them or their staff at the time.

After Jack, Clara came along quite quickly. Camilla had not produced any children, which was a worry for her parents, who were elderly by then. My mother often sat and read to Mrs Heathcote in the afternoons, and it was the old lady who said that Camilla's husband, Robert Pearson, was desperate for a son and heir. 'A lot of nonsense,' she had said to my mother. 'He should be ready to be parent to any child, whatever the sex, but at this rate it looks as though he won't have that privilege.'

On the occasions when I visited her, my mother would fill me in on all the latest talk from the big house. I remember her telling me that Camilla had been consulting the Queen's gynaecologist and that there was a great concern that she might not be able to have babies.

Once I met Camilla in the grounds when we were both visiting for the weekend. I was walking with Jack and Clara and introduced them. I never forgot the pained look on her face – it was almost a grimace – as she looked down at the babies I was showing off so proudly. I did feel sad for her then.

A year later, everything changed suddenly. First Colonel Heathcote died and his wife followed soon after. Camilla inherited the house and estate. Soon afterwards, I learned that I was going to have another baby, and my mother informed me that Camilla had recently announced that she was expecting. It has always struck me as sad that her poor dear parents did not live to hear the news or to see the birth of a grand-child. And if they had, how differently things might have turned out!

Sadly, my own dear mother died when I was eight months into my pregnancy. I arranged the funeral in the village church. There was a good turn-out, for my mother had been popular in the village. Even Camilla came, which I appreciated at the time, but I think it was only because she wanted to talk to me afterwards. She was looking blooming as she awaited the birth of her child.

After the funeral, when most of the mourners had left, Camilla asked if I would clear my mother's belong-ings out of the cottage as soon as possible because she had recently appointed a married couple as staff, and she preferred to have them living in the cottage rather than in the big house.

I was rather shocked and distressed by the speed at which she asked me to do this. I had hoped that she would wait until after I had had the baby. But I was in no fit state to protest, and it's not in my nature anyway, so I agreed. I said I would go down and sort it all out the following week.

As it turned out, it was an extremely difficult time for us back home. Your father had just started a new job at the piano factory and he was unable to take time off work. Fortunately Dolly kindly agreed to look after Jack and Clara while I went back down to Sussex to sort out my mother's affairs.

The journey down was exhausting to me in my condition, though I was fortunate to be healthy throughout the time that I was expecting. That helped me get through the ordeal. I was more than a little annoyed to find that by the time I got there, the cottage had already been cleared out and all my mother's belongings had been pushed into the carriage house. I was upset not to be able to pick through the things myself and hurt by Camilla's insensitivity at such a time, but I reminded myself of how kind Camilla's parents had always been to me over the years, and decided that was what counted most. Life had changed. One era had passed and another one had begun.

Camilla was apologetic and charming about what she had done and she invited me to be her guest in the big house. Everything was in turmoil: her husband was away in London and the new housekeeper had suddenly become ill with influenza. It seemed that most of the neighbourhood was down with it and I was worried about catching it myself. Camilla said she had hired a temporary maid from an employment agency to help in the house. She kept complaining about the expense and I remember thinking that her mother would never have complained in such a way.

I sensed that Camilla was glad to have my company, just in the way she had when we were children. I was better than nothing. Her confinement was closer than mine; in fact her baby was due the following week. We were both easily tired, but I have to confess that just a short time away from the demands of my little ones seemed to restore quite a bit of energy in a short time, even after a day of going through my mother's things.

We ate supper together both nights. I remember being struck by the way Camilla talked about her baby, referring to it constantly as 'he'. I thought at the time it was sad that her desire for a son was so blatant. Although her husband had been anxious for her to have the baby in a maternity clinic in London, Camilla had insisted on having it at home in Sussex with the family doctor in attendance. 'Dr Potter's father delivered me and my brothers,' she said, 'and I want Dr Potter to deliver my baby.'

In the middle of the second night, I awoke suddenly knowing that my baby was coming. I managed to ring the bell for the maid, who came and told me that Mrs Pearson had also gone into labour soon after going to bed. The district midwife was on her way. They had telephoned for Dr Potter but learned that he was in bed with influenza and unable to attend.

My labour was extremely short. By the time the midwife had arrived, the baby, a boy, had already been born. Although he was nearly three weeks early, he was well-formed and a good weight. He gave no cause for concern at all. The midwife checked that the baby and I were all right and then got the agency maid to clean us up while she concentrated on assisting Camilla, whose labour was longer and more difficult.

The third time round, it seemed so easy. I felt calm

and relaxed. I settled back in bed with my new baby and drifted in and out of sleep.

When I awoke in the morning, I learned that Camilla had given birth and that all was well. She had had a little girl.

The midwife checked over the babies and mothers for a second time and declared everyone fit and well. She said that she would probably be back the next day to check on us, and to fill in the registration papers. But with any luck, she said, the doctor would be well enough to come himself. I remember that she seemed a bit confused about who was who. She was new to the area and quite a young thing. I think it was her first job, and the idea of two babies being born on the same night in a private house was overwhelming to her.

Later that day I was in my room worrying about how I was going to get in touch with Frank to tell him the surprising news, when Camilla appeared carrying her baby in a shawl. After my initial elation, I had begun to feel a bit fuzzy-headed. The birth of the baby, coming so soon after my mother's death, suddenly took its toll. I certainly could not think straight, and I felt completely helpless and incompetent. I could not imagine how I was ever going to be able to get back to London and my family. I was feeling close to not coping at all.

Holding her baby, Camilla sat down on the end of my bed. She was looking wild-eyed and nervy. Then she burst into tears and started to talk in a choked voice. She told me that she was desperately upset not to have a boy and that she was scared for her marriage. She kept rubbing her brow and frowning, and she kept telling me over and over again how lucky I was to have a boy. I was

lucky to have a boy and a girl already, she told me, so
the sex of this third baby had never mattered at all. 'Can
you imagine what it's like,' she cried, 'to want something
for so many years and then get exactly the opposite?'

I began to feel sorry for her. She was right, I was
lucky to have a boy and a girl and not to care about the
sex of the next. But I don't think I ever cared very much
either way about whether my babies were boys or girls.
All I cared about was that they be healthy. But Camilla's
words began to eat into me until I began to feel guilty
for having what she envied me for. It was a strange feeling which I had never had before. In the past, I was the
one who envied Camilla.

She said that the doctor had telephoned earlier to say
that he would be coming that evening to visit both
mothers and babies. Camilla paused for a few seconds
and then she told me what she wanted to do. The reason
she had come into my room was to ask if I would
consider swapping the babies.

The tears had gone when she spoke, looking me
directly in the eye in the way she always did. 'We could
exchange babies and no one would ever know,' she said.

I was horrified at such a suggestion and I told her so.
It was a barbaric and ridiculous idea. But now Camilla
had started to cry again, as if she could not cope with
my refusal. I had hardly ever seen Camilla cry and I
found it disturbing. Camilla went on and on about her
fears and how miserable she was not to have a baby boy.
She talked about her beloved brothers who had died
and how her husband had wanted a son, how much she
wanted a son. She went on and on until I wanted to
clap my hands over my ears to shut out her voice. Then

she began to remind me of all the kindness her family had shown to my own parents. On and on she talked until I could bear it no longer. I was worn down. She was right, they had always been so kind to my family. I owed it to them to be nice to theirs. I felt sorry for her. And I wanted to help. I was completely overwhelmed. I could not withstand the pressure she was putting on me. I had never been able to stand up to her when I was a girl playing games with her, and I couldn't stand up to her any better then.

To my shame, Annie, I gave in. I finally agreed. I thought I would go mad if she did not leave me alone. She wore me down. She made me feel guilty for having exactly what she wanted and didn't have. Dear Annie, I am crying as I write this because it is the hardest part of the letter. I am reminded of what I did not only to you but also to my baby son. But it was the only way to stop her tormenting me. So I did it. I gave in. I agreed to swap my baby for hers. I handed over my boy and took her baby girl, you.

The moment I agreed, I knew that there was no going back. Camilla looked delighted. The moment she held my baby in her arms she seemed to be revitalized. She assured me that as long as we did not breathe a word to any one about what we had done, no one else would ever know. She had worked it all out. It was just her good fortune that the housekeeper was ill and that the only staff in the house was the temporary maid who was due to go that day, with a replacement arriving later. No one would ever be aware of anything untoward having taken place.

There was no going back once I had agreed and there

was certainly no hope of going back once we had lied to
the doctor about which baby belonged to whom and
signed all the necessary papers. No, there was definitely
no going back. The deed was done. This terrible sin
bound us together forever.

Camilla was happy to send a telegram to Frank in
London to inform him of the birth of his second daughter and that mother and baby were well. I remember
thinking at the time that for someone who had just had
a baby, she had a frightening amount of energy.

When Dr Potter came to the house, he only knew that
two babies had been born in the night. You were duly
registered as my child, and the boy presented as Camilla's
son.

Soon after the doctor had gone, Camilla's husband
arrived from London to take his son and heir into his
arms and celebrate. While a delighted Robert Pearson
held his son and talked about his plans for the future,
Camilla took me aside and kissed me on the cheek.
Then she slipped a diamond and sapphire brooch into
my hand. 'I'll be grateful to you forever,' she whispered
into my ear. 'It's worth a lot, that brooch.'

Camilla was glowing with happiness. Everything had
worked out perfectly for her. Extraordinary chance and
a fair bit of natural guile had enabled her to get exactly
what she wanted.

I returned to London with you in my arms. Frank
borrowed a car and motored down to Sussex to collect
me. By the time he arrived, I had already convinced
myself that I had given birth to a girl, that you were
mine. It was the only way, you see. I knew that if I were
to live with this lie, I had to convince myself from the

start that it was true. It is remarkable what you can make yourself believe if you have to.

And I did, I think. I did fairly well. I always, always thought of you as my child, my daughter. Away from Sussex, it seemed possible, especially now that my mother was dead. I had no reason to go down there.

For the first few years it was easy. I simply forgot about the circumstances of your birth. But then, inexplicably, I lost two babies in succession. Those deaths seemed too terrible not to have some meaning. Slowly the deed began to gnaw at my insides. At first it was just the occasional twinge but gradually over time it grew and grew to monstrous proportions. I fought against the notion that those dead babies were punishments for what I had done, but it was hard. When I started to get the symptoms of my rheumatoid arthritis I began to feel that I had poisoned myself with my deeds.

And, of course, however hard I tried to throw off such thoughts, there was always a reminder, a link with Sussex and my terrible misdeed in the form of the brooch, my payment. I stuffed it into the top of my wardrobe as I could never bring myself to touch it. I could neither wear it nor sell it. It seemed wrong to benefit from it in any way.

Then Bobby was born and everything seemed wonderful again for a while until my health got worse and then, of course, Bobby was taken away from me, my precious replacement boy. There is nothing I can say to describe the pain I feel about Bobby's death. And I know that I am largely responsible.

My conscience has burned for the past few years. My greatest regret is that I cannot go back in life and do things differently. I have felt tormented. I have felt so cut off and remote from you children. I was living a lie which grew to an unmanageable size.

The Reverend Richardson was helpful to me over the years. It was originally his suggestion that I reveal the truth to you, to lift the burden off me. He told me he thought it was your birthright to know.

I don't know if he was right, dear Annie, and I'm sorry that he passed away and is not here to talk to you about it. He was a wise man. Marion is also wise, and she will always be willing to talk to you if you need someone to talk to. She has been a good friend to me and a strong person. Watching her cope with the problems they've had in that family makes me feel that Marion would never have given in to Camilla as I did. That realization makes me feel worse, because for many years I had convinced myself that I had no choice, that anyone would have done what I did. Now I know that if I were a different character I might not have been so weak.

Apart from Marion and the priest, no one else knows. Frank does not know the truth. It is up to you, Annie, to tell him or not. But remember that if you tell him, he may want to search for a son he never had. It is a terrible burden and I'm sorry to place it on you. It was my weakness a long time ago that is responsible for all this now.

I shall be leaving you the brooch to do with what you like. I have never known what to do with it. I could never abide the sight of it but I could not get rid of it, either. I am leaving it to you because it will mean something to you, though that meaning will be different.

Perhaps after all you will be able to benefit from it in some way. It is worth a lot of money and should give you a start in life.

I know that I am not well. Over and above my arthritis, I feel there is something wrong with me and that it is serious. I feel such sadness looking at the state of the family as I shall be leaving it, with Jack now thousands of miles away in Australia, Clara married to a murderer and alone with her babies, however adorable they are, little Bobby in his grave . . . Poor Frank, abandoned by his happy wife many years ago. And now you, dear Annie.

I want you to know that I have always thought of you as my daughter, whatever my private agonies, and that my love for you is as strong as a mother's love can be. Although I regret what I did, of course, if I had not done it, then I would not have had the pleasure of having you as a daughter. And I would regret that.

I hope you will forgive me and that you find happiness in whatever it is you choose to do.

PS: At the end of this notebook you will find some photographs. They are of happier days to show that I was different once. I was happy with myself. Please remember, though, that I have always been happy with you. M.

That was the end of the writing. About a quarter of the pages remained clean and untouched. Annie turned to the back of the notebook. On the inside cover there was a small pouch with three photographs inserted into it. She pulled them out and laid them before her.

There was a grainy picture of her parents she had never

seen before. They both looked so young, standing close together with their arms around each other and smiling directly at the camera. Frank's curls were thick and dark, while Grace's fair hair was tied back in a French plait. Her lips were dark with lipstick. Annie could see now how much Clara looked like her, with her rangy limbs and strong, well-balanced features – widely spaced eyes, broad cheeks, full lips and small chin. It could almost be Clara standing there. There was also a photograph of a baby, a standard studio shot. On the back was written: 'Anne Turner aged six months'. Finally, there was one of Annie aged about eight. She had a page-boy haircut, and was wearing a dark tartan skirt, white blouse and a Fair Isle cardigan. On her feet were the Clarks sandals which she remembered so well. She was holding Rabbit and beaming into the camera.

'Oh, Rabbit,' Annie sighed, as she gathered up the photographs and slipped them back into the pouch at the back of the notebook. 'Oh, Rabbit, I wish we could go back and start again.'

Annie closed the notebook and stared at her long fingers spread out over the brown cover. She could hardly take in her mother's words. Her thoughts swirled around her head like leaves in the wind. She was not her mother's daughter. She was not her mother's daughter. She was not her father's daughter. She was nobody's daughter.

Annie felt battered by wave after wave of shock. She had barely absorbed the information her father had given her the night before. Mother was not her mother. Yet she was her mother, she was the only mother she had known. She had not grown inside her body as Jack and Clara had done. She had been born to a woman who had promptly rejected her just because she had been the wrong sex. It was not personal. It should not matter, but it did. Deep inside her a terrible wound had been inflicted on her for nothing. But this at last was the truth, and the whole truth. Now it all made sense – the brooch, the parentage.

Annie opened the journal again and gazed at the open page. She let her eyes slip out of focus, allowing her mother's writing to swim before her in a blurry haze. Her whole life seemed to pass in front of her eyes, with everything slipping into place as if by some pre-ordained pattern.

Now she understood all the mysteries of her childhood. She knew now why there had been that hint of sadness in her mother's dark brown eyes all the time. She winced at the thought that it was her very presence that was the cause of that sadness. Annie was a constant reminder of what Grace had done.

Now she also understood why she had been so different from the others, why she had a small, angular and delicate body instead of the strong athletic frames of Jack and Clara. Now she knew why she was tone-deaf when everyone else had a sharp musical ear. Now she understood why Mrs Pearson had made that puzzling remark about Tommy not being good enough for her when she and Tommy had gone down to visit in the middle of the war. Everything about her past was suddenly clear.

It was also very confusing. She just did not know who she was any more. A few years ago she had been Annie Turner, third child of Frank and Grace Turner, and for a while, the girlfriend of Tommy Smith, the boy who lived down the road. Then everything changed. First she was no longer Tommy's girlfriend; she was his half-sister. Just as she tried to get used to that idea, she learned than this was not, in fact, true after all. She was not Tommy's half-sister, as she had been told. Now she had learned that she was not the sister of Jack and Clara, either. Or that she was not the daughter of either Frank or Grace but of a man she had never met and a woman she had met only once in her life.

She could go back to being Tommy's girlfriend (if it was even possible) but only at the cost of her very identity. For who is anyone if not in relation to other people?

Annie certainly did not know what to do now. More responsibility had been heaped on her. Should she tell her father? Should she show him the diary? Deep down, she did feel that Frank remained her father, even though her real father was a dead lawyer she had never even met.

She did want to talk to someone, to ease the pain and the pressure. But she was also scared to. If she started talking, she might start something she could not stop. How could she talk to anyone? No one had ever told her anything until it was too late. Wasn't that a lesson to her now? It was impossible to make any decision about what to do except to decide not to act at all. That way, the information she had just learned could at least be kept under control, for a while.

CHAPTER 20

Beginning Again

IT TOOK SIX MONTHS for Annie to decide anything. When Frank cautiously asked if she had finished reading her mother's diary, Annie had simply said yes and ignored the questioning look in his eye, the look that begged her to tell him what had been in Grace's diary. 'I have finished, and it's private,' she had replied, unnecessarily sharply, she thought afterwards.

Since the night of her mother's funeral, relations between Annie and Frank had been strained. Frank was still ashamed of his behaviour and waited for Annie to forgive him. But she remained stiff and cold with him. They ate their dinners in silence and conversed about little. Annie did the housework and went out to work. Although she functioned enough to apply to art schools and get herself to interviews, she felt that she might as well be paralysed, so incapable was she of deciding what to do. Certainly she had ceased all sketching and painting. She had not picked up a drawing pad for weeks. When she was offered places at two art schools, she was unable to decide even then what to do. She did not want to reply to either, and then finally, after requests from the institutions themselves for an answer, she wrote to say that she was turning down their offers. No, she decided, perhaps she ought to forget about studying art and just stay at home and look after Frank and the house.

She also felt sad on the day of Tilly's departure for America, off to the New World to marry Hank Jackson, who was waiting for her on the other side of the ocean. Marion was quiet that evening, sad that her only child had chosen to live so far away, but she was philosophical about it. 'I believe people should do what they feel is right for them,' she said.

And even though Marion knew the truth and perhaps was waiting, hoping, for Annie to turn to her for advice, to become a surrogate daughter to her, Annie felt unable to do that. Perhaps one day, but not for a while yet.

Then Camilla Pearson's letter arrived. Soon after Grace's death, Frank had sent a death notice to Camilla Pearson, who had replied with a polite note of condolence, which Frank had not even bothered to show to Annie. Six months later, Camilla Pearson wrote a letter to Annie herself.

Annie's hands were trembling as she tore open the envelope, staring at the bold, confident handwriting. It was eerie to think that this was the handwriting of the woman she had been born to.

The letter was brief but intriguing. Camilla was inviting Annie down to Sussex again. 'Now that the war is over, certain developments mean that we have some matters of mutual interest to discuss.'

It was too tantalizing an opportunity to miss. Annie telephoned Mrs Pearson and arranged to catch a midday train the following Saturday.

It was a hot, steamy day with little breeze. The train was slowing down as it approached Pulborough Station. Annie had combed her hair and given her nose a quick powder. Peering at herself in the mirror of her compact, she hoped she looked more composed than she felt. It was an extraordinary journey. Here she was on her way to meet the mother who was not her mother, the woman who gave her up at birth simply because she was not a boy.

How different this all was! How different she felt this time! Last time, travelling down with Tommy, Annie had been excited by the prospect of learning the truth about the brooch. Now, six years later, she knew the truth about the brooch, and much more. There were no more secrets to be had, at least she thought there were no more. Perhaps in fact there were. Perhaps the final knots in the tangled thread were ready to be untied at last. What could the matters be that Camilla Pearson wanted to discuss? Annie's curiosity had, of course, made her respond to Camilla Pearson's request. She was also nervous about seeing Camilla again and seeing her in a new light. Knowing what she did now, she was not sure how she would behave towards her.

All her thoughts and feelings were topsy-turvy. She did not want to go but she also had a deep urge inside her compelling her to go. Go on, find out! A voice whispered constantly in her head. At last it will be over. Go, go!

She was met at the station by the chauffeur who led her into the big black Riley parked outside in the station forecourt. Annie sat on the beige leather seat at the back of the car staring out at the lush green foliage of the hedgerows and fields rushing by. The sun was hot. Hazy heat rose from the tarmac of the narrow roads. Annie's mind felt both full and blank. She did not know what to expect yet she dreaded what lay waiting for her.

The car swept into the driveway and took the side road down to the cottage where Annie's grandparents had lived for most of their lives. Camilla Pearson was standing by the front door. She was wearing a blue and white paisley dress and brown shoes.

'Hello, there,' she called. Two black labradors ambled over to Annie, pink tongues hanging out, as she stepped out of the car.

Camilla strode over and grasped her hand. 'Welcome,' she said. 'Have you had a good journey? How good to see you again.'

Camilla led the way into the sitting room of the cottage where she offered Annie a chair.

Camilla Pearson had changed considerably in the years since Annie had last seen her. She looked much older and thinner. Her hair was now grey and the eyes had sunk into their sockets. With her slightly drooping mouth, Camilla's once handsome demeanour had given way to a forlorn and sad expression.

'I was sorry to learn that your mother had passed away,' Camilla said, offering Annie some tea.

'It was mercifully quick,' replied Annie, repeating the words she had heard so many times from other people's lips over the last few months.

Camilla talked about the house. 'The army has left at last,' she said, 'but I have to say that they have left the house and grounds in a disgraceful state. I shall get some compensation, I hope, but it's going to be quite a struggle to restore it to the way it was.' She paused and stared out of the window. 'It needs so much doing to it.' Her words were hardly audible. 'I don't know if I have it in me now . . .'

Her eyes were suddenly glistening with tears. She turned to Annie, her lips pressed together in an unnaturally tight line. 'You know that my son Julian died . . .'

Annie shook her head. 'No, I'm so sorry, I didn't know.'

Camilla raised her hand. 'It's been over two years now. He was killed in his first week of training for the RAF. It was an accident, a stupid freak accident. The pilot who was training him had a heart attack while they were in the air. He had been perfectly fit up until then. Julian, unfortunately, was not experienced to control the plane in such an emergency . . .'

She sighed softly and turned back to look out of the window, into the gardens beyond the cottage. 'He was only eighteen. He was going to inherit the place, to bring it back to its former glory. We would have had parties on the terrace again, dances in the ballroom.' She smoothed her hair with the palm of her hand. 'It was going to be the way it used to be . . .'

Annie shook her head. 'I'm sorry,' she repeated.

Camilla turned to her now, her blue eyes staring intently at her. 'Anne, my dear, I have something to tell you which I know will be a terrible shock to you . . .'

Annie waited. She had decided earlier that she would not let on that she knew anything until she had to. She wanted to hear what Camilla had to say.

'The fact is, my dear, you are my daughter. I am your mother.'

Annie stared at her silently.

'We swapped, you see, your mother and I. I so dearly wanted, needed, a son because my husband had been quite desperate to have someone carry on his family name.

There were no other men in his family, you see. Your mother didn't mind. She already had a boy and a girl and she wanted to help . . . She was the kindest creature, you know.'

Camilla was talking fast now, almost gabbling, as though disconcerted by Annie's blank expression.

'It was good of her, very good of her. Grace was a good person, she always was . . .'

Suddenly Camilla broke down. A deep sob erupted in her throat and she hid her face in her hands. More sobs followed, her shoulders shook uncontrollably. 'I've lost my son and you've lost your mother, or the person who brought you up . . .' she added quickly. She raised her head. 'But you are my daughter, my real daughter, and now you can come and be mistress of this estate. I want to welcome you as my daughter and have you come and live with me here. I can promise that life here will be much more comfortable that what you're used to.'

She paused, waiting to see Annie's response.

Annie's nervousness had vanished. Now all she felt was a hard core of anger rising up inside her. 'I am not your daughter,' she said.

'But what I have just told you is true . . .' Camilla interjected.

'Oh, I know it's true to some extent,' replied Annie. 'In fact, I know it's true because my mother had already informed me . . .'

'She did?' Camilla looked surprised.

'She did, yes, because she loved me. She told me everything, all about how you bullied her into swapping babies.'

'That's nonsense!' Camilla sat back in her chair and frowned. 'That's unfair. Your mother agreed quite readily.

And she never changed her mind about it. She could have . . .'

Annie shook her head to silence her. 'You may have given birth to me but you're not my mother. My mother brought me up and loved me for being me. She was tormented by what you did, by what you made her do. You are only interested in me now because Julian has died and you want someone to take over your responsibilities. You said so yourself. Well, I'm not interested. I'm not your daughter.'

Camilla stared at her for a moment and then rose to her feet. She came over and placed a hand on Annie's shoulder. 'Dear child, please forgive me . . .' Her eyes were brimming with tears again. 'I'm so unhappy, so lonely.'

For a moment, Annie nearly gave way, nearly relented. But then she visualized her mother's journal, and the agonized expression of her mother's torment. 'My mother was unhappy, too,' she said quietly. 'For many years she was unhappy, and all because of you. I find it hard to say this because it goes against the way my mother brought me up, but you deserve to be unhappy. I don't want to have anything to do with you. Now, I'd like to go. There is nothing more to discuss. I'd like a lift to the station. I'll wait there for the next train back to London.'

The train home took a long time. Some children had dropped a boulder on the line from a bridge so there was a long delay at Horsham. Annie did not mind. While the other passengers sighed and rolled their eyes impatiently, Annie sat in the corner of the compartment lost in her own thoughts which raced about her head.

It was early evening by the time Annie had arrived back

at Victoria. By then she had decided what to do. She caught the Tube home and, with her jaw set in an expression of sheer determination, she marched round to the Smiths' house in Leverton Street.

First she knocked on the door, then she banged on it. No one was in. She knocked again.

Mrs Whelan opened her door and stepped into the street. 'There's no one home. The older folk have gone to the bingo in Camden, and Connie went out about half an hour ago.'

Annie nodded and thanked her, only slightly irritated by Mrs Whelan's busybody ways. But with her earlier intentions foiled, she felt deflated. She walked home dragging her feet. She felt almost overwhelmed by a sense of gloom and despair. She felt she would seize up if fate dealt her another blow.

As she walked in through the front door, she was surprised to hear the unfamiliar sound of laughter coming from the kitchen. She could hear her father's deep voice, animated and excited, and a woman's, a familiar woman's voice. It was Connie Smith.

Frank and Connie Smith were sitting at the table having a cup of tea. The remains of a seed cake lay on a plate before them.

'Why, it's Annie, my dear.' Frank leaped to his feet and hugged Annie tight.

Annie stiffened. She was unable to respond naturally to anything. She nodded hello to Connie.

'Connie made me a delicious cake.' Frank lifted the plate towards Annie. 'There's plenty left. Help yourself.'

'No, thank you.' Annie poured herself a glass of water from the tap.

'We've been talking about the old days, haven't we, Connie?' Frank laughed at Connie. 'We go back a long way, don't we?'

Connie laughed. 'We do indeed. I can't remember when I didn't know your father. How's your day been, then?'

Connie smiled at Annie in a kind way. She was the way she had been on that day when Annie had come over to see the mice with Tommy, warm and friendly. She was not at all cold in the way she had been since she didn't want Annie seeing Tommy. With her sparkling eyes and red cheeks, Connie was looking pretty.

'It was all right,' grunted Annie. 'But I'm tired. I'm going upstairs.'

As she climbed the stairs to her room, she felt a mixture of rage and relief. How could her father be laughing and joking like that so soon after her mother's death? How could he sit in Grace's kitchen and banter with Connie as though he did not have a care in the world. How dare he?

But as she walked into her room and shut the door, a voice inside her challenged her. Why shouldn't he? Why shouldn't he have some fun after all these months of misery? Months? Why, it had been years of misery for him. Everything had been so grim for such a long time, she should be glad that there was a change in the air.

The sound of the piano rose up the stairwell. Nobody had played the piano for years.

First there was music, her father playing so deftly, his fingers running lightly over the keys. Then she could hear Connie singing along in a lovely clear, pure voice that reached up to the top of the house. Then her father joined in, singing with Connie, his deep, rich voice circling and joining Connie's in the duet.

It was a lovely sound which took Annie straight back to her childhood. She lay on her bed listening. She suddenly felt a great weight lifting from her. Her father had a right to be happy. He also had the capacity to be happy. And if being with Connie made him happy, then she, Annie, would accept that. She realized then how much she loved him and how little all the recent revelations had really changed things.

She sat up suddenly. That was right. Nothing had really changed. Even if Grace and Frank were not actually her parents, her feelings for them remained the same. She loved them very much. She also loved Tommy very much, as much as she always had. And she, too, had a right to be happy.

Leaping to her feet, she went to the window and stared out at the view across London. The music from the hall was loud and constant, uplifting and exuberant at the same time. The view across to the Kent hills was for once clear. Annie's thoughts were suddenly very focused. Everything had fallen into place. She knew exactly what she had to do.

She went downstairs to ask Connie for the information she had wanted before.

The next morning Annie caught the bus down to Camden Town.

Clara was at home in her flat, to which she had returned some months before. She looked tired, and the children were running noisily around her feet.

'I can't stay,' said Annie. 'Here, this is for you.' She thrust a small package into Clara's hands. 'It's worth a lot of money. Sell it and get yourself a nice place to live. You need it more than I do.'

Clara was speechless as she opened up the paper to

reveal the diamond and sapphire brooch twinkling in the palm of her hand.

Annie reached over and gave her a great hug. 'I've got to dash,' she said. 'We'll talk about it when I get back . . .'

Hurrying away, Annie slapped her hands over her eyes. 'Please, God,' she prayed, 'please bring my big sister back.'

An hour later, Annie was sitting on a train again, this time heading for an address in Bristol which Connie had given her that morning. Tommy was going to be surprised to see her, she was sure, but she was also sure that he would be glad.

The train rolled along with a comforting clackety-clack, clackety-clack. Once again Annie thought of her mother's diary and what the revelations in it really meant to her. Her mother's voice in that diary had been strong and direct. Her mother had still existed right up until the end, even though for years she had faded away to almost nothing. She was still a person with thoughts and feelings, and love and hope.

Annie thought of her family and the happier times of her childhood. She pictured her mother smiling gently, bent over her sewing, while Clara and Frank sat at the piano playing their duets. She pictured the many family meals around the kitchen table, sometimes fraught, sometimes full of laughter, but always safe and containing.

She thought of Tommy, whose origins were, as it now turned out, so similar to hers. Was that why they had been drawn to each other in the first place?

Of course, Tommy did not know about his origins. Connie did not want him to know. Frank did not know about Annie's either. She had not yet been able to tell her father the truth. Telling him the truth would mean telling him that he had had a child, a son, he had never known.

Clackety-clack, clackety-clack. The train thundered on towards the west. Annie stared out at the green fields racing past, the hedgerows and trees, the hills in the distance, the cows and sheep standing mournfully in the meadows. If she wanted to stop with any one scene in front of her, she could not. The train was beyond her control. She would not say anything to Tommy, and she would not say anything to her father, either. It was not for her to pass on anything. But Annie knew that she could not control these things. Secrets work their way up to the surface, however long ago or however deeply they were originally buried. These secrets were no different, and would no doubt work their way out at some time in the future too.

But in the meantime, she was not going to let secrets spoil her life. She would push them to the back of her mind and only look forwards from now on. She was going to write back to the art schools and see if they still had a place for her. If not, she would reapply next year. Frank did not need looking after, and even if he did, it wouldn't be for her to do it, not now.

She sat back and breathed a soft sigh, letting her body roll gently to the rhythm of the train. There was Annie Turner, a pretty young woman going to meet up with the man she loved, a light smile on her lips, an excited sparkle in her eyes. For that moment, at least, she was ready for anything.

AWAY TO THE WOODS
Lena Kennedy

'Lena Kennedy is a natural storyteller . . . Dickensian
energy, a huge range of vivid characters, and clear delight
in telling us about them' *Daily Telegraph*

Lena Kennedy was sixty-four before her first novel, *Maggie*,
was accepted for publication. Having lived in the East End
all her life, she was able to use her knowledge of the area
and its people to great effect, writing with tremendous
energy about the characters and times she had known and
experienced there.

In *Away to the Woods*, she looks back on the formative
influences that shaped her career, such as the idyllic
summers spent at her family's 'holiday home' in Kent,
where among the 'shack-dwellers' of the woods and the
simple beauty of the countryside she began to realise her
growing need to express her feelings through writing. Lena
also vividly describes the long search for a publisher; her
joy at finding success, and the setback late in life that
nearly robbed her of many years' work.

Lena Kennedy died in 1986, and some of her books have
subsequently been published posthumously. *Away to the
Woods* is a significant addition to this bestselling collection,
and, told in her inimitable style sheds much light on the life
of one of Britain's best-loved novelists.

WARNER
0 7515 1602 3

NELLIE WILDCHILD

Emma Blair

The Glasgow Nellie Thompson had been born to was a city bled colourless by poverty and despair, and divided against itself by religion and class. A city where appearances meant more than the truth that might lie in a person's heart . . .

Nellie knew what it was like to be hungry and hopeless; to live a bitter lie with a man she hated. But still she held on to her dreams. Somehow she would leave those grey and violent streets behind. Somehow she would make her own life and her own world – even if she were forever denied the comfort of love.

WARNER
0 7515 1669 4

☐	Away to the Woods	Lena Kennedy	£5.99
☐	Queenie's Castle	Lena Kennedy	£4.99
☐	Kate of Clyve Shore	Lena Kennedy	£4.99
☐	Nellie Wildchild	Emma Blair	£5.99
☐	Hester Dark	Emma Blair	£5.99
☐	The Blackbird's Tale	Emma Blair	£5.99
☐	Elle	Maria Barrett	£4.99
☐	Dangerous Obsession	Maria Barrett	£4.99

Warner Books now offers an exciting range of quality titles by both established and new authors which can be ordered from the following address:

Little, Brown and Company (UK),
P.O. Box 11,
Falmouth,
Cornwall TR10 9EN.

Fax No: 01326 317444.
Telephone No: 01326 317200
E-mail: books@barni.avel.co.uk

Payments can be made as follows: cheque, postal order (payable to Little, Brown and Company) or by credit cards, Visa/Access. Do not send cash or currency. UK customers and B.F.P.O. please allow £1.00 for postage and packing for the first book, plus 50p for the second book, plus 30p for each additional book up to a maximum charge of £3.00 (7 books plus).

Overseas customers including Ireland, please allow £2.00 for the first book plus £1.00 for the second book, plus 50p for each additional book.

NAME (Block Letters) ....

....

ADDRESS ....

....

....

☐ I enclose my remittance for ....

☐ I wish to pay by Access/Visa Card

Number ⬚⬚⬚⬚⬚⬚⬚⬚⬚⬚⬚⬚⬚⬚⬚⬚

Card Expiry Date ⬚⬚⬚⬚